FORBIDDEN WISH

SCARLETT FINN

I0713776

Also by Scarlett Finn

TO DIE FOR...
TO DIE FOR TRUTH
TO DIE FOR HONOR
TO DIE FOR VIRTUE
TO DIE FOR DUTY
TO DIE FOR LOVE

GO NOVELS
GO WITH IT
GO IT ALONE
GO ALL OUT
GO ALL IN
GO FULL CIRCLE

KINDRED SERIES
RAVEN
SWALLOW
CUCKOO
SWIFT
FALCON
FINCH

**LOVE AGAINST THE ODDS
STANDALONE COLLECTION**
SWEET SEAS
HEIR'S AFFAIR
RESCUED
MAESTRO'S MUSE
GETTING TRICKY
THIRTEEN
REMEMBER WHEN...
RELUCTANT SUSPICION
XY FACTOR

EXILE
HIDE & SEEK
KISS CHASE

THE EXPLICIT SERIES
EXPLICIT INSTRUCTION
EXPLICIT DETAIL
EXPLICIT MEMORY

WRECK & RUIN
RUIN ME
RUIN HIM

MISTAKE DUET
MISTAKE ME NOT
SLEIGHT MISTAKE

NOTHING TO...
NOTHING TO HIDE
NOTHING TO LOSE
NOTHING TO DECLARE
NOTHING TO US
NOTHING TO SAY
NOTHING TO GAIN
NOTHING TO YOU
NOTHING TO THIS

**THE BRANDED
SERIES**
BRANDED
SCARRED
MARKED

**RISQUÉ & HARROW
INTERTWINED**
TAKE A RISK
FIGHTING FATE
RISK IT ALL
FIGHTING BACK
GAME OF RISK

LOST & FOUND
LOST
FOUND

**FORBIDDEN
PREQUEL DUET**
ALL. ONLY.
ONLY YOURS

THE FORBIDDEN NOVELS
FORBIDDEN DESIRE
FORBIDDEN WANT
FORBIDDEN WISH
FORBIDDEN NEED

ONE

"I STILL DON'T BELIEVE it. It's like living in a nightmare."

"You are living in a nightmare, Mila," Imogen Stratford said. "No one should have to endure this."

Four days ago, cops pulled the body of Mila's roommate from a dumpster. The bereaved friend stood fixated on the coffeepot. Blank. Aimless. Completely on pause. Grief had a way of sucking the oxygen from a room. How did someone process such a devastating event?

Three days ago, she'd come to the apartment for the story no one else wanted to tell. No one cared. No one except her. As an investigative reporter with The Chronicler, it was her job to be intrigued by a puzzle, but this case was more than that. Since meeting Mila, a much more profound sense of duty thrummed within her. They were the same age. Had so much in common. The victims could be her friends. Her cousins. Could be her.

"When Steph was missing, I thought I'd do anything just to know, you know?" Spoon in hand, Mila stared into nothingness. "Now, knowing, hope's gone. Just pulled right out from under me. I didn't think it would feel like this. She's dead. I know she's dead, but… What her family must be going through."

Stephanie Weet, the deceased, wasn't close with her family. They were middle class. Respectable. Stephanie was a paralegal. Good job. Nice apartment. Nothing in her history suggested substance misuse or addiction. Law enforcement hadn't released her cause of death, but she had it on good authority there was foul play. Not that she needed official confirmation. The victim hadn't died in her sleep. A dumpster was not somewhere a person like Stephanie died naturally.

"It's a terrible time for all of you," she said, stroking Mila's back in comfort. "You need time to grieve. Did she have a boyfriend?"

Mila snapped from her daze. "Cops said they talked to him. I don't know, it's just… He came around looking for her, you know, when she was missing? He avoided the cops though. I don't know how they found him."

Wouldn't be the first time a perpetrator stuck close to a victim's loved ones, despite knowing they were already dead.

"Maybe they knew him. What's his name?"

"I only knew him as Bryan," Mila said, picking up her phone to scroll through it. "They were going out a couple of months, but he never spent time here. Not much time. Overnight every once in a while. She could've done so much better. He wasn't even that hot." She handed over the phone. "What do you think?"

"Uh…" In the screen's foreground, Stephanie smiled, wearing glasses… Her new glasses, that she'd picked up from the optometrist less than a week before she disappeared. In the background, a frowning guy in profile held a phone to his ear. "Nothing special."

"Right?" Mila said, looking at the screen, tears gathering in her eyes again. "I can't believe she's really gone."

"Oh, honey." Compelled to pull her into a hug, someone had to do the job of comforting Mila, now Stephanie wasn't around to do it. "They'll find the bastard who did this."

If *they* didn't, she would. Somehow.

"People keep saying that, but…" Pulling away, Mila wiped her eyes with a sleeve. "Do they ever? I mean, can they ever be sure they will? If it was some crazy, spur of the moment, wrong place, wrong time thing, at least we'd know it was a crime of passion or some psycho lost control of himself, but… The injuries she had…" Shaking her head, the grief became disbelief. "They tortured her. Whatever happened to her wasn't quick."

Details had not been fully released to the press or the public. Those closest to the victim were provided more information. She understood why it was that way, that someone might want to know what their friend or family member endured. But did it make it easier? She wasn't sure.

"I'm sorry for her pain and for yours."

"Why would someone do that? What kind of sick animal would…? And Stephanie? Why Stephanie? She's the kindest, sweetest… was the kindest…"

Another daze.

The least she could do was pour the coffee. She eased Mila aside to do just that. The woman may not drink it, coffee wouldn't ease her grief, but it was something. Something to fill the void of futility. Still, somehow, it didn't feel right to do something so mundane given their topic of conversation.

"Stephanie didn't deserve it." She pushed a coffee to Mila. "I know some cops. I can try to find out more."

The family was best placed to get further details about Stephanie. Often loved ones had to pester the precinct and assigned detectives for broad strokes, but they usually got them in the end. Most of the time. Specifics were harder to come by. Good thing she had a lot of practice finagling things from cops. Anything she learned could take them closer to nailing the perp.

One thing she hadn't shared with Mila was her own hunch.

This wasn't a random killing. It wasn't an isolated murder. Other women had died in the past few months under similar circumstances. The cops hadn't put it together, wouldn't put it together despite her bringing it up more than once. It wouldn't be fair to scare or upset Mila with her theories. Not until she had evidence.

"Has he been back? This Bryan guy? Have you seen him since they found Stephanie?"

Since they found her body.

Mila picked up the coffee and wrapped her hands around the heat of the mug, propping a hip on the counter. "No. I haven't seen him at all."

If he was a real boyfriend, a genuinely concerned boyfriend, she'd expect him to pay his respects. To send flowers. To be near others who knew her like he did. Then again, two months wasn't exactly a lifetime. Could be he didn't feel it was his right.

"Do you have a number for him? Maybe he could help piece together what happened. When did he last see her?"

"She left here to go meet him. That's what she said. He said she never showed up. Cops said he's got an alibi."

Had they checked it out? If she could talk to him, get him to give her the info, she could follow up herself.

"Do you know where he lives or works?" she asked. Mila shook her head while raising the coffee to her lips. "Where he hangs around? Any of his friends? Did they go to a certain bar or restaurant more than once?"

Identifying a regular haunt would be the quickest way to find this Bryan.

"No, I…" The woman's whole affect changed in an instant. Putting the coffee down, Mila pushed away from the counter to pass her and go into the living room. "We shouldn't be talking about this."

What just happened?

She went after Mila. "Why not?"

"It's dangerous."

Something juicy hung in the eaves of that statement. "Why is it dangerous?"

Mila put the couch between them. More than bereaved, conflict was written all over the pretty young woman's face. "She swore me to secrecy, I can't… It doesn't even matter, she said she'd never been there, but…"

"But what?"

"She said Bryan had connections. That he could get them into some club."

"A club?"

"Yeah, but if he had connections… could those connections have gotten her into trouble? Is that why she's dead? Maybe she saw something. Heard something."

And the murderer wanted to shut her up? Possibly.

"What kind of connections are we talking?"

Politics? Drug kingpin? Strung out celebrity?

Toying with her fingers, Mila's conflict appeared to eat at her. "You ever heard of…" Saying nothing, she waited for the woman to continue. Silence could be the greatest prompt. "I shouldn't even be talking to you, should I?"

"Hey…" She went around the couch to take Mila's upper arms. "You don't have to tell me anything. You can kick my ass out in the street and demand I never come back. This is about what you need."

"I need what's best for Steph… If she was here, I'd talk to her and… She swore me to secrecy, said Bryan would be so mad if he knew she'd told me."

"I don't care about him. If this is tearing you up, you need to get it out."

"You said you were going to help. That you wanted to find who was responsible."

"I do."

"This isn't just… it's not some sleazy story to me. She was my best friend." Mila sighed. "I want to do what's best for her… I told them about Bryan, the cops, I mean. They said they'd check him out, I don't know if they ever did…"

"I can check him out."

Shaking her head, Mila wrapped her arms around herself. "It could be dangerous. I don't want anyone else to get hurt."

"No one will get hurt," Imogen said and smiled. "My brother's not the type of guy anyone wants to mess with. He'd go to hell and back for me…" She bobbed her head to the side. "He'd probably tell you he already has."

Mila managed a brief laugh. "He'll look after you?"

"Yes."

It took another few seconds, but the young woman relented. "Vex Manzani… do you know who he is?" Only too well. Youngest son of mafioso don Silvio Manzani. She nodded. "He has this really super exclusive club… Hustle. It's invitation only. Do you know it?"

"No," Imogen said. "But I know a man who will."

TWO

HEATHER LANTRY.

Michelle Cadlow.

Stephanie Weet.

Their names were all she thought about. How did no one else see it? Others didn't want to, so they wouldn't. People loved to kid themselves.

Someone had to pay attention. Someone had to care. If she had to solve the mystery herself, that was exactly what she'd do.

I can do this.

That's what she'd told her editor, Steeple, he hadn't been so sure. She'd talked him into it. Sometimes it paid to have good skin and a great rack.

Asking questions was her job. In the name of getting to the story, risks were part of the process. Hadn't all the greats gone undercover to get to the truth? Okay, she was no hardened crime reporter… or even a jaded detective, but this was worth it.

Someone had to put the pieces together.

Right then, that someone was her.

Her brother lived and worked at Jagg's Autos, her next stop. Ford would be reasonable, wouldn't he? Someone had to listen to her, why not her brother? First her colleagues shrugged her off, then her boss was dubious. Even the cops shooed her away. Family was her last hope, and she'd choose her brother over her father any day.

The dark gray corrugated metal fence around the vast warehouse site didn't offer any glimpses inside. Being Friday afternoon, the guys may have closed for the day already. If they had, she'd need to go to her father's… She shivered. That was one line of questioning best avoided.

The wide sliding gate was open. Good start. Now on to locating her brother.

Cars and bikes lined up under the covered parking area, running the width of the site. The glass doors at the front meant to be the main entrance would be locked. She didn't need to peek through the glazed frontage showcasing the beauties inside to know that.

The real magic happened around the back. Unless someone had an appointment, there was rarely anyone in the showroom.

At the side of the building, a black door led to the front desk of the service department. Yeah, custom paint jobs were the biggest money, but they catered to all kinds of customers.

All kinds.

Standing around waiting for service wouldn't get her anywhere. Patience was not a virtue she possessed anyway. Nor was reserve or restraint. The sound of masculine laughter didn't deter her from rounding the corner of the massive building or striding across the painted concrete floor toward her brother at the back with a bunch of guys.

Whatever they all did around there, it was car related. Hence the vehicles on ramps or in various states of dismantled. People didn't concern her. Ford was her focus. She walked right up to him, ignoring everyone else.

"We have to talk."

"Whoa, shit, who's the hot-ass babe?" one of his buddies hooted.

His friendship group expanded and contracted all the time. Those who'd stuck around a few years, she knew. Those who hadn't were apparently idiots. No surprise. Jagg, the owner of the garage, had a habit of cutting breaks for guys down on their luck. Sometimes it panned out, sometimes he wasn't so lucky.

"His sister, asshole," Sutherland said before someone got smacked. "Show some respect."

"Yeah, off-limits," Coakley added.

"You say that like you asked, Coak," the guy with the big trap said.

"I did."

More laughter, but she didn't flinch. Ford didn't either, he studied her expression and must've concluded she was serious.

"Come here."

The door by them went to the corridor that ran from the back shop to the showroom. From there, he took the second on the left into their breakroom. One of the three doors in the far corner was open an inch, but she had no idea what was back there. Jagg was his best friend and had been forever, but it wasn't like she hung out there or ever went exploring.

Curiosity would wait. "I need your help," she said, getting to the point as soon as Ford closed the door they'd just come through.

"What's up?" he asked, coming in close. "You're amped."

"Yeah, I am," she said. "Do you still do work for Evander Manzani? Vex they call him, right? Never mind, I know you know people. I need to get into his place."

"What place?"

"He has a club."

"More than one. Vex likes to have a good time." Her brother used the mafioso's street name. Everyone did. "His family has a lot of business interests. Why do you want to get mixed up with a guy like that?"

"I don't care about Manzani. I care about getting into his club."

"Why?"

"None of your business."

"It's one of your stories, isn't it? You wanna write about Vex Manzani? Do you have a death wish?" His fist went to his forehead for a second before it leaped out into the air. "No. I won't help you."

"I will do this with or without your help. Showing up with my brother, who does work on the side for the club owner, I might be saved from pawing hands or crazy gangsters."

"Not going at all saves you from both."

She shook her head. "Not an option."

"Me coming with you is not an option," he said and came to lay a hand on her shoulder. "If Dad found out—"

"If Dad found out you abandoned me there…"

His head relaxed. "You spoken to him yet?" She said nothing. "Hard for him to find out if you don't speak to him."

"It's complicated."

"No, it's not. It's about the cop."

Not entirely. Her brother didn't know about her latest run in with their father. And she didn't have time to loop him in.

"You know, you don't have to call him that," she said. "He has a name."

"Never learned it while you were with him, don't plan on learning it now."

"And it's that kind of attitude that drove a wedge between me and Dad."

"Mom didn't like him either."

"How would you know? You never visit her."

"I don't like leaving the city."

"Yeah, it's like you're worried you'll die without the pollution, crime, and overcrowded-deprivation infecting you every second."

"I like the pollution and it likes me," he said, sauntering around the kitchen island to the counter in the corner. "Want coffee?"

"No. If you're not going to help me, I need to find someone who will. I don't have time for coffee."

"Just once, little sister, pause and pay attention." He turned his back on the coffee to fold his arms. Great. Lecture time. Her dad did the same pose. "Vex Manzani is dangerous. Not in your league. Not even close."

"How would you know?" she asked, going closer. "You don't know anything about my league."

"I know it includes cops and Manzani is so far away from that—"

"Lachlan might be a cop, doesn't make him a saint," she said of her ex. "And who was talking about sex?"

Her brother flinched with instinctual disgust. "No one. What the hell, Im?"

"I had sex with Lach. I dated him. That's not related to what I want from Vex Manzani. I don't even want Vex Manzani; I just need to get into his club."

"Which club?"

"Hustle."

His brows rose. "And you want *me* to go with you?" He snorted a laugh. "Good call, sis."

When he returned to making his coffee, her irritation spiked. "You spend so much of your time judging me, you never listen."

"You think I judge you?" he said, filling the machine with water.

"Yeah. We came from the same place you and me. You and your friends look down on me—"

He laughed and spun to face her again. "Down on you? Want to know how many of us rejected the Ivy League?"

Why was he always like this? Always determined to piss her off. "What's that got to do with anything?"

"You had a chance to make something of your life, little sister. Something far away from here."

"I didn't want to be far away from here."

"You should be far away from any conversation that involves Vex Manzani. You should be far away from that shitty local section, far away from that boss of yours that sends you on these insane, dangerous jobs—"

"He didn't send me," she asserted. "I found this story. I want this story. No one else has even noticed. I noticed. And I am not going to let it go because yet another man is short-sighted. People are dying—"

"And I don't want you to be one of them!"

Why did they fight so much? It hadn't always been this way… had it?

"Forget it," she said after a tense pause. "I shouldn't have come."

"Im," he said when she turned for the door. "Immie, I'm sorry, don't run out of here." She stopped. He sighed. "You're my kid sister. I don't want you near guys like that."

"I'm not looking for a date. This is my job. You don't think it's important, I do."

"If you think about writing a story on Hustle or the Manzani—"

"It's not a story about the club. Why would I waste my time writing about that?"

Scrutinizing her, he took his time. "Aren't there people better suited to this type of thing? What about the woman that wrote that other Manzani story? The one that's been all over. She's gotta be the go-to gal for shit like this."

Her eyes cut to him over her shoulder. "Your father is my father, Ford."

Shaking his head, he approached. "I was raised with Dad. Dad's way. You stayed with Mom." They'd made their choices when their parents separated. Having been only five, she didn't remember, but that's what she'd been told. At that same time, ten-year-old Ford was already a handful. He only wanted to be with their father: famed thief and general scoundrel. "This isn't your world. Dad and me worked hard to make sure of it."

They fought. They were different. Both true. But she loved her brother and never doubted he loved her too.

Breathing out, she let her shoulders fall, showing him what he wanted to see. "You're right." He smiled. "I get into these things and… I just want to be good at my job."

"I get that," he said, resting his hand on her shoulder again. "You're a good person, Immie. One who should stay away from the scum of this world. Rule of thumb?" An offer of advice, she raised her head like she planned to accept it. "If you need my help to get to a story, it's not a story you should be anywhere near."

She laughed. "Okay."

Pulling her close, he kissed the top of her head. They'd come from the same place, yet he thought she was made of glass. She wasn't. Whatever it took, she'd get the story. She'd get justice. One way or another.

THREE

SEXY WOULD DO IT.

In theory. Her choice of a circle miniskirt gave her plenty of room to move… though it barely covered her ass. If Ford had believed in her and come along, displaying so much skin wouldn't have been necessary. A strip of midriff showed between waistline and the halter top held on her body by three thin straps across her back and one at her neck. Skin. Rack. Those were her only chance of getting inside.

The cab dropped her off at the front. Maybe. There was no sign. No lights. No glitz and glamour. In fact, it was dark and more than a little creepy. Super exclusive, just like Mila said. A few people hung outside, didn't look like they were getting in.

A chain hung across the entrance, an actual chain. Not like red velvet or a rope line, nope, real chain. Behind that, two thugs, almost wider than the doors, had already noticed her. Probably because it was cold and her chest was saying hello in its own way.

Widening her smile, she was subtle about arching her spine and pushing back her shoulders. At least, she thought it was subtle. That's right, fellas, nothing threatening here. Cute and harmless or femme fatale? Her ruby red lips matched her skirt. By the look of the club they were apparently protecting, white may not have been a good choice for her top.

"Evening, gentlemen," she said, stopping at the chain. Those loitering to the side noticed her too, but men's egos tended to have a specific bias toward boobs. "I'm meeting someone."

"You've met him. I'm right here, beautiful," one guy said. "Man, you're a classy chick."

With a sly half smile, she did an innocent little shoulder raise as her chin went toward it. "Am I?"

The guy laughed, drawn in, perfect. "Guess we could audition her."

His partner came closer. "Know a few of the guys who would."

"And you wouldn't?"

"I fucking would. I will… Boss's got rules though."

Okay, they were talking about her as though she wasn't there. A journalist's dream. It was so much easier to gather information when people dismissed her as inconsequential.

"Yeah, we can't let you in, baby," the first guy said, touching the halter of her top, drawing his fingers down.

Was he just going to grope her right there? If she wanted to get in, she'd smile through it. Thank God her brother wasn't there.

"We can take you round the side," the second guy said. "Security guys hang there and at break—"

"Much as I'd love to, I really am meeting someone inside."

The guys looked at each other. "What's your name, darlin'?"

Did people bluff their way in all the time? She couldn't see a physical list anywhere. Could it really be that exclusive? She had money in her clutch. Might be time to see if a little grease would help.

"My name?" she said, sliding her purse from under her arm to open the clasp.

"Yeah."

A name? Did she want them checking her out? Her hand slipped into her clutch. How much was too much? She didn't want to insult them either.

"Dunn."

That word came from nowhere. Swinging around, she didn't expect to see her brother's best friend, Jagger Dunn, moseying toward them. Her mouth dropped open. Ridiculously tall. Ridiculously built. Mothers warned daughters about bad boys like Jagg. Dangerous. Brooding... Perfect for a place like Hustle and exactly the kind of guy who could get her in.

Hot was relative. No one could deny his appeal in those grubby jeans and heavy boots. In contrast to her extra effort, it didn't appear he'd given any thought to his attire... or even changed out of his clothes from the day.

"Dunn," the first guy said, and appealed to his colleague. "Did anyone—"

"No one said you were back in the game," the second guy said.

"I'm not," he said, tossing a heavy arm over her shoulder. Resting against the side of her neck, it just hung there in front of her body, urging her against the solid guy at her back. "You gonna move..." he sniffed, "or you want me to move you?"

Both guys took a second before laughing. "Yeah, right," the first guy said, unhooking the chain.

"If I was gonna get my ass handed to me by anyone…" the second guy said, reeking of hero worship.

Jagg walked, like she wasn't even there, propelling her along in front of him. Providing she kept her body connected to his, it was surprisingly easy to move that way. With her own form of human outerwear, Jagg sure made for an amazing security blanket. Just be invisible. Be an extension of him and no one would notice her.

New plan.

Good plan.

The second guy came hurrying over to open the door. The darkness within wasn't welcoming. Enveloped by it, consumed in shade, the door behind them swung shut.

"Breathe in, Genny," his voice rumbled against her back.

The door in front of them opened, light flashed across them. The music was loud, bassy, definitely heavy, yet it wasn't like any other dance club she'd visited. Her eyes hadn't adjusted yet. White and electric blue lights flashed up and around, but the room wasn't completely dark. Light stuttered in corners, keeping the illumination jumping and dying in a rhythm that went with the bass of the dulled music.

Still trying to take it in, she was swept forward when Jagg walked again. Going with it, the motion took them inside. It was only when they were there that she got her first look at the people… and what they were doing.

Benches lined up back to back, side to side, against the walls, in the middle of the room. Rectangles. Circles. Podiums. People occupied them all. And… yeah… she didn't have to worry about showing too much skin.

She swallowed. Hard. Both were definitely relevant in this room.

Least she'd kept her sense of humor.

Sex. Everywhere. In every form. Right there. In front of her. Raised on the split level. Standing up. Sitting down. Lying. Reaching. Touching. Men. Women. Together. In threes. In groups. In every position and demographic that ever existed.

"Want to leave?"

Jagg's voice made her jump. Right there. Above her ear. She dropped her head as a shiver went through her. Fuck. Why did she have to be there with a walking sex dream? In sex fantasy land, who else should she be with?

Though the music wasn't deafening, it covered most of the sound going on around them. Thank goodness. Rather than try to talk to him, she twined her fingers between his in front of her, and advanced deeper.

This wasn't the time to be squeamish. Women were dying. Heather Lantry. Michelle Cadlow. Stephanie Weet. The victims gave her strength.

Bar to the left, occupied though not overcrowded. As she got over the surprise of the theme, details formed in observations. Bartenders, servers, male and female, wearing only panties or briefs in black or white. Patrons did have some tables to sit and drink at. Few conversations seemed riveted, those people were watching… or foreplaying.

Okay. Not what she was expecting. But this was good. No one was taking names or pictures. She could watch. Wait until she found what she was looking for, then pounce.

The room opened up to reveal a protruding stage area, a mass orgy zone, with podiums at different levels for those who wanted to put on a show. On either side? Double doors. Interesting. Security protected. Exactly what she'd expect for a mafia son. To get in, Bryan had to know someone. Could he be in that secure room with his contact?

Rather than go the intriguing way, Jagg kept going forward, taking her with him, around a few more tables and benches… beds, to the wall occupied by one guy.

"Move," Jagg said to him and bent over, her still in the cocoon of his body, as the guy scurried off.

He flipped the mattress like it was nothing then sat them down. The bed was narrower than a twin, so it wasn't totally unlike just pulling up a chair in a bar. Thankfully, it had a sort of headboard separating them from the guy being serviced by two women next to them.

Their spot against the wall was perfect. Prime placement. With a view of those double doors.

No one was going in and out over there. The doors were closed. Did they go to the same space? Did it matter? Left or right?

A long finger hooked her jaw, dragging it around. Her eyes were the last thing to follow. They blinked a few times, taking in the dark ones scowling down at her.

"Will you buy me a drink?" she asked Jagg, hoping to keep him busy.

"Would, 'cept if I leave you alone, you won't be alone when I get back."

"I will," she said, widening her eyes, aiming for innocence. "I'm not going anywhere. I'll wait right here."

That was just a lie. If she could get—

"You lied that easy to Ford today too." Was his voice always so unimpressed and growly like that? "You get a good look around, spy? 'Cause this is not a place a woman like you should hang out."

"I am not a spy," she said, pushing his hand from her face. "And I've got all the same parts these women have. Probably done all they're doing too. Are you shy, Jagg?"

His jaw moved as it tightened. Good. He should be pissed off. She was too. Not because he'd come to get her in. No, he got points for that. Beaucoup points. But for treating her like glass, like her brother, yeah, that cut him down a few.

"Good thing you're not," he said, his face coming closer to hers. "'Cause there are rules here."

"What does that mean?"

One of his brows rose. "Didn't think of that, did you?"

That performing may be required? No, she hadn't. Though she did know why her brother had laughed when she proposed they visit Hustle together.

"No one will notice what I'm doing," she said. "Take a look around, everyone else is occupied."

"Everyone?"

When he tossed a subtle nod toward the room, she took her own advice and looked around... at the nearby faces. Oh, boy. Shit. They were being watched. Her? Him? Both of them? Together? What did people expect? A show or a shot?

FOUR

SHE BREATHED IN and pasted on a smile. Thank God she was good at faking it. "Okay…"

His voice warmed her ear again. "People notice a knockout. Men can sniff that shit out from a thousand yards." What did she care if they were watching? Let them stare. She wanted to do a little of that too. At those doors over there. "You're new. Newbies get special attention. VIP treatment. A full service."

Oh, ding, ding. Was that how to get through those doors? Wait. That was information, yes, but no grand prize. She had to fuck her way through those doors? If the guys out front were any indication of the kind of men in the chain of command…

Suddenly, her legs were scooped up. Jagg! Did he have to keep interrupting her thoughts? Surprising her. He draped her across his lap. Good. Yeah. If people thought this guy kept her occupied, maybe she could do a little surveillance without being bothered.

Like before, his finger hooked around her jaw, forcing it to move. All she wanted to do—why was his face so close, looming there above her?

"One rule, Genny," he said, skimming his finger to her chin. "We never breathe a word of this to your brother."

What was he—his mouth closing over hers erased all thoughts. Was he kissing her? Why was he…? Oh, God, it was incredible. Hot, steady, getting hotter by the second. Releasing her purse on the seat, she parted her lips and coiled her arms around him.

Did her tongue seek his first… or was it the other way around? Who the hell cared? His broad shoulders offered the perfect anchor for her elbows to dig in and leverage higher. His hard thighs were a better seat than the mattress… and they'd offer a better vantage point.

Vantage point?

Right. Shit.

She wasn't there to make out with sexy white knights. The club. The murders. The contact.

Pulling her mouth from his, she didn't even look him in the eye while twisting around on his lap, positioning herself back to chest, like he was a part of the furniture. Yep, the doors were so much clearer from there. Still no movement. Stroking her palms down Jagg's arms, she guided them until she clasped the back of his hands, closing them around her breasts.

If those in proximity wanted a show, she needed cover, and God, he was good at it. Tossing her head to the side, she pulled the pin from her hair, letting it cascade free. And with a little direction, like her winding her arm around Jagg's head, she urged his mouth against her neck.

Over by the stage, a guy walked up to speak to one of the guards. Pushing higher, she scrunched her hand in Jagg's hair, moving in time with the caress of his tender lips on her carotid. Man, the guy was good. First, he showed up to save her and then gave her more intimate attention than she'd had since Lach.

What were those guys over there talking about? Did the guy want in? Maybe. Who was behind those doors? Manzani, that was pretty much guaranteed, but who else? Bryan? Could be someone back there wanted to talk, wanted to reveal enough to tantalize her with the next clue.

A tremor of pleasure moved her hips, flipping her stomach too. Shit, her hormones didn't know this was just an act. Pretend. They were playing a game so she could get a better angle for... Was that his cock?

Pushing back harder, she hooked her spike heels on the edge of the bed, rising to get right up close, right up to that... Oh, shit, it was, he was hard. Incredibly hard and incredibly huge. Mmm... A groan of... something, shook all of her as it left her lips.

Don't forget they were being watched. Voyeurism had never been her thing. She didn't think... had she tried it? Not something that presented itself as an opportunity all the time. Their cover was important. If anyone suspected they weren't really there to take part, that could spell trouble. That was why her pelvis undulated faster, why her hands snuck around to grab the wooden frame running between Jagg's back and the wall.

"Jagg," she whimpered, doubting he heard it.

But as she got higher, her head went further onto his shoulder, opening up her collarbone, her throat. His hands slipped under fabric, squeezing, teasing, testing her limits. Oh, limits be damned.

Rolling her hips, her weight braced between her perched feet and clinging hands. Still steadying herself with one hand, the other snuck its way around between their bodies. That lump in his jeans was impressive.

Tempting. Her curiosity needed an outlet, it needed to be satisfied. Shit, yes, she had to be satisfied.

Pressing hard against him, she did her best to rub him through frustrating denim. His teeth grazed her jaw. Her mouth jumped in instant response, seeking the gratification of his eager tongue's invasion. Maybe something else could invade. Something longer, hotter, harder. Maybe it could go so much deeper, sate the hunger heating and tormenting her.

Her arm tightened around his head again as the other tried to loosen the buttons of his jeans. One of his hands left her breast. One she hoped would help her. But that wasn't its mission. Oh, fuck, it wasn't heading for the apex of his thighs. No. It was heading for the apex of hers.

Dipping under her skirt, he grabbed her leg, squeezing her hard. His strength. Solidity. Determination. Jagg didn't apologize for who he was or what he wanted. Never had. Even when her mom ranted at Ford that his friend was bad news, Ford didn't listen. Yeah, Jagger Dunn was bad news in the worst kind of bad boy way, but no woman could be blamed for giving him everything he wanted when it felt so damn good.

Dragging his hand higher, he stroked her over her panties. Stupid panties. Why had she thought they were a good idea?

Releasing just enough pressure on his mouth that her lips could move, she exhaled one word, "yes."

When she licked her lips, they were so close to his that her tongue met both. A breath passed as his fingers slipped into her panties, caressing her clit with such deliberate control, the world slowed. Man, that… the pressure. The need. Was it all her? Did she…? Should she…?

Flashing between darkness and light, their lips were still in touch when her blind, drowsy, mesmerizing stare met his. Were they looking at each other? Were they kissing? Yes. No. Neither was right. Neither wrong. Awareness only wrought a deeper panting between their mingled breath when his fingertip dipped into her. It went further, slow, oh, so fucking slowly. Her jaw relaxed with each millimeter of his advance.

The second he got knuckle deep, her arm clenched and her mouth grabbed his, devouring the man meant to be her cover. An advance had never been more welcome. Wherever they were, whatever was… How was he doing that? Finger fucking her and massaging her clit at the same time? She didn't care. The man worked with his hands for a living, obviously he was good at it. Damn. Shit… Uh…

Her kiss paused. Her whole body froze. Every muscle tightened; every nerve pounced closer to the surface of her enlivened skin. Oh, shit, she was… Her attention on him lagged. Neglecting him would be bad form if he wasn't the reason she…

A yelp of climax jumped from her mouth to his. She couldn't… His head bumped hers, pushing it against his solid shoulder, giving her permission to experience every single incredible second… It kept on going and he twisted his hand, suddenly taking a different approach, swiping her clit the other way and… Oh, God, it was—

"Dunn."

Dunn? What? Who said…?

Blinking fast, she couldn't see straight as she lifted her head. There was a guy there. Two actually. Standing right there.

"What?" Jagg snapped, out of breath. "What the fuck do you want?"

"He wants you," the guy said, eyeing her chest.

"Does it look like I give a fuck?"

"Looks like she's about to get one," the guy behind said.

"Boss gets what he wants. You know he does."

"Shit," Jagg exhaled.

"Leave her here for us. We'll finish her for you."

"Yeah, right," Jagg said, raising a knee to boost her onto her feet. "She stays with me."

FIVE

WOBBLING IN THE unexpected upright position, it was Jagg standing to flop his arm over her again that kept her balanced.

"My purse."

She managed to think straight long enough for Jagg to hand it over, somehow without taking his arm from her.

As she looped the wrist strap around her hand, they walked, winding through people and tables and… other stuff.

Looked like they were getting through those doors after all. Someone had to be watching out for her… Wait, no, she didn't want anyone watching what she'd just been doing with Jagg. Especially not a higher cosmic power.

The guys stayed close, leading the way. Seeing between them was difficult. Jagg could see right over the top of them. If only she were so tall. She could just climb up on him, not like anyone around there would care.

Adrenaline and anticipation merged with endorphins… and the couple of tequila shots she'd taken at home earlier. Her fingers threaded between Jagg's. For grounding, her other hand clasped that connection tight. As the security guy opened one door for them, she sucked in a deep breath.

Time to work.

Stark darkness in the space wasn't lit the same as the main room. Yellow dusky spotlights illuminated a raised bed to one side. They were led forward to a desk and the guy perched on the front of it.

"Fuck me," he said. "Jagger Dunn."

Evander "Vex" Manzani. She'd never met him, but everyone knew his face. From pictures in newspapers, online, and in cop files she may have seen lying around Lach's apartment once in a while.

"Manzani," Jagg said in response.

There were others around. On couches to the right, some next to the bed occupied by those entertaining the mobster. The music was much quieter there, so they weren't spared the grunts and moans of overt passion.

"I almost didn't believe it," Vex said, standing up. "You want a cut?"

"I'm not back."

"Sure, you are. And thank fuck, none of these bastards know discipline. Thirty percent of opening night. Twenty after."

"No."

"'Kay. Forty-thirty, but that's as high—"

"Vex—"

"What about her?" Vex asked, checking her out. "Private or community?"

"Private," Jagg said. "No one touches her."

"Ah..." Vex said, sauntering closer, sharpening his scrutiny. "Got a woman to support. Course you need the work. If she belongs to you, she'll get our fullest protection." His smile was too sly, too sinister to reassure her. "Welcome to the family, sweetheart, you are a beauty."

"Thank you," she said only to be jolted when Jagg yanked her harder against him.

Vex laughed. "Discipline a problem in your house, Jagg? Never struck me as the pussy bitch type."

"We're getting the fuck outta here."

Jagg pulled her back but Vex raised a hand and a bunch of guys closed in around them.

"Night's just getting started," Vex said. "Got a live one, if you're interested."

When he nodded to something behind them, she tried to see what Jagg twisted to look at, but he jerked her back before she could get a good view.

His hanging hand rose from in front of her to grip her shoulder, so his arm was hooked around her neck.

"Not interested."

"Then I've gotta wonder…" Vex strolled around his desk. "What would Jagg Dunn be doing in my place if it isn't to work?"

"Didn't know I was unwelcome."

"You're always welcome, but after the way we left things…" He sank into his chair, lounging as he examined the couple. "You want to make amends?"

Shit. What had she got him into? Her brother and Jagg ran with the Manzanis and other unsavory characters for a long time. They'd been free of that for years… her brother had. And she didn't know how they got out.

Vex Manzani didn't appear to be the kind of guy who'd give up on what he wanted.

"I want to take my girl home."

"Hmm," Vex said, examining her again. "What do you like, sweetheart? Danger? Violence?" She didn't know how to answer. "You like it rough?"

"Watch it," Jagg snarled.

This wasn't good. Those who'd been occupied were over the orgy and fixed on the unfolding drama at the desk. Faces. People. Anyone she knew? Anyone she was looking for? It was difficult to focus while under such unwelcome scrutiny. Doing her best to absorb the features male and female of those in Vex Manzani's inner circle, this pressure couldn't be for naught. She had to make it count, make this encounter worthwhile.

"You were never good at sharing, Jagg," Vex muttered. "Weren't good at commitment either… What's special about her?"

"I wanted to try it," she said, grabbing for a believable lie. "Watching… being watched."

"And now she's over it," Jagg said, strengthening his arm. "We're done." They turned toward the exit, but the loitering thugs hadn't let-up. "You looking for a show, Manzani?"

"Always," he said. "The woman's like one hand tied behind your back… Could be interesting." She couldn't see Jagg's face. Whatever passed between the men, Manzani relented and waved at his posse. "Don't leave it so long next time, Jagg…" They were already heading for the door. "Come back and visit us any time, sweetheart!"

They departed and crossed the main floor so fast, she didn't have time to process. Different goons guarded the door. Not that it mattered. They didn't linger there either. Jagg took them across the street and around the corner. Lights flashed on a car, then he was pushing her into the passenger side and jumping in the other one himself.

"I don't know your address."

Right. Pulling her focus, she took a deep breath and corrected her posture in the seat. "Just keep going straight. What was that about?"

"What about?"

"With you and Manzani."

"Nothing. Unfinished business."

"You could've finished it," she said.

"Like he said, I was at a disadvantage."

Because of her. "Thank you for coming. I mean, I didn't get what I was looking for, but…"

"What were you looking for?" he asked. "Going in there alone was crazy."

"I didn't know it was a sex club. How could I have known that?"

"If you don't know, you shouldn't go."

"It's not as easy as that."

"Do you know what could've happened to you in there? How much trouble you could've gotten into?"

"With the cops?"

His eyes cut her way. "With Manzani. He's a sick fuck."

"I believe you," she said, tucking her skirt around her thighs. "Take a left… I didn't go there looking for Manzani."

"You sure?" he asked as they turned. "'Cause you were damn interested in his security."

"Why did you come? Why would Ford send—"

"You think your brother sent me to…? I heard you two talking and can spot a liar easier than Ford; when it comes to his kid sister anyway. I've known both of you a long time. Maybe you weren't paying attention. I was. Ford always thinks the best of you."

"So you thought you'd do the opposite?"

He glanced her way again. "I was right, wasn't I?"

Okay, he won that round. "Did you tell him you were coming?"

"If I told him I even thought about it, he'd gut me…" On a gruff exhale, he dropped his wrist to the top of the wheel. "I'm going to hell."

"Think we already knew that anyway," she said, raising a shoulder in a half shrug. When he looked at her again, she smiled. It was a joke, geez, the guy didn't have to take everything so seriously. "I appreciate what you did tonight. Looking out for me… getting us out of there."

"You wouldn't have been near Manzani if it wasn't for me," he said. "Been a long time since we stood eye to eye."

"How long?"

"Long time," he said. So specific. And so frustrating. Time was absolute. Straight questions should get straight answers. Though he wasn't the story, it wasn't her right to pry. "Your brother was right, by the way, writing about the Manzanis will get you killed."

"Obviously, you don't pay that much attention because I told Ford I'm not writing about Manzani… I don't think so anyway. Just up here…" She pointed at her stoop. "With the red door." He pulled over and put them in park. "Thank you again, Jagg."

"Want me to walk you up?" he asked as she reached for the handle. His eyes closed. "What the hell is wrong with me?"

She laughed and grabbed for the shoulder of his chair to boost herself over to kiss his cheek. "Cut yourself some slack, Jagg." Her smile grew as she sat down and reached for the handle again. "I'm hot, baby."

Slinking out of the car, she didn't look back while running up the stairs and unlocking her door. The car didn't move. As she slipped through the door, she peeked over her shoulder just as he upped the revs a few times. Funny. Who knew Jagger Dunn was funny? Maybe there was hope for him yet.

SIX

OKAY, SO HUSTLE hadn't worked out, but she wasn't ready to give up. There were other avenues to explore.

Women were dying. That wasn't something she planned to forget. Thankfully, there hadn't been any new homicides reported to the office that morning. The Chronicler got a daily bulletin from law enforcement. That day's report contained nothing of interest to her investigation. Steadfast in her pursuit, she'd meet Lachlan later to see if there were any updates.

That would come after her trip to the most recently deceased woman's apartment. Her roommate, Mila, had been the one to give up Hustle as a location for Stephanie's boyfriend. Hustle was keeping its secrets for the moment. If she couldn't talk to Mila again, the club may make it back onto the to-do list.

No one answered the buzzer. She didn't have to wait too long for the door to open as someone exited. The trick was to appear like she belonged there. Most things could be bluffed if you exuded confidence… Something she'd learned from her father.

Jogging up the stairs, her eagerness fueled her desire to know. It wasn't just the mystery. Yeah, those always bothered her, but these women deserved more attention than they were getting.

Mila had just lost her best friend. It was understandable that she didn't want to answer the door to anyone. She expected to go up and knock, to call through the door and appeal to the woman she'd got along with so well.

As she approached the apartment, it became obvious it wasn't going to play out that way. First came a spike of concern, the door hung open a couple of inches. She considered calling the cops. Intrigue took her closer. Her fingertips drifted across the wood, heading for the handle. Before they got there, the door opened.

She gasped.

A tall, glaring man stood on the other side, trash bag in hand. "What do you want?" She blinked at his bark. "You gonna pay the rent?"

"Am I... what?"

"You know her? You a friend?"

"Of Mila's?"

"Yeah," he said, crowding her out of the doorway. "Know where she is?"

Panic hit hard. "She's missing?"

The guy gave the door a shove, opening up the view of inside. "Bitch ran out on her rent." It was empty of furniture. Possessions. Everything was gone. "The first went and died, then the other one bails on me."

"Stephanie didn't mean to die," she said, though there wasn't any evidence to prove that either way... so far. "It's a traumatic time for Mila. She won't be thinking straight."

"Yeah, she's running out on everyone."

Everyone? He'd headed down the hallway, so she scurried after him. "Everyone?"

"You, me, the boyfriend that came around this morning."

Mila didn't have a boyfriend. That had come up in their first conversation. About her lack of support, and her fears over what Stephanie went through coming back to bite her.

"He didn't happen to leave a card or a name or… anything?"

"Wasn't the kind of guy who carried cards," he said as they descended the stairs. "Didn't ask either. Mean looking fucker. I wasn't getting into it with him. Asked him for rent though…" He paused on the landing, peering down his nose at her. "He gave me a hundred and asked the same questions."

Widening her smile, she recognized the shakedown. "And you gave me the information for free. Thank you."

"Wanna know what he looked like?"

Yes, she did. Damnit. Satisfaction crept onto his expression.

She opened her purse and offered him a fifty. He took it but kept his hand open until she slapped another one on top.

"Spill," she said, shoving his hand toward him.

"Had a tattoo on his neck. A snake with like a Chinese thing."

That didn't help. "A Chinese thing?"

"A dragon or something. I don't know."

Distinguishing. Interesting. Had she seen anyone at the club with a snake-dragon tattoo? Not that she remembered, but it was dark, and she'd been distracted. In Mila's picture of Stephanie's boyfriend, there hadn't been a tattoo like that… had there?

"Anything else?" she asked before realizing the guy had started down the stairs again.

"Yeah," he called back to her. "Next time come back with rent…" He paused at the top of the next flight down to the basement. "Or pussy."

Her smile was tight, but she kept descending, one slow step at a time. "My boyfriend carries a badge… and a gun… sure you want to proposition me?"

Ex-boyfriend, but whatever. That was splitting hairs.

He shrugged and continued. "Never hurts to ask."

"No," she muttered, pausing on the first floor, the light from the entrance flooding the foyer. "It never does."

Snake-dragon tattoo. How could she find him? If she couldn't find Stephanie's boyfriend, she had to find this Snake Guy. Still pondering, she went out the front door and paused on the street to look around. She needed eyes… into the past.

A camera on the store opposite provoked another smile. Undoing a button over her cleavage, she pulled her shirt down a little. She just needed a quick look, so she'd offer another in return.

SEVEN

"I DON'T KNOW HIM."

Sitting at the bar next to Lachlan, she was showing him the still picture of Snake Guy she'd got from the store camera.

"Are you sure?" she asked, lifting the phone closer to his face. "Doesn't feel like you're looking at it."

"I'm looking at it, babe. I don't know him."

She exhaled and scrolled back a few pictures. "Do you recognize this tattoo?"

The same one all the deceased women had.

"Where'd you get that?" he asked, taking her hand to angle the phone.

"From a guy I know."

His attention went from the phone to side-eye her. "I told you to stop using my name at the precinct."

"I don't need to use your name," she said, inspecting the tattoo picture. "They know me."

"And they give you information because they think I've sanctioned what you're doing," he said. "Which I haven't, by the way, I don't."

She put down the phone and picked up her drink. "You made that clear… many, many times… Did you ask for the case?"

"I've got enough on my plate," he said. "You wouldn't be any easier to deal with if it was my case. If any of them were my case. And I'm vice. Not homicide."

"It's just one case."

"There are three dead women," he said. "Three cases."

"They're linked."

"So you keep saying," he said, tipping beer into his mouth. "Show me proof."

Frustration was grating. "Which is what you keep saying," she said. "Trust me, they're linked. I don't know how you can—"

"The MO's different," he said, putting down his beer to count on his fingers. "Location of the bodies, different. State of the bodies, different. Cause of death, different."

"Manner of death, the same." Murder. "And they all have the tattoo," she said, pushing her phone toward him.

"Doesn't mean anything."

"Why not?" The way he sealed his lips piqued her interest. "Why doesn't it mean anything?"

He returned to his drink. "Just trust me. It doesn't."

"You won't trust me, but I should trust you?"

"There are things I know that I can't share with you," he said. "You know that."

Yeah, because being on the outside had been a sticking point in their relationship.

Persistence was the only route to potential victory.

"They're the same age," she said.

"Roughly."

"From similar backgrounds."

"Approximately."

"None of them had debts or vices."

"That you know about."

"This is suspicious. There's enough similarity to consider a connection," she said. "Tell me I'm wrong."

"You're wrong," he said, his lips curling around his bottle as he drank. She just sneered at him, which earned her a laugh. "Okay, look, I don't know. Maybe they are connected."

Hope. Finally! "You think?"

"No," he said with a single head shake, then leaned in to kiss her temple. "Work the only reason you wanted to meet tonight?" She shrugged, propping a hand under her chin to hold up her head. He sighed. "You want me to get into it?" Dubious, she wouldn't be fooled a second time. Was he serious or not? "I can ask some questions. No promises."

Grinning, she threw both arms around him. "Thank you."

"No promises. I still don't think they're linked."

"I know," she said, reassured that someone was listening. Lachlan was a good start. "I don't want promises. I want evidence, just like you. Next drink's on me."

She gestured the bartender over to ask for another round.

"You talk to your dad yet?" Lachlan asked when the guy walked away.

Well, if that wasn't just a mood killer. "I changed my mind about the drink."

"He can't change who he is, babe."

"And I can't change who I am," she said.

"You love your dad."

"So? That doesn't mean he gets to make my choices or run my life."

"He's looking out for you. It's what he's supposed to do."

"No, he's supposed to love me no matter what," she said. "Ford's getting worse at it too. What is it with the men in my life that they think they can dictate every detail of my existence?" His head twitched in response to the accusation. Uh huh, let the truth be free. "You did it too, don't deny it."

"I don't want to dictate anything to you, Im. I'd say they don't either. They care about you. I care about you. We want to look after you. Unfortunately, you're blessed to be surrounded by men who prefer you safe and healthy; better than no one giving a shit."

"I can be safe and healthy and do my job. It's everything, everywhere, all the time… All of you forget that Kurt Stratford is my father, just the same as he's Ford's."

"Ford's…" What was that? Why did he trail off? Twisting around, she set a questioning glare on him. "Your brother is bigger than you." So not where he'd been going. "He can take care of himself and spars with Jagger for fun. That guy's undefeated. He's never gone down. Not once."

"And that would be really relevant if I had any intention of ever fighting anyone."

"You don't have to go looking for it," he said and scoffed. "'Cept you are with this case. Be careful; you don't know what thread you're pulling on. Maybe it leads somewhere you can't get out of. Somewhere dangerous."

"Or it leads to justice."

"Say you're right, say the three cases are connected. Let's say dragon guy's our perp."

"Okay."

"You think he'll be happy you're asking questions? You think he'll want to answer them?"

"Maybe I don't have to talk to him. Maybe I just have to know where he hangs out, who he associates with. You should know, sometimes bearing witness is enough. If the opportunity comes up, and it's safe, yeah, I might talk to him. Right now, I'm just looking around..." She widened her eyes. "With my eyes... not my mouth."

"Okay, remember that. And call me when you get into trouble."

"When?"

He smiled and swung his bottle toward his lips. "Yep. When."

EIGHT

TROUBLE.

If there was one person who'd know about trouble…

The next day, she delayed her visit to Jagg's until after lunch. Her brother would be in a better mood with a full stomach. That and Steeple held her up with questions and warnings. Her updates weren't exactly enlightening. Filling out her answers wasn't easy while also trawling previous crimes and the internet for talk of a guy with a snake-dragon tattoo.

Jagg's Autos didn't usually land on her itinerary. Not this often. It just so happened the information she needed might be available there.

Going around back, she didn't expect anyone to be working on a Sunday. The floor was clear of cars, but there was light in one of the three spray booths at the back. Walking up the ramp to the window just as whoever was inside stood straight, she tapped on the door, getting their attention.

Jagg took the mask from his mouth, leaving it hanging around his neck as he backed up and flicked a switch on the wall. The doors opened wide, presenting the opportunity to make an entrance.

"Ford's at your dad's."

"Okay," she said, admiring the red and black over blue design on the car. "Looks good... Vinyl?" Bullseye. The flash of offense on his face told her she'd hit her mark. She laughed and touched his arm. "I'm kidding... You're an artist. I know. It looks amazing. Why are you working on a Sunday?"

"What else would I be doing?" he asked, cleaning up. "Need a ride to your dad's?"

She restrained a groan. Just barely. "You trying to fix us up too? Ford, Lachlan, and now you. Is there something in the guy code about fathers and daughters that I missed?"

"I figured you wanted to see your brother."

"Oh... right." Duh. Not an inaccurate assumption. She brought her purse around on her shoulder to dig inside. "Good guess, but you'll do."

"I'm flattered," he said, deadpan.

Bringing up her photos app, she found the one of Snake Guy. "Do you know this guy?" she asked, turning the phone.

His expression didn't change at all, not even the tiniest flicker. "No."

He went to a bench at the side to get a bottle of water. Hmm, did she believe him? He'd turned away fast, gone to do something else, a physical replacement for a subject change.

"I think you do."

"You're still on this Manzani thing?" he said. "It's dangerous."

Opening her arms, she gestured to the room. "So is huffing paint."

He pointed at the mask. "I wear protection."

"I carry protection," she said, going closer. "I have a cellphone and a rape alarm."

"Neither of which will help if you need it," he said. "If you end up on Vex's radar—"

"I don't plan to end up on his radar."

"You are on his radar. Remember the other night? Did you forget what I said about knockouts like you?"

She shook her head, dropping her phone back into her purse. "Did you forget he said I have Manzani protection?"

"As my girl. You get their protection because anyone who messes with you has me to answer to."

She smiled. "There we go. Problem solved. Thank you for your kindness."

He wasn't moved. "I don't do private security anymore."

Since he'd sort of brought it up, she had to ask, "Is it true you're undefeated?"

He frowned. "Who you been talking to?"

"Are you sensitive about it?" she asked, reaching for the hip pocket on his coveralls. His hand jumped to snatch hers before it got there, startling her eyes to his. "You are."

Why was he so... tense?

"It's a past life," he said. "Ancient history."

"Okay." She chose not to push. Although... "Are you seeing anyone?"

Immediately, he dropped her hand. "Why?"

She shrugged. "A guy like you can't have many opportunities to get your thoughts and feelings out. If my brother is your only outlet, I'm surprised you haven't gone crazy already. If you're not seeing anyone and ever want to talk..."

His muscles loosened. Just a little. "Only if I'm not seeing anyone?"

"I don't think a girlfriend would like me butting into your business."

"You do have a habit of butting in," he said, holding the line for a second before one corner of his mouth ascended. "I don't need to talk, Genny. Neither do you. You need to stop talking to people… especially people connected to Vex Manzani."

He left her to head over to the back of the booth, still dealing with his tools.

She was getting sick of hearing that. "You might get your wish. I'm hitting dead end after dead end. Lachlan's on it now though, so either he comes through for me or I have to go sleep with a slimy landlord."

He whipped around so fast she recoiled. "Someone's pressuring you? Why didn't you call Ford?"

"I don't call my brother every time a slimeball sleazes on me, geez. Besides, I'm not an easy woman to pressure," she said, righting the strap of her purse. "I'm not that desperate yet and the slime was useful… I also told him I was dating a cop. That's always a useful nugget…"

"Thought you and the cop were done."

"We are."

"But you still have sex with him?"

"No," she said, drawing out the word as she started a slow progression his way. "Why do you care who I'm having sex with?"

"I don't," he said, tossing some metal thing onto a box of tools.

"Kinda sounds like you do," she said, successful this time when she reached for his pocket. Tracing the line of stitching, her finger slunk to the zipper on his coveralls low on his abdomen. "You didn't answer my question about your current status."

"No, I didn't," he said, taking a deliberate step back. "Because this isn't on the table."

"Who said that?" she asked. "Did you talk to Ford about us at Hustle?"

"We're never talking about that again. That was the deal."

"Okay," she said. "Whatever makes you happy."

"You're my best friend's kid sister."

"Okay," she said, offering a smile. "I'll get going. Got hunting to do."

He nodded, so she spun around to head out. Aware of every hair on her body, she chilled while heating from the inside. The movement of her shoulder accentuated the figure he couldn't see. But it wasn't just her chest, her hips flirted with each step she took. Every inch of her tingled with zipping anticipation. Her body wanted something it hadn't been promised. One taste and, apparently, her pussy was hooked.

He wasn't even touching her, yet every part of her felt him… maybe that was wishful thinking.

Pausing on the threshold of the booth, it hit her just how open she was to the idea of Jagg. Of her and Jagg. Like more than open to it, she was—

"Keep walking, Genny."

Her smile grew. That edge in his voice. That rough rumble… She wasn't the only one open to it. Maybe it would never happen. Maybe he'd never figure out how open to it he was. Still, it was nice to know she wasn't the only one still thinking about Hustle.

NINE

MORE THAN JUST thinking about it, she dressed and got herself back to Hustle's location. Almost to the location. She got the cab driver to drop her off a block early. That way she could walk by, try to get a better look at those waiting outside.

The doormen had said security hung around at the side of the building. Jagg had recognized Snake Guy. He had. Without a doubt. Lachlan hadn't recognized him. If Snake Guy hadn't crossed Lachlan's radar, but had crossed Jagg's, it stood to reason the latter ran in the same circles. At some point.

Jagg had also gone straight to Manzani after seeing the picture. Hustle was key. The next piece of the puzzle was in there... or at least connected to it. If she could just get at it, then she could progress to wherever it led.

"Hey, baby!" a guy shouted from the club the moment she came into view. Men shouted. Especially drunk ones, late at night. But this wasn't a drunk guy, it was one of the doormen. "Your date beat you to it tonight."

"Excuse me?"

"Dunn's girl, right?" he asked, unhooking the chain as she approached.

Disguising her surprise wasn't easy. "He's inside?"

"Has been a while. Hope you're not the jealous type."

Oh, God. What would she walk into? The guy expected her to go inside. If Jagg was there, how could she not? If he was with someone, she'd never find him. Even if she did, what was she supposed to do? Tap him on the shoulder? Stand and wait patiently until he finished?

The dark area between the entrance doors was like an airlock. The doors in front only opened after the ones behind closed. Stopped prying eyes outside seeing the truth of what went on in the exclusive space.

The lights, the action, the music, it was all just like two nights ago. Except she was alone and didn't know where to look. Would he be where they'd been the last time? Figuring that was a good place to start, she didn't get more than a step before he caught her eye. Sitting at the bar. The only person there not watching the action going on around them. The only one wearing a dirty scowl.

Going over there, she tightened the wrist strap of her purse and slipped in front of him, into the wide vee of his thighs, winding her arms around his neck.

"Am I in trouble?" she asked, appreciating how the stool brought him closer to her level.

Her lips were almost on his. When his hands skimmed from her waist to her ass, she closed the last of the space between them and gave into the kiss she'd craved earlier in the day.

The heat of his rock-solid body would be a comfort wherever they were. There, surrounded by all Hustle offered, it meant more than physical reassurance. The fact he'd waited for her, that he wasn't overcome by his animal urges or pounced upon by a pack of eager women, was a miracle.

Kissing him was a treat she hadn't expected. The power in his tongue betrayed either desire or anger. Was he mad at her for coming back? How had he known…? Or had he opened himself like she had that afternoon?

He tipped his head back, taking his mouth from hers. "You lied to me."

"I did not," she said, pushing deeper against him. Was he hard? She had to know. Like had to. The compulsion was crazy. It shouldn't be important, but she wanted to know if that kiss was as good for him as it had been for her. "I didn't say I wouldn't come here."

"You can't come here, baby," he said, stroking and squeezing her ass. "It's dangerous and now they know you're connected to me."

What was he worried about? That some old enemy would use her against him? They couldn't do that. Her editor checked in regularly. If she got in trouble, he'd notice fast. Then there was Ford. No one would want to be in her brother's crosshairs.

"This is important."

"Not this important," he said. "I need you to listen to me on this. If anything happened to you and your brother found out I knew you were into this… that they'd put us together."

"So put word out we're over."

"That's worse," he said. "At least now you have some level of protection. Take me out of your equation, it'll be carnage."

"I don't understand what you want me to do," she said, putting her hands on his shoulders to push out of his arms. "You want me to give up?"

"It's a story. Not one worth your life."

"It's taken the lives of at least three women so far. They're someone's sister, child, friend, too. They're people. How many more will die if someone doesn't do something about it?"

Glancing left to right, his scrutiny was wary. "We can't talk about this here."

Planting her hands on the bar, she got the attention of a bartender. "No one cares what we're talking about."

When the bartender reached her, Jagg's hand slid across her stomach as he stood up. "She's good."

Pissed, her ire flashed on him. "You dictating what I put in my body now?"

He ducked lower. "You wanna talk it out? We'll talk it out. We can't do it here."

She hadn't expected that. Was he really interested or just trying to get her out of there? Could go either way. But if he knew Snake Guy, he might be the next piece in her puzzle. That was a chance she couldn't pass up.

Interlinking her fingers with his, she gave him the benefit of the doubt.

TEN

HE DROVE THEM to an all-night diner by the river. In a shitty corner of town. It wasn't a surprise he knew it existed. It was a surprise she'd never been there.

Dump-diners were a specialty of her father's. Often childhood visitation meant touring the city for rhubarb pie and vanilla milkshakes. Maybe the eateries weren't the most hygienic, but her dad knew the best spots. That's what those visits were: pie and shakes. And laughter. He'd always been able to make her laugh. Damn, why was she thinking about that?

"Coffee," Jagg said to the waitress, who came over as they slid into opposite sides of a booth in the darkest corner, far from the window. "Want anything, kid?"

"Coffee's good," she said, offering the woman a smile.

Couldn't be easy to keep the faith if life meant coming to this place every night, spending hours on your feet, serving society's less-than-finest.

Jagg plucked the menu from its slot at the end of the table. "Want something to eat?"

"You don't have to babysit me," she said. "We've left Hustle. It's done. Okay? You did your duty, you got me out of there." Way sooner than she'd wanted to be done. "Good job."

"This means something to you," he said, tucking the menu back into its slot. "Why?"

"Why not?"

The server came over with two cups, filled them from her pot, and disappeared again.

"What's special about these women or this story?"

"Everything," she said, hooking her cup closer to her body. Letting out some optimism, it wasn't easy to be the only one giving a shit all the time. "Did you finish that car?"

"You don't want to talk about the car," he said. "Tell me about the women."

For a second there it sounded like…

Suspicious, she met his eye. "Why?"

"This means something to you," he stated again. "I'm serious, Genny, talk to me."

"I…" He was asking. Actually asking. Sitting up straighter, she pushed the coffee aside. "It started almost two months ago. For me. Every day we get bulletins from the districts. Updates. Usually nothing exciting, one thing or another. I write for a local section, so I can investigate whatever I want providing it's…"

"Local."

"Right," she said, breathing out a smile. Crime and murder weren't her typical field. "Michelle Cadlow was found… by the river… She didn't have defensive wounds, but there were suspicious marks on her body… They couldn't tell how long she'd been in the water… But she has this tattoo…" Retrieving her phone from her purse, she found the picture and pushed it across the table to show him. "They all have the tattoo. The cops say it means nothing—"

"It doesn't," he said, sitting back, drinking his coffee.

She deflated. "Lachlan says it like that too. How can you possibly know—"

"It's the Manzani mark," he said. "All their girls have that tattoo."

At least he explained it. "All of them?"

"Manzanis mark women as property. Once they're on the books, they're in for life." The Manzani family didn't have books for the women who worked for them, not literally, but she got his meaning. "It on the front of their leg? On the seam where the thigh meets the torso?" She nodded. "Yeah, they're working girls."

"But they're not," she said, infused with certainty. "These women are good girls. They're respectable. From good families. With good jobs. Great prospects. None have substance or addiction issues. Their friends and family reported no erratic behavior. No indications they were mixed up in anything suspect."

"How'd you get to Hustle?"

"The last victim…" she said, "she told her roommate that her boyfriend could get them into this exclusive club. They didn't know anything about it. I didn't know anything about it."

"She used Vex's name?"

Why in the hell would he ask that question? "I thought you quit working for him."

"I did."

"Then why are you talking to me like that? Like you'll run back to him with whatever I say."

"I don't give a shit about Manzani, except he's dangerous," he said, resting his elbows on the table to lean closer. "This contact of yours needs to be careful."

"And I would tell her that if she hadn't disappeared." Saying it out loud struck a chord of fear. "Oh, God, you don't think something happened to her too, do you? That's how it happens. They disappear, for a couple of days or a couple of weeks, then reappear dead."

"Cause of death?"

"Never the same. Heather bled out. I don't know how. Lachlan said I didn't want to know. Michelle was blunt force trauma. Stephanie, they haven't released that yet... and Lach hasn't told me, which suggests it's something really bad."

"He just gives you this information?"

On a glare, her head dropped to the side. "I sucked the guy's cock for three years, Jagg, so, yes, he just gives me the information."

His semi-shrug was maybe supposed to be an apology. "Figured there were rules about that shit."

Her smile quickly became a laugh. "And you're all about following the rules."

"Wasn't passing judgment on the guy, just saying, some crims aren't all bad, and some cops ain't all good."

"He's good," she said, scooping up her cup. "In all the ways that matter... Lach's probably the most honorable man I've ever known."

"Not much of a line for that medal, Genny. Your dad and Ford were breaking rules before you were born... And the asshole your mom married..."

"He's not an asshole. Is that what Ford says?"

"The dude made Ford wear a tie to dinner at Christmas."

The memory switched her mood. "Yeah, that was funny," she said and laughed. "I have never seen him so mad... in a situation that didn't end in bloodshed."

"I was in the car on speed dial. We were ready to take on him, his preppy son, and their posse."

Sometimes her brother went looking for a fight. Jagger was always there, no questions asked. Their friendship was more like blood brothers than buddies.

"Ted doesn't have a posse. I can't believe he took you away from your holiday. That's so rude!"

Sinking down on the bench, he laid his forearms on either side of the coffee cup. "Not much of a holiday person."

He was right. It wasn't good to admit it, but fuck, he'd been right. "Have I not been paying attention?" The question was so genuine, it seemed to startle him. "You said 'maybe you weren't paying attention' the night you took me home."

"I was just talking, kid."

"I haven't been a kid for a long time, Jagg," she said, folding her arms under her breasts before leaning across the table, plumping them for his visual consumption. "I grew up."

"I see that," he said, admiring her cleavage just as she'd intended.

Sinking back, she supported her head on a hand. "You know I'm twenty-seven now. I've been legal for ten years."

"Okay," he said, scrubbing a hand across his forehead. "We're not talking about this."

"I don't know why it makes you uncomfortable. Why is it suddenly such a big deal? I have sex. I like sex. I'm good at it too… certain things. I have boobs and a pussy and—"

"Im," he said, opening a hand. "Don't."

"Okay," she said on a sigh. "I just don't get it."

"You're Ford's kid sister." Something she'd been her whole life. "You're my best friend's sister and… this isn't on the table."

Except her body tingled again. A specific part of her body. A very specific part.

"We've never done this," she said, her eyes slinking left and right. "Hung out alone and talked like this. Shit, you've been inside me and we—"

"Hands don't count." When they both looked at his on the table, he was quick to drop them to the bench at his sides. "They don't."

"Hmm," she said, slipping her foot from her shoe as she slid lower in her seat to run her toe up the inside of his leg, past his knee, to his thigh and on. "What about feet?"

He caught her foot and held it tight without pushing away or recoiling.

Though he did cover his eyes, supporting the weight of his head. "Why the fuck is this happening now? Last week you were Immie. I'd have gone to war for you 'cause you're my buddy's family…"

"And this week?" she asked. "You wouldn't go to war for me?"

He peeked over the edge of his hand. The darkness in those eyes. The mystery wasn't in the details. It wasn't in his unknown past or the question marks over his character. Those would apply with a stranger. This man wasn't a stranger.

"Genny…"

"I always knew you were attractive, that's obvious, but…"

"Yeah," he said, letting his arm drop. "Not like I never heard guys talk about you… or beat on some of them with Ford."

"You beat on guys for me?"

"Just the disrespectful ones."

Was that adorable or hilarious? Both.

"You never struck me as the kind of guy who'd stand up for a woman's honor," she said, bobbing her head in a side-to-side nod. "No, you did… But you also seem like the kind of guy who knows how to enjoy a woman."

"Yeah. There are available women and then there are…" He drew an invisible line with the side of his hand and pushed it back. "Off-limits women." He gestured at her. "Which you are. Off-limits."

"Is that what it is? I'm forbidden fruit?"

"If that's what it was, I'd have wanted you like this ten years ago."

And there it was. Out there. He wanted her. Relaxing, she let herself look into him. Let herself be tempted by his dark demons and shadowy past. He was more than any man she'd known. More complex. More broken. More forbidden.

"You know, you'd be doing Ford a favor if you dated me."

Sensing her joke, his jaw rose. "Oh, yeah, how's that?"

"He's never liked any of my boyfriends. Never one."

"Some of them he's liked right up until the moment they became your boyfriend. You never noticed that?"

Her hair fluttered around her upper arms when she shook her head. "Nope. He'll like one of them one day."

"Always were a dreamer," he said. "Always an optimist."

"Wasn't always easy," she said. "A part of me got left behind when we left the city. When Mom met Ted and… Everything I knew was here, it was my home. Ford was my home. His routine. His strength. His presence. His buddies… Sometimes I think…"

Maybe it wasn't the time to get deep. Not the first time her thoughts got ahead of her mouth.

"Sometimes you think what?"

Well, he was asking.

She smiled and surrendered. "It hurt more losing him than it did losing my dad… I was always sort of invisible to Strat," which was what people called her father. "I was his princess. His angel. Yeah, but that was like this ethereal thing. Intangible. It wasn't real. It wasn't me. He stood up for his little girl because that's what men like him do."

"Strat loves you like you wouldn't believe."

"I know," she said because she didn't doubt that. "But it was Ford's bed I crawled into when I got scared at night." His placating smile gave her a shake. What the hell was she doing sitting there going on about her childhood? "Shit, I'm sorry."

"It's okay."

Taking her foot from his lap, she sat up straight. "You were nice to me and I… Thanks for letting me ramble…" She shifted to the end of the bench. "I'll get a cab."

He reached over to catch her wrist before she could fully stand up. "No, you won't." She didn't get it, but relaxed back down when he gave her a tug. "You haven't told me about the case yet. Tell me everything you know."

"Why? Why do you care?"

"Because I've asked you not to do it. Ford's asked you not to do it. Probably the cop too, and you're still on it. When Genny Stratford gets the bit between her teeth, she doesn't let go. One of my many observations."

She smiled. "There are others?"

"Oh, yeah."

"Like what?"

"Like when you smile because you think it's what people want to see," he said and her smile faded. "You do it all the time. With Ford. With Strat. With me. It's your shield. You're so scared to be vulnerable, to show anything but strength. You don't want to let anyone down. You smile because it's what people expect and you don't want to disappoint them."

"Please," she said, picking up the coffee, using the prop as a distraction. "Haven't I already delved deep into the abyss of ridiculous childhood traumas enough for one night?"

He exhaled a laugh. "Fair enough. But you're still going to tell me about this case... and why it's so important to you."

"I've met the victims' friends. Their families. These are good people. Like we're good people, Jagg. These women are my age. They have nice families like Ted's family. They have educations. The first woman, Heather, she went to Princeton the same year I was accepted."

"Why didn't you go?" he asked. "Ford and Strat were so proud. Wouldn't shut up about it and then you didn't go. Why?"

"These women could be me, Jagg," she said, avoiding the question. As she'd said, they'd delved into the past enough for one night. "If this happened to me, would anyone care? Would they shrug me off as a working girl? Unimportant? Inconsequential? Like I'd been asking for it or got what I deserved?"

ELEVEN

"YOUR FATHER AND BROTHER would raise an army for you, Genny," Jagg said. He was the only one who ever used the end of her name as an endearment. Pronounced "*Ginny*" it was unusual without being weird. "This would never happen to you. Ford would never let it happen."

"Bet these women's families said the same thing. I bet they thought they were protected and loved… If I'm wrong, then who cares? They were random killings and the only one looking dumb is me. I'll take it. I can handle that. But if I'm right…" she got closer, "if I'm right, there's a maniac out there killing people. A serial killer, Jagg. Killing women. Right here under our noses. And he's banking on everyone being too stupid to see it. I don't want to be the sheep he expects. I am the kink in his plan. The variable he never saw coming."

Studying her, the glint of his wonder was obvious. "He's not the only one," he murmured.

"If you don't want—"

"Where were they found?" he asked, tugging a napkin from the holder. "Miss?"

Imogen glanced around because he hadn't been talking to her. "Who are you…?"

The waitress was already at the table.

"Can we borrow a pen?" Jagg asked.

The woman actually sagged in disappointment and plucked one from her apron to hand it over. Jagg was at least nice enough to wink at the server, pepping her smile.

"How does she know I'm not your girlfriend?" Imogen asked once the woman was gone.

He got busy drawing on his napkin. "Why would we be out here in the middle of the night if you were my girlfriend?"

"People go out on dates, Jagg. It happens all over."

"To a place like this? At this time? Only reason a couple comes to a place like this is if they're lost or fighting. We're obviously not fighting. If it was the first, we'd be sitting on the same side."

Would they? Wow, he viewed things from a specific angle. "I don't think people get lost anymore. Doesn't everyone have their phone all the time? They're twenty-first century security blankets."

"Okay," he said like maybe he hadn't been listening and turned the napkin toward her. "Give me an area."

"An…" There was the city laid out in front of her. Not every single street, but landmarks and enough detail that she could tell exactly what was what. "Geez, you really are an artist."

He put the pen on top. "Think you can figure it out?" She could and took the pen to ponder and mark three crosses. "Are you sure there were only three?"

Shaking her head, she pushed the napkin back to him. "There are at least five others that I considered. They could be linked, but without knowing what puts them together…"

"It's difficult to tag everyone," he said, examining her marks. "You know what's right in the middle of this…"

He connected the marks in a triangle.

"What's in the middle?" she asked, eager to hear his thoughts.

"I don't know. I'll need to check it out."

"No, tell me. You can't take me right to the… Satisfy me, Jagg."

Her pleading obviously broke through because he glanced up. "The Manzani's own an old hotel in that area. They don't use it as a hotel… or they didn't. I've been out of the game a while. Maybe they sold it. Could be anything now."

"But it could be something." Bouncing to the edge of her seat, optimism bloomed again. "Thank you. I will check it out."

"No, you won't," he said, an almost sarcastic snicker in his words. Once again, he reached over the table to curl his fingers around her wrist. "Don't run in blind, baby. What do you plan to do in a whorehouse at this time of night?" Hmm. Good point. "What do you think women do there?"

"We could go," she said, wiggling her arm to loosen his grip and join their fingers. "Together."

"You want us to go there?"

Nodding, her certainty was absolute. "That way you can watch my behind if it's going to be so dangerous and—"

"What do you think guys do at a place like that at this time? At any time?"

Huh, he'd have to… Jagg was not the type of guy who had to pay a woman for her time. Even if he was willing to humiliate himself like that for her benefit, she wouldn't want to stand by while other women fawned over him… or worse.

"How long were you in Hustle tonight before I got there?"

"Half hour maybe," he said. "Last time I waited out in the cold, praying I was wrong. This time I knew better… It's warmer inside." His gaze trailed over her upper body. "You'd probably freeze anywhere in that."

"I wasn't cold when you were holding me. Come to think of it, I've never been cold around you. Guess something about you gets me hot."

"You've gotta stop talking like that. It's funny now, then next time you forget and your brother's standing there…"

"What do you think would happen exactly? I'm flirting. It's fun. I enjoy it."

"Ford has no sense of humor when it comes to guys sleazing on you."

"I'm the one sleazing on you," she confessed. "If I take it too far, you can walk away any time."

Except he'd said the words. He wanted her. It might make sense for them to keep their distance. To ignore what had happened between them and how it had ignited a potent attraction neither of them knew existed. But in her line of work, she was often reminded that life was short.

"And if I take it too far?" He shook his head. "Shit, what I did at the club was way, way too far."

So much for not talking about it again. His rule. She didn't mind. She thought about it so often that it was nice to have someone to talk to about it.

"I gave you my consent, Jagg. I told you yes. You gave me what I wanted… More than I wanted," she said, sure her cheeks were heating, not in embarrassment, but at the memory. "I have never come so fast with a guy. Hell, I don't think I ever came so fast on my own either."

"It's not on the table."

"Okay," she said, holding her hands up in surrender, dropping against the backrest. "Way to take a compliment."

"Thank you."

"Most guys like knowing they're good in the sack."

"We weren't in the sack."

"And the difference matters in this context?" No, it didn't. "You don't want Ford to know, I get it." He picked up his coffee to drink some. "Plenty of guys are afraid of my brother."

He gulped once more, then paused and lowered the cup. "What?"

"I'm saying it's okay to be afraid of him. My brother can be a scary guy when he's mad. I'm not afraid of him myself, bu—"

"I'm not afraid of Ford."

She shrugged. "Okay."

"Why would I be afraid of him?"

"Because he's big… and strong… and, you know, doesn't like men who play with my feelings."

"I didn't play with your feelings. When the hell did feelings get into the equation?"

"You'd rather I said 'men who play with my pussy'?"

A beat passed. "Let's stick with feelings."

Her lips curled. Being there, with him… It wasn't odd or awkward, didn't feel like their first time choosing to be in each other's company. Jagg had been in her life for… as long as she could remember. He'd just always been… there.

Their time near each other usually revolved around her brother or father, or some city event or location. This was different. Just them. In the night. It felt… right.

"Is this where you bring all your women for a first date?"

"All my women? This isn't a date."

"Good, because any guy who brought me here on a first date would not get a second."

"'Cause you're a high-class chick, baby."

"The guy on the Hustle door said that too," she said. "Is that an insult? It's not like I'm dripping in diamonds."

"It's not about money. It's the way you carry yourself, Genny. With class."

Glancing down, she made a point of looking at him and at her cleavage again. "My chest is hanging out."

"Which is okay with guys. High-class or hooker. Always okay."

She laughed. "Yeah, I'm sure."

"What's wrong with this place anyway?" he asked, bobbing his chin toward the room, though his eyes stayed on her. "Prefer surf and turf?"

"No." The dark eyes, the rough voice, Jagg was a glimpse into every society. A slice of life. "Like you said, it's not about money. I just wouldn't feel comfortable here with a guy on a first date."

"Why not?"

"Chances are, I won't know him well if we're just going out," she said. "It's creepy around here. Shadowy. There's a bridge over us. I don't know the area. If a guy brought me here, it would send a message."

"What message?"

"That he wants us to be faceless, anonymous, unnoticeable," she said, and suddenly his choice of location made sense. "You're scared Ford will find out about this, us spending time together!"

"I'm not scared of your brother."

"Why didn't you take me to your place then? Jagg's is Ford's permanent address." Though sometimes he stayed with their dad or a girlfriend or wherever. "We would be safe behind your security gate."

"You feel unsafe here?"

Licking her lips, another truth tightened her chest. "I would… if you were anyone else."

"I'm not sure you're safe with me, Genny."

His arms lay on the table again, the coffee between them as he toyed with a torn corner of the napkin between them.

Sitting up, she clasped her hands over his. "I think about kissing you… way more than I should think about kissing you."

"Gen—"

"I know, it's not on the table. The last thing I'd want to do is get between you and Ford. You've been through everything together."

"Yeah. More than you know."

"In some ways, I know everything about you. In others… I don't know you at all." Something she had to remedy. Had to. So much was becoming a must around him. "Your mom died when you were a baby."

"Mm hmm," he said, freeing his hands from hers to fold the napkin.

"Your dad was violent. Drunk or sober. He beat you. Sometimes just for fun."

"I take it back, you have been paying attention."

When he dumped the napkin in his coffee, he inhaled like maybe he intended to get up.

She took his hands again before he could. "Tell me something I don't know about you, Jagg."

"I spent more of my first ten years sleeping at your place than I did my own."

Which she already knew. And that he'd basically moved in with her brother and father after she and her mom left town. Whenever Strat had visitation with her, Jagg was around, whether Ford was there or not.

"Where is he now? Your dad. Do you still see him?"

"Once in a while. He's around," Jagg said. "I hear from him less since I cut ties with… my past life."

"Bet he still comes around when he wants money." His response was a single brow raise that relaxed again just as quickly. "You deserve better than the hand you were dealt, Jagg."

He glanced up from his coffee. "My cards were just fine. I have skills that make me money. A roof over my head. Friends I can rely on. Family is a label that has nothing to do with blood."

Bending over the table, she laid her cheek on her hands, still in his. "You think it's too early for breakfast?"

"Way too early, baby," he said, though scanned in the direction of the counter. "Hungry?"

"You really want to hear everything I have about the case? Every theory? That's a lot of ground to cover."

And not just professionally. If she hadn't been paying attention before, she sure was now. Jagg was more than just her brother's best friend; he was a staple in her life. One she'd stop taking for granted.

TWELVE

"OH MY GOD. Oh my God! He does not!"

"True story," Jagg said, bobbing his head in confirmation.

Her mouth was open in outrage, yet she couldn't contain her laughter. "My brother thinks I lost my virginity with my horseback riding coach? He was like forty years old!"

Which didn't seem that old at her current age. When she was fifteen, on the other hand…

"He said you wouldn't tell him."

"Because it's none of his business! Why would I tell my brother something like that? Why would he even want to know?"

"To beat on the guy."

Spoken like that was the most natural and obvious reason in the world.

"He doesn't have to beat on every guy I get sexy with. If one of them hurts me, yes, but I have him on speed dial for that."

"You ever called your brother to take care of a guy for you?" he asked but answered his own question. "No, you haven't."

"How do you know? Maybe I have."

"Because I'm his wingman, Genny. It's my job to have his back… and provide an alibi."

"You two are ridiculous," she said as her purse vibrated against her thigh. Her phone. Who would call at that hour? When she read 'Steeple,' she answered fast. "Steep—"

"You missed the Monday briefing," he said in her ear. "Where the hell are you?"

"I missed the…" Scanning around, when did the diner get so busy? And the light from outside. They were… Was this the morning rush? "Oh my God, I'm sorry!"

"You alive?"

"Yes, I'm alive," she said, grabbing Jagg's arm to twist it around and look at his watch. Shit. She'd definitely missed the meeting. "I'll be there A-SAP. I'm sorry."

"Yeah. Yeah," Steeple said.

The line died.

"I'm sorry, Jagg," she said, sliding to the end of the booth. "I have to go. I'm super late for work. Guess it pays to be your own boss."

No one called Jagg to chase him down… though that meant no one was keeping tabs on his movements either.

Opening her purse, she pulled out some bills, but Jagg was two steps ahead. He'd put money on the table and was standing up, his hand out toward her.

"I'll give you a ride."

Cheaper and faster.

"Thank you," she said, taking his hand to hurry out into his car.

The morning rush was thinning. Late was very late. Sitting up all night in a crappy diner with an incredible man had been a welcome, if unexpected, diversion. Jagg was… She didn't know what he was… or what she was to him. They were friends, more now than they had been yesterday.

When he pulled up outside her office building, she was tugging at the neckline of her dress.

"Here," he said, reaching into a gym bag on the backseat. He produced a tee-shirt, which he offered her. "It's clean."

"I don't care," she said, putting it on, tying the end into a knot on her hip. "So long as I don't have to go into work dressed for a night of streetwalking, I appreciate it." She pulled the sleeve down one arm to expose her shoulder. Casual and obviously not her attire, but better than before. "Thanks."

"You're welcome."

His attention slunk back to the windshield. Say goodbye and walk away. Just open the door and… She grabbed his shoulder to boost over and kiss his cheek. The smart thing would've been to walk away… Sometimes the smart thing was overrated.

As his head came around, she opened her door. Better to turn her back on his reaction than be told again to cool her jets.

With one leg out, she was ready to go. Something caught her eye. Someone. In the alley by her building. Pacing, nervous, the woman clearly had something on her mind.

"What's wrong?" Jagg asked, obviously noticing her delay.

"Will you stay here a minute?" she asked, distracted by the anxious beauty. "I know I've already monopolized your—"

"I'll wait."

Had he registered what she was looking at, or was he just being a good guy? She was more interested in the unexpected visitor and got out to head over.

"Mila?" she asked when within a few feet.

"Imogen." Mila rushed over to grab her into a hug. "Oh my God, I can't believe it."

She couldn't believe what?

Returning the hug was polite and if the woman needed comfort, that was fine, but...

"What are you doing here? What's wrong?"

"I think there's another one. I think he killed someone else."

Her jaw loosened, absorbing the revelation. "Who?" Checking out Mila's crumpled clothes and wild hair, it was clear she hadn't been taking care of herself. "How long have you been here? Where are you staying?"

"Bryan called me," Mila said. "He wants to meet."

"When?"

"He said he'd email me. I don't know what to do. Do you think Vex knows? Did you tell anyone what I told you?"

Only Jagg and she didn't doubt him.

"Are you scared? Do you think he's coming for you?"

"I got a note through my door, at the apartment, after you left on Friday. It told me to leave, to get out of there. I moved that afternoon, packed what I needed and put everything else in storage." With a tight grip on her arms, she pulled her closer. "I think someone is cleaning house... I could be next."

"Okay." Imogen cupped the woman's face. "First we need to get you safe. You need food and sleep... and a shower."

"Where is safe?" Mila asked, shaking her head. "Nowhere is safe. I don't know what to… I don't know who I can trust."

"You can trust me."

"You can't protect us. If Bryan finds me—"

"You don't have to worry about him." Imogen turned her around to point out Jagg in the car. "See my friend over there? He won't let anything happen to us."

"I don't… I'm not…"

"I am," Imogen said, showing her a smile. "Come on, let's get you off the street."

She'd hogged Jagg's night and now his morning too. If he accompanied them to a hotel, somewhere safe, and she got Mila settled in one piece, then she'd let him go. She didn't mean to keep relying on him, she didn't, but he was safety. Security. Certainty. Right now, Mila needed all three… and she did too.

THIRTEEN

"I'M SORRY. I've taken over your day."

"That girl's messed up," Jagg said.

Mila hadn't said a word in the car. Not one single word directly to Jagg. Until they got to the hotel anyway. Once they'd checked in and gone upstairs, Imogen started to ask questions. After that, the dam broke and Mila wouldn't shut up.

She'd paced, saying bits of one thing and parts of another. Speaking in fragments jumbled together. There were facts in there. Though making sense of them wasn't straightforward.

At the end of the liberation of energy, it didn't take much to convince Mila to get washed up in the bathroom. The woman needed her sleep. They all did.

"You can go," she said, alone with Jagg in the hotel bedroom. "I mean I'm not dismissing you. I appreciate you sticking with us, but you have a life to get back to."

"She thinks she's in danger."

"For what she told me," she said, conflicted by her own guilt. "And what I might have passed on to Lach. If she's in danger, it's because of me."

"This is not your fault. You had to tell the cop."

"They still don't see it as a single case. How can they not see that these women are linked? Mila said there's someone else. Another victim."

"Who?" Jagg asked.

She shook her head and sank onto the end of the bed. "I don't know. Remember I told you I thought there were others? I just couldn't pick out which was which. This is my first time as lead detective on a serial homicide case. I'm figuring this out as I go along."

The quip was intended to be funny, ish. It was also true. Being the only one who recognized the pattern, she was the only one on the case. Or had been. Before Mila joined her.

"You have to be careful," Jagg said. "If this Bryan works for Vex, it's a setup."

"We don't know that. Maybe he knows something. Someone warned her to leave her apartment. Someone's watching her back."

It could be this Bryan. Whose side was he on?

"Don't assume that either. See her behavior? The way she is now? Paranoid and tweaked. Everything you said the victims weren't. They set it up like this, make her paranoid. Scared of what goes bump in the night, so she's acting crazy before she disappears. Then everyone says they should've seen it coming. That she'd lost her mind since her roommate died."

"How do you know that?" she asked. "How do you know they operate that way?"

"Because I was one of them. I did this kinda thing."

"Driving people nutty?"

"She needs rest."

He didn't intend to answer the question. That much was clear from the finality of those words.

Curious as she was, it wasn't the time to satisfy herself. "We all do," she said, standing up. "You too. You should go."

"Because you think I'm working for him? That I'm a spy for the other side?"

The accusation clanged around her skull, unfair and untrue.

"If I said yes, wouldn't that make me paranoid and tweaky too?" The inhale and half roll of his eyes that preceded his chin descending didn't fill her with confidence. "Hey…" Getting up close, she laid her hands on his waist. "I know you're no saint. You have a past. Big deal. Who doesn't? Just because I ask questions doesn't mean I'm judging or doubting you."

"You should. And you should stay away from guys like me. That's what Strat and Ford would tell you."

"I've never been good at doing what I'm told." Sliding both arms around him, she nestled in close, sinking into his strength. "I feel bad sending you away when there are two beds right here… But I'm not sure I'd trust myself in bed with you."

He caught her chin on a finger and raised it up. Her body was still wrapped around his, but his discerning eye probed for something more.

"Bad boys were never your thing. Growing up you had plenty of opportunity with Ford and Strat's crews hanging around. You never fell for that shit."

No, she hadn't. People said women went for men like their fathers. That hadn't been her experience.

"Maybe I don't see you as a bad boy. You're a good man. Legit. On the straight and narrow. You run a business, look after those important to you. Don't you see? You're a stand-up guy."

"This isn't on the table."

"So you keep saying," she said, closing her eyes to enjoy his fingers as they caressed her cheek.

"I have to remind myself."

If he kissed her there, in that room, while they were alone, they'd end up in bed. Urgency pooled and spread low in her belly. There wasn't a rush, shouldn't be a rush, and her claim she didn't want to come between the men was genuine. They were friends, brothers, their friendship was solid. Why should she rock their foundations?

"Genny—"

"I know," she said, taking his hand from her cheek to step back. "It's okay."

And she smiled. Except it didn't feel real. It was. She wanted him to know that she was okay. That they were okay. But his observation about her faking it changed its hue.

"I can stay," he said. "If you want someone around while you rest."

Unlike Mila, she wasn't in fear for her life. Though it was sweet of him to offer.

"We'll be okay," she said, linking their hands to lead him to the door. "You need to sleep too."

"Yeah."

"I mean it," she said, opening the door. "Go home to bed. I might need you tonight."

She doubted it and had no intention of dragooning him out later, but if it got him to relax, a little lie was worth it.

"Okay," he said, hooking a hand around the back of her neck to pull her in and kiss her hair. "Call me if anything changes." She nodded in agreement, but he raised her chin up to meet her eye. "Genny?"

"Yes," she said. "I'll call if I need you."

Her body might argue she needed him then and there. Her head, her heart, her libido, what was really in play?

As she closed the room door, the bathroom one behind her opened. Mila came out in a hotel robe. Looking much better… if exhausted.

"Who was that?" Mila asked.

"I sent Jagg home to rest," she replied, locking the door then hooking an arm through hers. "Which is what we're going to do right now."

She'd have to call Steeple, let him know she was still breathing. And Lachlan. They hadn't checked in with each other, and she wanted the cops to spend time solving the murder cases, not worrying about her. Her ex had said he'd ask questions. Maybe he had some crucial answers for her.

FOURTEEN

"THANK YOU FOR believing me," Mila said.

"Of course I believe you."

Funny that she'd spent most of the past few weeks being disbelieved by everyone who heard her argument. The power of belief gave strength and encouragement. Giving back to Mila was a no-brainer. Whether they were right or wrong, supporting each other got them closer to the truth. Mila also didn't catch onto the fact that her revelations validated both of their theories.

Anna Emin.

Another name to add to her list of the unforgettable. Someone needed to get justice for them. Mila seemed as determined of that as her.

"It's horrible that she died, but…"

"We have to consider the future, not just the past."

Over their breakfast tray, they pondered their next step. Sure, it was after lunch, but their day was just beginning.

"There could be a woman out there right now," Mila said, "someone going through what Steph and Anna did."

Yes, because the women always went missing before they turned up dead. Autopsy reports confirmed the victims had been alive for some time between their disappearance and discovery. Usually, the Medical Examiner's Office put time of death within twenty-four hours prior to their bodies being found.

"How can we figure that out? How would we know who—"

"We need to look at recent missing persons reports," she said, finishing her coffee. "Come on. I know what we have to do."

***

SAUNTERING INTO THE police precinct with Mila at her side, it was a relief to see a familiar face.

"Look who came to visit."

"Hey, Lou," she said, going up to the desk.

"What can we do for you? I don't think McLeod's in—"

"That's okay," she said. "Any chance we can have a look at missing persons reports for the last couple of weeks?"

He frowned. "You lose someone?"

"Maybe."

"Can you narrow it down for me?"

"Women. In their twenties. Pretty. College educated."

"This that murder thing again?" he asked, typing.

Laying her forearms on the counter, she leaned over them. "Maybe… Just playing it through to the end."

"By starting at the beginning," Lou said, reading his screen. "Got three hits for you."

Oh, that was good. Not good that three people were missing, good that they were making progress.

She took her phone out and opened her notes app. "Can I have their socials?"

He let out a single short burst of laughter. "I shouldn't even give you their names."

"I know," she said. Not like she wasn't known for taking chances or pushing the boundaries. "Hit me." He read out their names and first line of address. It was a start. A good start. "Thank you."

"Don't you be thanking McLeod for my hard work later."

She laughed and offered a salute. "I promise." Spinning around, she rushed along with Mila. "Now we have our beginning."

***

"SHOULDN'T WE START by talking to friends and family?" Mila asked as they settled in their research room at the library.

"We will. That comes after we find out what we can. We have to know what to ask, don't we? Who's telling the truth or hiding things?"

"I guess."

"Okay," she said, reading the profile of their first potential victim. "Social media is an investigator's friend. People post all sorts of… huh."

Huddling closer, Mila's attention zeroed in on the screen. "What?"

"She's quite…"

"Depressed," Mila said.

"Yeah."

A lot of posts preceded her disappearance. That didn't exclude her completely, but one thing about the mystery killer's victims was their lack of warning signs before vanishing.

"Do you think…?"

"Let's check the others."

The next one was more promising. Happy, positive pictures of a filled social life. Pictures of her and the boyfriend she'd had since grade school were less convincing.

"Do you think she's another victim?" Mila asked. "That he took her?"

"Maybe." Imogen copied the boyfriend's name to put it into the search bar. Bringing up his information quickly solved that mystery. "Wow. Not so missing anymore." The second potential victim's picture was on the boyfriend's page. Both of them sported brand new wedding bands. "That mystery's solved."

"That's so sweet," Mila said, sorrow in her voice. "I wish Steph's story ended that way."

"Except from what you've said, Bryan was no picnic." Imogen searched the third name. "When does he want to meet?"

"I haven't checked my email. Oh, God, do you think we missed it? I didn't check it before we left the hotel."

"I'm sure it's okay. If he wants to meet and genuinely wants to help, he won't judge you for missing it."

And if she had, there was nothing they could do about it, so no point making her feel guilty. If the guy wasn't genuine and wanted to hurt Mila, he'd be back in touch. Without getting a feel for him, it was tough to assess his motivation. The last thing she wanted was Mila to be disappointed or worse.

"Yvonne Ingham," Mila said, checking out the page with her. "No pictures of a boyfriend."

"No, but she talks about seeing someone." Imogen pointed at the post she was reading. "A guy named Bryan."

They made eye contact.

"That's him. It has to be! That's it."

"Maybe," Imogen said. "Unfortunately, it's a common name. That's not enough on its own." Lachlan would not go to bat for her with his colleagues based on that evidence. When she took it to him, and to Steeple, she needed a slam dunk. "If there was a picture…"

Opening the page's media stalled her.

"I don't see any guy," Mila said. "Scroll down." When she did nothing, she got a nudge. "Imogen? What is it?"

"I know her," she murmured, scrutinizing the pictures. The woman didn't have herself in the profile picture, but she was in others. Either that or she really liked this particular friend in half a dozen pictures on the first page.

"You do? How? Are you friends?"

"No, but I know her face… I've seen her before."

"Where?"

And it hit her. "Hustle."

That woman, the one right there, had been in Hustle the first night she and Jagger visited the club. In Vex Manzani's private suite. She was sure of it. Positive. That was a face she remembered.

"Oh my God, you went? Alone? How did you get out alive? What's it like? Can we go there?"

Hustle was definitely back on her to-do list. Right along with finding the hotel Jagg spoke of and tracking down this woman as well.

"Let's find out what we can about her and then go to her apartment."

They read some more, clicking through the profiles of friends and family linked to her page that they could access.

"Her family really misses her," Mila said with a quiver.

Putting a comforting arm around her, Imogen gave her a squeeze. "You don't have to do this." It had to bring back all kinds of memories. "You can go back to the hotel if you want. I can handle this."

"I want to help," Mila said, grabbing for resolve. "And you shouldn't be out on your own. Not if this is Manzani related. If I'm in danger for what I said, they won't like you digging around."

So far, according to what she knew, the Manzanis wouldn't be able to pick her out of a lineup. She hadn't asked questions at the club. Not directly about the murders. And she hadn't printed anything either… though she hadn't read The Chronicler that day. Maybe Steeple put something in there. She doubted it; her editor would've warned her.

"Let's go to her apartment."

Moving targets were harder to hit than static ones. Investigating might help Mila stop dwelling on her own heartache. She'd have to process her grief, that was healthy, but while in fear for her life, focus needed to be on keeping her own, not on those already lost.

They got out of there and into a cab before her phone rang.

Lachlan.

Of course.

"Hey, honey," she said, widening her smile. "Miss me?"

"Ever think about calling first?"

"I didn't use your name," she said. "I didn't even say your name."

"Yvonne Ingham's the only one who matches your victim profile."

"We came to the same conclusion."

"Who's we? The blonde you came in with?"

"Yes," she said, not surprised he had the details. "We're backing each other up." Which should, hopefully, make him feel better about her sleuthing. "We're going over to Yvonne's place now."

"She lived alone," he said. "She was reported missing on Saturday, hasn't been seen since Tuesday."

Except she'd been in Hustle on Friday night. Should she tell Lachlan that? She trusted him and wanted as much help to find Yvonne as possible. But if the cops went poking around Hustle, that could lead the Manzanis to her... and Mila.

"If there's no one at her apartment, we'll try her workplace."

"I have her colleagues' statements. No one knows anything."

"Some people don't like talking to cops," she said. "They'll tell me things that they won't tell you. Do you know if her Bryan boyfriend is the same as Stephanie Weet's Bryan boyfriend?"

"We're still trying to trace him. As I said, she lived alone and didn't tell people where her boyfriend lived. No one's even sure how long they were seeing each other or how serious it was."

"Not very serious if it is the same guy," Imogen said. "Do you know where she was last seen? Who reported her missing?"

"Her mother reported her missing. She'd been trying to call and got no response. Colleagues said she was at work on Tuesday, spoke about meeting her boyfriend for dinner. No one's seen her since she left work. No one we can trace."

Bracing, she pushed the boundaries. "Any activity on her cards?"

"Babe," he warned.

She exhaled. "I know… I know, but you have access to certain things we don't… I could probably find a computer geek to seduce and—"

"Let us do our job," he said. "I know you're worried about this girl."

"I am worried about her." With good reason. "You would be too if you knew what I knew."

"Babe?" he said with more weight in the word. "You can't keep me in the dark."

"I won't. I'll tell you everything, I just… I need a little more time."

"Dinner?"

"Can we do it tomorrow?" she asked, swiping hair from her brow. "It's been a long couple of days."

"Okay. But when you get into trouble—"

"I know. Call you. I will."

"Be safe, babe."

They hung up and she put the phone back in her purse.

"Who was that?" Mila asked.

"A friend. A very supportive, very patient, friend."

If she told Lachlan about Mila and her fears, he'd go into overprotective mode. As soon as she let the cops in on their Manzani suspicions, the secret would be out. The targets on their back would grow tenfold.

As it stood, she wasn't sure the Manzanis themselves were involved. Maybe the killer just picked his victims from Hustle. But why would the women have the tattoos? She needed more information. Jumping to conclusions could drop all of them in hot water that wouldn't be easy to escape. Even if the Manzanis weren't involved, they'd want to punish her and Mila for suggesting they might be. No one would get away with drawing police attention to the infamous family. The Manzanis faced enough scrutiny on that front without anyone adding to it.

They had to be careful. They had to be smart. They had to be sure.

FIFTEEN

A MODEST OFFICE SUITE, Yvonne's workplace was on the first floor of a taller building. Some training day on the opposite side of the city had stolen most of Yvonne's colleagues. Great, no answers. Frustrating. They resolved to go back the following day.

The delay worked in their favor. By her reckoning anyway. Pushing Mila too far could be disastrous. For this story, risks were necessary. That was her prerogative. Her decision. Somehow, tying someone else up in her choices didn't sit easy. Mila might say she was okay, but the trauma of losing her friend couldn't be underestimated. In grief, her judgments weren't necessarily rational.

That was why she left her new friend sleeping in the hotel to sneak out alone that night. Some choices were impossible to explain. Why was it acceptable for her to take the risk while barring Mila from the same route? Her conscience wouldn't tolerate risking someone else. Mila had lost too much already. If she got into trouble, a call to Ford would bring him to her rescue. In a real pinch, she could call her dad, but that would be a last, final, doomsday sort of event.

The map napkin in the diner hadn't been exact and disappeared with Jagg's coffee. Still, the internet was a wonderful thing. Turned out there was an actual website that could triangulate a central location when given three points on a map.

Just in case of trouble, she stopped at home to change out of her slut-wear and went with skinny jeans instead. She didn't want to draw attention to herself, hence the lack of purse and choice of hooded sweatshirt. Yes, she'd have to explain the change of attire to Mila, but that was a problem for tomorrow.

Like her last trip to Hustle, she asked the cab driver to drop her off a block early and walked in. Getting a lay of the land was easier with a wider approach. Information and her life, those were the two things she wanted to leave with.

The street wasn't busy. People milled around sporadically. The people you'd expect to see in that kind of area. Groups of guys hung around in doorways. The younger ones called at each other from an alley.

No one ever scared her.

No, that wasn't true. She never showed anyone fear. Bravado could come off as arrogance, that was where the innocent thing came in. If she got a little too haughty, she could switch and draft. Her father and brother may not have wanted her to be part of their world, but it had infected her young.

They'd consider that a bad thing. She didn't. With her father in the city, her mom in the suburbs, and her stepfather's high six-figure salary, she was as comfortable in the company of paupers as kings.

Most people weren't bad through and through. Those who meant harm were usually easy to spot. Anyway, if someone got too close, she'd pick her brother's name or her father's depending on the age of the perpetrator. One of their reps would mean something to an assailant.

Yet on approach to the group of women smoking outside the hotel entrance, it wasn't her relatives' names in her head.

"Hey," she said, tucking her hood back from her forehead a little.

"We're on break."

"It's information I need, not service," she said. "Is there someone inside I can talk to?"

"You can talk to whoever you want, honey," a blonde with crimson lips said. "If it's got a dick, pull that zip down and they might even talk back."

She smiled at the laughing women and carried on through the darkened doorway. Broken lights above and on both sides suggested it was once a well-illuminated space. The painted walls and gouged floors spoke to the lack of upkeep. The current occupants didn't care about the décor and their customers were more interested in the look of other things. Like the product.

The point was to get inside. To get an idea of what went on in that building. Talking to the women outside was a respect thing. She wouldn't walk past people like she was better than them. Offending the home team on their own turf never ended well.

Lights around reception showed exactly where customers were supposed to approach. A woman behind the desk didn't even look up. Key hooks above the mail slots were occupied or not, depending on who was busy, she guessed. Rather than mail, each of the slots held a picture... a boutique shot... clothes, it appeared, were optional.

"Whoa, hey! Lookie, lookie..."

A guy, she hadn't seen, swung from inside the room behind the desk. Beyond a bunch of women sat around what had to be a kind of breakroom.

"Hi," she said, aiming for a pleasant, unthreatening smile.

"Never offered my services to a client before," he said, sauntering over. "But, baby, you want a good time—"

"Put your tongue back in your head, Kenny," the woman at the desk said.

"More like his dick in his pants," one woman called from the back room.

Laughter followed those words, though his scowl didn't see the funny side. "If you got time to joke, you've got time to walk the street," he said, whipping around to storm into the back.

"What do you need?" the woman at the front desk asked, ignoring the squawking and arguing going on behind her.

"I need you to whisper in my ear," she said, slapping her hands on the desk. The woman's brows just rose. "Has my guy been hanging around here?"

The woman's mouth opened in understanding. "If you're gonna cause trouble—"

"Not for you," she said, widening her smile, hoping to appeal to the woman's sense of sisterhood. "If there's something special he likes that he's not getting at home…"

The hostess was kind enough to subdue her laughter. "This ain't a how-to, show and tell gig, babes."

"I know, I—"

"You got a picture?"

No, she didn't. Why didn't she? "I don't but—"

"We don't take names and addresses here." Her head dropped to the side. "You think your guy—"

"I'm seeing Jagger Dunn."

A complete lie. Jagg was right, she did lie easy. Except, technically, it wasn't inaccurate as far as the Manzanis were concerned. Would Jagg be mad if he found out? No, how would he find out? Wasn't he the one who kept saying he wasn't part of this world anymore?

Stalled, the woman took a second before her grin came with a burst of laughter. "Oh, honey, if Jagg asked, there'd be a line of women around the block waiting to serve him…" She ducked closer, "and I'd be right at the front of it. No payment required." Her smile warmed. "My advice? If Jagg's playing away, let him. Some guys just need to get their kicks that way, you know?"

Interesting advice. "He's a good guy."

"He is and raking it in from what I hear. If him and Tav join forces, there'll be a lot of sad crooks on the street, I tell ya."

She didn't know what that meant but nodded along. "You must see all kinds of guys in here." Nodding at the pictures, she looked closer, checking if Yvonne was in any of them. "Do the girls live here full-time?"

"Some of them."

"Do they see guys off the books?"

"Ask Jagg straight out," the woman said. "He's the type who don't do well with subtle. He really don't."

How would she know? From experience? "I don't want to be the crazy, clingy bitch."

"But he's going out nights…" she said, nodding slowly. "They got their own world. Men are like… they never grow up. They want fun, easy, commitment-free women… You want a ring or something?"

"No! No, I… He's not the only one with prospects."

"Ah, is that where we're going with this?" She scoffed. "You got a better man than Jagg sniffing around? Grab him with both hands. What's his type? He rich or something?"

"A girl's not getting any younger."

"Even from here I can see you've got a figure," she said. "Play the field, baby, and put Jagg out for the rest of us to share too."

"Would you tell me if he was coming here?"

"Confidentiality is important to our clients... So probably not."

At least she was honest. "Can I talk to the other girls?"

"You start knocking on doors and Kenny will bust something. Boss is on his ass already. Supposed to have finished the work on ten and the plumbing's still fucked. Don't think he needs someone else riding his ass."

"Sure."

"But come back," the woman said, wandering to her seat. "Any time. If Jagg's here, you wait long enough, you'll see him around."

Good point and just the excuse she needed. The more time she spent there, the more she'd learn... and they'd be more open as they got to know her.

"Thanks," she said, putting her hood back up. "I'll do that."

Damn, well, that wasn't as informative as she'd hoped it would be. If Yvonne's picture was there, she could call Lachlan and save the woman straight away.

Marathon. If it was a marathon instead of a sprint, she could only hope Yvonne had enough time. With every second that passed, the woman was enduring more pain, more torture, more... she couldn't even imagine.

Hope.

Yvonne better be holding on. They needed time... would they have enough?

SIXTEEN

IN THE MORNING, they trawled the newspapers with breakfast. Nothing on more missing persons. Nothing on bodies found. Good. That was something. No other women had died. As far as the cops and the papers knew anyway.

Mila didn't even ask about the jeans, so she didn't offer an explanation. Wardrobe was low on the list of priorities.

Getting to Yvonne's workplace was higher on the agenda.

That lunchtime, the building was bustling. People came and went. Commandeering colleagues on the street or in dark alleys may be more discreet, but they had to go inside to ensure they talked to the right people.

"Hi," she said, projecting confidence in her voice. "I need to talk to someone about Yvonne Ingham."

The startled receptionist glanced at Mila, then back at her. "Are you with the police?"

"I just have a few questions." Not a denial, not a confirmation either. "I'd really appreciate it if someone could help us out… We can wait… as long as we have to."

Something no business would want. People loitering around for all to see. People interested in the employee who'd gone missing under suspicious circumstances. Maybe she added that last part, but it was true.

"Let me see if I can…" Though the receptionist was hesitant, she picked up the phone. "I'll see if her supervisor's available."

"Thank you."

Reversing a step from the desk, she held her chin high. Confidence. She was a Stratford. Her father's daughter. Her dad could talk his way in anywhere. The Ritz? No problem! A back-alley dive bar? Would be his home within the hour. Her high school French teacher's panties? Easy as pie… or was that easiest pie? That had been a hell of a parent-teacher conference. Especially with her mom and Ted there too… But she got an A, which, come to think of it, she'd never thanked her dad for.

The receptionist jumped up as a door in the corner opened. The guy who came out didn't look happy to see them. Could be a lead. Maybe this guy was their perpetrator. Did he and Yvonne have a thing? Had he wanted them to? Had the young beauty told him no one too many times?

Jagg came to mind. Hadn't she told him she wasn't the paranoid tweaker? Now everywhere she looked, there were clues and duplicity… Her father would be proud. *"Suspect everyone"* was one of his mottos. Though *"always make friends with your enemy"* was his favorite. How did those gel?

"Hello," the guy said. "I'm Simon Langspring, Yvonne's supervisor. What's the problem?"

"No problem," Imogen said, pleased to see the starch leave his shoulders as his eyes flicked between them.

That's right. Just two pretty ladies, innocent, unthreatening… felt a little like drawing the fly into her web. Was she a predator? Some might say. Jagg, for example.

"You have questions? Come this way."

He took them into a glass-fronted conference room and closed the blinds while gesturing at the long table.

"Sit down," he said. "Is there news? Do we know something?"

Oh no, had she given this guy false hope?

"I don't," she said, seating herself next to Mila. "Sorry."

"You have questions? Yvonne was a hard worker. Smart. Comfortable with clients… not too comfortable. Good at her job. I didn't know her much outside of work. She came to functions, she was closer with other members of her team… Everyone spoke to the cops."

"I know," she said, addressing his confusion. "We just want to go over a few details. Did she leave at the normal time?"

"Yes, everyone was out on time. There was talk of meeting later for a drink. Everyone, you know, not just her and… She spoke to her boyfriend. He said they were going out for dinner."

Interesting. "Did you see him? Did he come here to pick her up?"

"No, she called him on the phone." Damnit. "On the street, while Yvonne flagged a cab, Claudia invited her to come for a drink later. Them, I suppose."

Yvonne and the boyfriend. "And did they? Come for a drink later?"

He shook his head, clasping the back of a chair. "I don't believe so. I didn't go out with my colleagues that night. I have a wife. A home." So even if he wanted to party with any of the underlings, it might be forbidden… The bead of sweat on his brow gave the impression his wife held that leash tight. "None of this is good for our company's image. I hired her. I thought she was… I never got the impression that she was flighty."

Blaming the victim? In his defense, he didn't know she was a victim. They didn't either. Confirmation would be difficult to come by without a body, and they didn't want it to get that far.

"We have no reason to believe she intended to cause anyone distress." Again, neither true or false. "Or that her disappearance was premeditated."

"Claudia would've known if Yvonne planned to leave. They were close… as close as colleagues are, I suppose. I believe it was her who first raised the warning flag."

"The warning flag?"

"That Yvonne was unreachable… Her family was immediately worried, I'm sure."

Was that fact or fiction? "Would it be possible to speak to Claudia?"

"She's off this week. I gave her some time… seemed the reasonable thing to do."

"Yes."

"Her number should be in your files."

If they were cops, it would be. "Thank you," she said, standing up with Mila at her side. "We appreciate your time."

They started for the door, which Langspring opened for them.

As they passed, Mila stopped. "Before she disappeared…" Mila said. "Was she different? Did you suspect anything had changed in her life?"

"No," he said, though he maybe wasn't the best man to ask. "I didn't."

Mila's expression didn't change as she walked out. Imogen offered a smile and hurried after her.

She caught up to her on the street. "What was that about? Was she different?"

"I worry, you know," Mila said, slipping her phone from her pocket. "Maybe I missed something."

"You can't do that to yourself," she said. "You were Steph's closest friend."

"And I didn't see anyth—"

The abrupt stop concerned her. "What? What is it?" Her friend fixated on the phone screen. "Mila?"

"He wants to meet," she said. "He wants to meet today. Now."

"Who?"

"Bryan," Mila said, turning the phone around. "We have to go."

Yes, they did, but when Mila grabbed her hand to pull her down the street, she held back.

"Maybe we should tell the cops… even unofficially. If they want to talk to him—"

"They talked to him before. That means they must know how to get in touch with him if they have to. They don't need to talk to him, we do. We can't waste this chance."

They merged into the crowd crossing at the green. "Let me call Jagg…"

She couldn't remember his number being in her phone, but the shop had to be in the book. Ford was an option too. Though too many new faces might spook her friend, never mind the guy who could be wrapped up in the plot.

"We don't have time. He's there now."

"Where?"

"A coffee place Steph loved. That's a good sign, right? A sign he's still thinking of her."

Or that he got some sick kick out of putting his victim's friends through the pain of enduring constant reminders of their lost loved one.

"Mila, we have to be careful," she said, tugging her friend to a stop. "Let's think about this. Just for a second."

"He's there," Mila said with a predictable impatience. "We have to go. We have to get there before he leaves."

"If he wants to talk to us, he'll wait. How far away is this place?"

"Less than two blocks. Five minutes and we'll—"

"How did he know we were here? That you were so close?" Glancing around, suddenly, nothing felt safe. "Does anyone know where you are? Your family? Friends?"

Mila exhaled annoyance. "We have played this your way so far. Have I complained? Have I argued with you? I trusted you."

"I know and I appreciate that—"

"I want you to be there with me because you know about this stuff. You have a knack for it, I guess, for putting people at ease. This is important. Steph is important."

"Yes, she is, but she wouldn't want you hurt."

"We don't know if Bryan is involved in what happened to her. Maybe he's just a guy. A heartbroken guy. We won't know unless we go there, unless we talk to him."

"Okay, we just have to be careful."

"Careful. Right," Mila said, guiding her over to the crosswalk. "But we have to be quick."

Did they? A heartbroken guy wouldn't decide to meet and then back out less than twenty minutes later.

Her awareness stayed keen as they walked the next block. When her phone rang, she slowed.

"Wait a second," she said, stopping when she read her boss's name. "I have to take this."

"It's right there," Mila said, pointing across to the midpoint of the opposite sidewalk. "We can just..."

She answered. "Steeple?"

"Still haven't shown up, Stratford."

"I know, I'm sorry. It's been a nutty few days."

"Still on this murder thing?"

"Yeah, and I'm making progress, I—"

A horrified scream on the road brought her attention around just as the sickening thud of metal on a human body ended the sound. Mila. Mila! On the road, she was, they had...

Taking off, the car spun its wheels with an urgent squeal. Horns blared, people called out, but she ran to her friend. Ran into the road. Over to the woman sprawled at all the wrong angles.

"Mila," she whispered, stroking her hair from her face. "Mila!" She swallowed, ignoring those gathering around her. Her friend was... She was... "Call 911!"

Others echoed her plea. Cars stopped; people held a makeshift cordon that crowded way too close. Her friend had... They were... The danger had known exactly where to look.

SEVENTEEN

"…FOR A FEW DAYS."

Lachlan had been at her side for… She didn't even know how long. With no idea of the time and no inclination to check, numbness clawed at her insides.

"I'm fine."

"You're not fine," he said, tucking her hair from her face, which was turned down toward the floor. "You need to look after yourself. You had a close call today."

"I didn't." They weren't after her. They got their target. "I'm fine."

"If not me, stay with your brother."

"No," she said, closing her eyes. "He doesn't need to… He has enough going on."

"He might have something to say about that."

Blinking around at him, she exhaled. "You called him, didn't you?"

Lachlan nodded past her, signaling to the other end of the corridor. Ford. Sealing her lips, she inhaled. Damnit. Now that he was there… Her eyes watered, so she closed them again, begging the tears to stay at bay.

"I am a Stratford."

Whispering the reminder as Lachlan stood up, she hoped he didn't hear it. Except when she opened her eyes to face her brother, the situation only got worse. Jagg. There, behind her brother. Double damnit. Blowing out a quick breath, she stood up, her back to the men, pulling on every ounce of resolve, swiping at the ridiculous tears staining her cheeks.

When she turned to see her brother and Lachlan shaking hands, she almost lost it. "Stop it," she said, lunging over to pull their hands apart. "You don't even like each other."

"Tragedy brings people together, Squirt," Ford said. "What the hell do you think you're getting into without calling me?"

"I didn't get into anything," she said, pleased for the anger; it was so much easier to express. "This was an accident…" Except, even as she said the words, they poisoned her tongue. It wasn't true. It wasn't an accident. She didn't believe that. "It just… happened."

"You know this shit she's into?" Lachlan asked.

"Yeah, and I thought you were smarter than to let her into it."

"I told her to stay out of it."

"So did I."

"She doesn't listen to anyone," Lachlan said. "Always thinks she knows best."

"Stop agreeing with each other," she said, glaring at one man then the other. Jagg got nothing, not so much as a sniff. "*She* is all grown up and makes her own choices. Not everyone has to agree with them."

"Almost got you killed today, Squirt."

"Stop calling me that." He only called her that when he was really scared, which just stimulated the tingling in her sinuses. "Did you call Dad?"

"No!" her brother was quick to answer. "Call Dad? Fuck, no! You want the goddamn army out here?" Would be an army of miscreants, but an army all the same. "Be happy it's just me you're getting."

"Yeah, well, I say she can't stay in her own apartment while this is going on."

"Agreed," Ford said.

"I offered to stay with her but——"

"No, she's staying with us," Ford said. "'Til I can get her out of this damn mess she's caused."

"I didn't cause any damn mess," she said, opening her arms. "I wasn't even the victim! No one was aiming for me!"

Her brother's chin tipped to the side. "Thought it was an accident."

She sneered at his goading. "I'll show you a fucking accident…"

When she raised her fist, aiming for his arm, she fully intended to make contact. Jagg caught her mid-swing as Ford and Lachlan made some nodding motion and disappeared to the other side of the corridor.

"Manzani?" Jagg asked under his breath when they'd put distance between them.

"I don't know," she said on an exhale, her shoulders and head dropping. "It was a setup. I told her it was a setup."

"You can't make someone hear you if they don't want to."

"I know," she said, not sure she believed it.

"Look at me…" he said, the heat of his body crowding in closer to her as his finger slid under her chin to raise it up. "You are not responsible. But you are in danger. Don't fight Ford on this… Come stay with us until this is over."

"No, I won't give up… Mila's not dead, she has a chance… just like Yvonne Ingham. Maybe she's still alive."

"I didn't ask you to give it up," he said. "I asked you to come stay at mine… I need to know you're safe… please, baby."

Shit, that soft pleading, that tender need. The only thing in the whole world that could make everything okay would be the taste of the lips begging her surrender.

"I needed you," she confessed the truth that would never have been voiced if it wasn't for the trauma of the day. "I told her I needed you and… I should've gone with my gut."

"I'd have been there."

"I know."

When he got even closer, too close for polite distance, her eyes closed again. Just being in his orbit set a heady concoction of hormones and heartache swirling through her bloodstream.

"Say yes, baby," he murmured, his voice more timbre than words. "If you don't, I'll move into yours. I'll be your shadow. Everywhere you turn, I'll be standing there watching your ass."

"I thought you were more of a rack guy," she said, feeling something other than despair for the first time since the accident.

"That too."

Her head fell back, loose on her shoulders. "How would you explain that to my brother?"

"I don't give a damn. Let him ask. I'll tell him the truth. You're mine and I'll do whatever it takes to protect you."

When he edged back, the tilt of his eyes betrayed Ford and Lachlan's return.

"You're staying with us," Ford said, standing shoulder to shoulder with Jagg. "Scream at me, fight all you want—"

"I'll stay," she said.

Fighting him would be spite. Yes, she liked her freedom, but he wasn't telling her she had to stay inside forever, just sleep where he could keep a better eye on her. With what had happened that day, and the level of evil she was dealing with, it wouldn't be a bad thing to have a safety net.

"That was easier than I thought it'd be," Ford said, glancing behind her. "Thank you… for looking out for her."

"Always will," Lachlan said, squeezing her shoulder. "Take care of her."

He kissed her head and his hand drifted away as she departed between her brother and Jagg. Two protectors, three, it didn't matter, Mila was the one in a hospital bed, her body in pieces. If she made it out alive, there would be a long road to recovery. Anyone else might take the crash as a sign to walk away. Not her. Yes, it was difficult, and of course it shook her up, but she needed justice for Mila now as well as the others.

EIGHTEEN

THEY BROUGHT HER to the breakroom of Jagg's Autos. Not so much brought. Her brother stayed in the doorway to finish the conversation, planning to depart again.

"I'll grab whatever," Ford said. "Clothes and shit. I'll stop at a store too. Anything you want?"

Because he intended to limit her need to leave again?

"I don't see why I can't come with you to my own apartment."

"You stay here. With the guys. Where it's safe."

"I'm not your prisoner," she said.

"Not yet." He backed into the hallway, holding the door. "You make my life difficult? I'll make your life difficult."

She just sighed. "Am I supposed to be afraid of you?"

"Yeah," her brother said, his gaze intensifying. "'Cause if I call Dad, he'll be here in minutes. He'll put you on full lockdown. You want to explain how you got yourself in trouble?"

No, she didn't want to talk to her dad at all. Ford knew that, which was why he was using it against her.

"I need my phone charger. And shampoo. Conditioner too. Don't forget the conditioner. And don't be afraid of my underwear drawer. You don't have to search anything, just grab a handful of whatever."

"Why would I be afraid of women's underwear?"

"Your sister's underwear," she said. "I don't care, just don't forget anything. Call me if you need help."

"Yeah. Yeah," he said, the door swinging shut when he let go.

His footsteps receded, and then there was silence. Space for her thoughts to rattle. The most prominent took her focus to Jagg, standing a few feet away, watching her. He had warned her of that.

"What does that mean?" she asked because it had been on her mind since he said it. "You said I'm yours, like… I don't know. What does it mean?" The question wasn't meant to reveal her uncertainty. Where they were concerned, there'd been nothing but question marks for days. "Because it's been a tough day… I don't want to…" He started toward her. "I just have to be clear what that means and what you want—"

Scooping her face into both hands, he pulled her up as his mouth descended on hers. They weren't in Hustle. Didn't have the excuse of kissing for cover or because it was a game used to protect them.

Her arms went around him as his hands glided down her back to boost her up onto the counter. The breakroom wasn't the sanest choice, but who gave a damn? With his lips on hers, his tongue giving hers meaning, nothing else mattered.

He pulled her close, right to the edge of the counter, and bowed forward, supporting her braced weight in his capable arms.

"Jagg," she whispered, her fingers losing themselves in his hair.

His mouth trailed down her throat. He planted one hand on the counter at her back, giving her a leaning post, freeing up the other to explore. Squeezing her breasts, he kissed each of the mounds and boosted back up to kiss her mouth again.

He wanted her. He'd said the words, and now she was experiencing their meaning. Fuck, she'd never wanted something more, never wanted someone more. Winding her legs around his hips, she locked their bodies together, rocking and writhing against the thick promise behind his fly.

Without hesitation, he lifted her up, distracting her mouth as he carried her to… wherever. It didn't matter. They could go to the back workshop and do it there on the floor in front of all his employees. Chances were, she wouldn't notice anyone but him.

He lowered her into the soft cradle of a bed and rose just enough to take her top off over her head. They'd never got naked with each other, but as he hooked the neck of his tee-shirt with two thumbs to pull it off, there was no mistaking their destination.

Time to enjoy him, to admire him, was snatched away by his hands on her body and his mouth returning to hers. Their kiss deepened, pushing her further into the abyss of arousal. All of her sang for him. Every single inch beckoned with a siren call meant only for his ears.

"Jagg," she said again, writhing beneath him.

Kissing her cheekbone, her temple, her ear, his breath came before his words. "Want me to stop?" Already she could hear the pant in his tone, the desperation, the same aching need that lit her passion. "You're vulnerable, it's—"

"Don't be a good guy now, Jagg," she whined.

Experiencing this softer, more intimate side of him tumbled her into falling harder.

"You're all I care about," he said, rising to run his fingers from her throat, down through her cleavage to her belly. "I can wait for this."

Grabbing the buttons of his jeans, one hard yank opened them all. "I can't. I can't wait…" Her body bowed, arching up, begging for him. "Please, baby."

The burden of his concern lifted, relaxing his brow and he climbed backward off the side of the bed, removing her jeans in the process.

Naked.

She was naked.

And he was… looking.

Jagg. The man standing there, drinking her in, was Jagger Dunn. Tough. Unyielding. Determined Jagger Dunn.

As his gaze devoured her, she absorbed him too. Shirtless. Jeans open. Definition in that chest. The muscles of his stomach. He was in shape. Always had been. Much better shape than any regular guy. Was that because of the fighting? The life he used to live? If his past misdeeds loitered around every corner, threatening his life, he had to be ready for anything.

She raised her arm, holding out her hand, wishing for his. Though it was flattering to be adored from afar, she wanted him closer, wanted his body above hers. In hers. Taking her hand, he slid a knee onto the bed, using it to part her legs further as he came down on top of her, returning to their languorous kiss.

Jagg was more than what people thought of him. More than the reputation. More than just some thug or a guy who did whatever he wanted to earn easy money. Those days might be gone, but his rough edges endured. It wasn't easy to shrug off a checkered past, just as it wasn't easy to erase the scars it brought with it.

None of that mattered. Nothing outside that bed could get to them while they bathed in each other, submerging themselves in the speed of their fervent passion. She couldn't bear to be without him anymore. The burden of desire needed to be lifted with release. Yes, release, relief. Moving beneath him, winding her legs tight around him, she needed him to complete her. All of him. Inside her. Completing her being with his.

His hips rose as her fingers tangled in his hair, aching to pull his mouth to hers. But he couldn't. They couldn't. Not while he… The push of him between her legs diverted her thoughts from his kiss. The dull throb of pressure rose to a zap of discomfort that he must've noticed.

"Baby—"

"Don't be gentle," she gasped, smiling through her haze of need.

With one hard shove, he gave her what she wanted. The overwhelming, torturous pleasure sent a clear signal of ownership throughout her. This man. This…

"Jagg," she whined, her body writhing beneath his. "Oh, God, Jagg."

The feral glint of satisfaction in his eyes also tainted the smile that twisted his lips. "How does that feel?"

"More amazing than you'll ever know."

She couldn't keep still, even as he slid back to bow and kiss her, his cock only just remaining within her.

"Doesn't feel as good as you around me," he growled and slammed into her again, pleased to take her breath as his body consumed hers.

Life wasn't the same. Would never be the same. Being joined with him revealed a secret, one she'd never known existed. Jagg was her other half. The moon and the sun and the whole goddamn—

"Jagg," she yelped when orgasm hit. The word escaped her lips, probably too loud, but the whine of bliss that followed couldn't be contained. "Oh, shit…" Another climax as the first climbed down. What he was doing to her, with his dick, with his fingertips, with those eyes locked onto her, it almost didn't seem right. It didn't seem fair. "Baby…"

With a grunt, he shunted up into her, gritting his teeth, summiting his own gratification. Shit. Goddamn. Fuck. She couldn't think. Couldn't even see straight.

As he exhaled and dropped onto his back beside her, the afterglow sent shivers of pleasure through her.

It must've been at least a minute before she even thought about attempting speech. She hesitated. He hadn't said anything. Was the gravity of what they'd just done sinking in? He'd asked if she wanted to stop because she was vulnerable after her trauma. Wasn't he vulnerable too? Caught in the emotion of fear for her safety, it might have clouded his judgment.

They could forget it ever happened. Erase the memory and… except that wasn't what she wanted. Whatever was happening between them, wherever it might go, it felt worthwhile. Profound. Like more than just a one-night stand or sex for the sake of sex.

But she was in his home. He'd offered it to her for protection. She couldn't now make him regret that decision by pressuring him. His friendship with Ford was the most enduring of either of their lives. She didn't have a friend like that. One she'd known her whole life who'd go to the ends of the earth for her. Both men meant so much to her, but she couldn't damage or diminish what they meant to each other by getting between them.

"You're quiet," he said, his deep voice gruff. "What's in your head?"

"Ford," she said because it was honest. "I don't want this to hurt him. To hurt your friendship. You'll resent me. Both of you will."

"Yeah," he said, surprising her with his agreement. "If we screw around for fun, it will fuck our friendship."

"He never has to know," she said and sat up. "We'll swear to each other it won't ever happen—"

"Hey," he said, catching her wrist before she could rise, sitting up next to her. When their eyes met, he scooped a hand around her cheek. "I made a choice."

"It shouldn't be that. I don't want you to choose me over him."

"I choose both of you. This doesn't end anything, it begins something. This is the start of us. Yeah, it might be rough going for a while… And we should be on a steady footing before we tell Ford, so he knows this isn't just hooking up without commitment…"

"Is it?" she asked. "Because if that's all you want—"

"What do you want, Genny?"

That was a helluva question. Way to put her on the spot. One thing was certain.

"I don't want that to be the last time we do that," she said, fixating on the plump temptation of his lower lip. "I don't want our last kiss to be our last…"

He leaned in to kiss her slow. "That's what we start with."

"You're so calm."

"Freaking out won't change anything," he said. "Want to lie down?"

How long did they have? Probably not long. They couldn't take the risk of anyone discovering them. If she'd made as much noise as she thought, their secret may not be a secret anymore.

In answer to his question, she crawled across the bed to lie on the far side while he settled next to her.

"So this is Jagger Dunn's bedroom?" she asked, glancing around.

"Yeah, I guess."

Smiling, she couldn't believe how important it felt to be there when just last week, she'd never even thought about it.

There was a stair up to the bed, and no headboard. Everything was basic, simple. Not austere, just as required, nothing more than that.

A few clothes on the chair in the corner might indicate a guy in a hurry. The few bottles on the dresser spoke of a man who knew what he liked. She wouldn't call him sloppy. No way, not Jagg.

"It's crazy how much I want to be here," she said, swiping her hair from her face, wondering which door led to what. "How much this means to me. How did this sneak up on us?"

"Maybe it didn't," he said. On his side, looming over her, he stroked her stomach. "You're hot. Any guy with eyes can see that."

True, as she'd told him, his attractiveness wasn't exactly a secret either. "You were in this box. Like this never gonna happen box."

"Hustle opened the lid and let that all out."

Yeah. She ran her fingers from his cheek up to his hair. "I have to go back."

"To Hustle?"

She nodded. "I know you think it's dangerous."

"It is dangerous."

"And you'd prefer I didn't go there, but it's really important to me that I find out the truth. Mila's in a coma, her brain's swelling, her bones are broken. I can't just give up. I can't stop—"

"Did I ask you to?" His interruption silenced her. "Wherever this came from, whatever it is, we'll figure it out. One good thing about our history, about how long we've known each other, we know what we're getting into. I know you, Genny. You don't give up. Doesn't matter if it gets hard or dangerous, you keep going."

"You're okay with it? With my investigation?"

"I'm worried about you, that comes with the territory. Nothing will change that. But I'm not interested in changing you or making your choices. You can make your own decisions, and you have to let me make mine."

"What do you mean?" she asked, almost offended. "I would never stop you from doing anything you wanted to do."

"Good," he said. "Because whenever you go to Hustle, I'll be right there with you. I won't stop you from going, so you can't stop me either."

Touché. Did she want him with her? She'd be safer. Yes, she'd worry, but he was right, it was his choice.

"I guess you're good cover," she teased, curving a hand around the back of his neck.

Although she tried to pull him down for a kiss, he hesitated. "No other guys, Gen," he said, intent on her gaze. "Not for anything. Yeah, it's a good idea to keep this quiet from Ford for now, that doesn't make you a free agent."

"Understood," she said, her fingers trailing to his chest. "But at Hustle you can't..."

He tipped her chin up. "I can't, what?"

"Distract me," she said, stroking his body. "That first time we were there, I forgot completely why I'd gone in the first place. All I wanted to do was..."

Though she silenced, her smile bred his smirk.

"What we just did?" She nodded. "You've got those powers of distraction too, baby. I went to keep you safe and ended up being the biggest threat to you."

"You're a threat I can handle."

With a little pressure and his acquiesce, she got him onto his back and climbed over to straddle him.

After a moment of admiration, something more discerning came over him. "I was sitting right next to him when he got the call," Jagg said into the silence. Ford, when Ford got the call. "An accident. You were in hospital… All the way there, I couldn't stop thinking it."

"Thinking what?" she asked, her fingertips tracing up and down his torso.

His eyes met hers. "That we'd missed it. Our chance… I couldn't even remember why I'd talked myself out of it."

"Why you took this off the table." It was on the table now. One hundred percent on the table given what they'd just done. "I'm sure about this." Even if it was lightning speed. "Now it just feels like…"

"Like what?"

"We wasted so much time."

"We had to get here. Everything had to come together just right or it wouldn't have happened," he said. "You were with the cop a long time."

"Three years."

"If you're still getting over him—"

"Lach and I are done. He knows that. We both do."

"You loved him."

"Yeah," she said and wouldn't ever deny it. She didn't believe love was restricted to just one someone. Losing Lachlan didn't erase her chance of finding love again. Being with him taught her a lot, taught them both a lot. Their love served that purpose, it granted them valuable experience. "You're right about everything coming together. I learned a lot about relationships and guys with him."

His smirk became almost a laugh. "Not sure how much I have in common with the cop."

"You might be surprised," she said, laying down, resting her cheek on his chest. "What about you? I never paid much attention to your love life."

"Pay attention now, 'cause you're it."

"I'll tell him." Her eyes sank shut. "When we decide it's time. I'll tell Ford."

"Probably better coming from both of us."

"Yeah, but you're afraid of him so—"

"Afraid?" He rolled them over, pinning her on her back, stifling her mouth with his. "Not a chance."

Jagger Dunn. Hot? Yes. Capable? Yes. Smart? Funny? He checked boxes, and some part of her had always known that. Maybe she'd put him in the "never gonna happen" corner too. But this was it, it was happening. However it went down, there was no backing out now.

NINETEEN

"BABE, YOU'VE GOTTA GET UP."

She didn't want to move. With her face buried in his pillow, she wanted him there next to her. Except it felt like he was pulling away.

Satisfied and tired, slumber begged surrender. "It's been a long few days."

"I know," he said, his lips warming her temple. "Ford's on his way back."

She sighed without opening her eyes. "Why do you have to live with my brother?"

"I've lived with your brother my whole life. One way or another."

Which probably meant she wouldn't get much alone time with Jagg when Ford learned of them.

"Okay," she said, stretching and rolling over, still without opening her eyes. "I'm awake."

Kind of. But what did the guy expect after ravishing her so thoroughly numerous times.

"I've gotta show you where to sleep."

Yeah, because her brother would've expected his friend to do at least that. What else would they have been doing in the interim?

"That means I have to get dressed."

Wandering around naked while Jagg's other buddies and colleagues ambled in and out wouldn't be on her brother's list of house rules.

Jagg jumped out of bed and into his jeans. "Not something I'm proud of."

"Being with me?"

"Asking a beautiful woman to get out of my bed."

"I assume…" she said, sitting up, "that you own whatever bed you intend to put me in."

"If I was getting into that bed with you," he said, coming to raise her chin on a finger to kiss her, "this wouldn't be so difficult."

Already it was foreign to be leaving his bed and getting dressed. It had been so long since she'd started a relationship that she was more used to sharing her life with her lover than living her own separate one.

Heading for the door, Jagg caught her on the way, tucking her in front of him, the way he had at Hustle.

"I got it so wrong," she teased, tipping her head back.

"Got what wrong, baby?"

"Thought bad boys were supposed to keep their women naked, ready for use."

"Don't need you naked to put you to good use." He guided her into the breakroom again. "Bathroom's the door next to mine."

"Been a while since Ford and I shared a bathroom. Hope you've trained him better than Strat did."

They went into the perpendicular room. "This is your room."

"Close to yours," she said as he switched on the light. "I approve."

Regular double bed, closet at the far end of the room.

"Anything you need, knock any time."

"I have to knock? What if I want to see you naked?"

Snagging her wrist, he spun her to the edge of the bed and pulled her to him, clamping their joined hands at the curve of her back.

"Start without me. I'll catch up."

"You don't have to knock before you come in here."

"I'll be watching that the other guys do. I'm getting a lock for this door."

When he tried to withdraw, she grabbed him back. "No."

"No?"

Draping her arms around him, going backwards, she lifted one leg then the other to rise on her knees on the bed.

"You're going back to the bed with all the memories, don't leave me here without any."

In a slow advance, he gave her a kiss to savor. Long, slow, racing until she was in his arms, her legs coiling around his hips and—

"Fuck," he spat and kissed her again.

"What?" she whispered, brushing her lips across his. "You don't want this?"

"I want it too much, Genny."

"Immie!"

Her brother's call from the breakroom parted them. She climbed off the opposite side of the bed to slide open the closet door. Lucky that she found sheets there and a pillow on the shelf overhead.

"What are you doing in here?" Ford asked from the direction of the door.

"I can't reach the pillows."

Good cover. Jagg rounded the bed and touched her waist as he reached over her to retrieve the pillows. In that contact, she got his approval.

"Woman's friend is laid up in hospital and you didn't even make the bed for her."

"I can do it," she said, shaking open a sheet over the mattress. "You think I can't make a bed?"

Ford dumped a holdall by the door. "I don't know," he said, coming to grab the other side of the sheet to tuck it in. "If I had to put money on it, I'd say the cop was the neat freak in your relationship."

"You've never been in a relationship with a cop, have you, brother?"

He snorted. "Not a fucking chance. Never have, never will." The pillow appeared at the head of the bed, one, then another. "Unpack your shit." Her brother backed toward the door. "I'm ordering pizza. We'll chill before you get some rest. When the adrenaline's out of your system, you'll crash and might not eat for a while."

Ford disappeared into the breakroom, and she couldn't even manage a smile. A duvet landed at the end of the bed. Jagg was somewhere behind her at the closet.

"This is wrong," she whispered.

His fingertips trailed down her arm until they twined with hers and he came in close, giving her something to lean on.

"Us?"

She sighed. "I have a brother caring for me. A boyfriend looking out for me. Protecting me." Her eyes closed. "And Mila's laying in a hospital bed all alone."

"She has you looking out for her."

"What a lot of good that did her today." Damn, she wanted to punch herself. "I knew it was dangerous. I knew—"

"Genny…" Turning her around, he set both hands on her shoulders. "What happened to her is not your fault."

"We're having sex and sleeping together, talking about pizza. Life shouldn't just go on. I told Mila we'd find whoever killed her friend and instead the same people got to her."

"There's nothing you can do for her tonight. We'll go see her tomorrow."

They. We. The concern in him only highlighted Mila's isolation.

"Do you think she's safe? If they meant to kill her—"

"I'll send a couple of the guys over," he said.

"What's the hold up?" Ford's voice joined them again.

Peeking over her shoulder, he only leaned into the room.

"Genny's worried Mila might still be in danger."

"If they meant to kill her, she might be," Ford said. "I'll send a couple of the guys to the hospital."

As her brother disappeared, her smile caught on Jagg. "You are so alike."

"Not in the ways that count."

He surprised her with a quick kiss, then spun her around to guide her out of the bedroom, his hands on her shoulders.

In the breakroom, Ford tossed his phone onto the island. "Done."

"Did you send real men?" she asked. "People with actual focus. Not the idiot who hit on me when I came to see you."

Walking past her, Jagg paused. He and Ford made eye contact.

"Dime," Ford said, answering his friend's unasked question. Wow, talk about attuned to each other. "He didn't hit on you, and he'd go out with a wingnut if he could stick his dick in it."

"You two really employ the best, don't you?"

She went to sit on the couch.

"We only have beer," Jagg said.

Ford already had three. One for Jagg, and he popped the cap off hers before handing it over.

She didn't really want beer. She didn't want anything. Except her phone. Dragging her purse across the coffee table, she plucked it out.

"Did you send Sutherland?"

"Yeah, how'd you know that?"

"He's the one you trust when you can't get Jagg."

"I'll go up there," Jagg said, putting his beer on the island. "If it will make you feel better about—"

"No, I want you here."

"Yeah, 'cause the assholes might move onto her next," Ford said. "You need your own security team."

"I'm calling Lach," she said, scrolling to his number, ignoring her brother.

"We not enough for you? The cops didn't do much to protect you today. Doesn't your boyfriend know what you're into? He just let you out there to—"

"Lach is not my boyfriend anymore," she said. "Don't you remember? Didn't you and Dad throw a party?"

"Look, if the guy took care of you, I wouldn't have a problem with it. But his head is in the job and that job could get you hurt."

"That's not why you had a problem with him."

"No, it's not." Ford propped himself against the kitchen island. "It's bad enough we have to deal with cops on the street. Who wants them in their house?"

"Lach and I never hung around with you and he never dug into your business." Which, given his department, he could've done, if he chose. "You ever think sometimes it's good to have a cop on your side?"

Her brother's head shook as he slurped his beer. "No. Never. What good can a cop ever do?"

"Watch and learn."

Dialing Lach's number, it only took him two rings to pick up. "Babe?"

"Mila could still be in danger."

"I know. I'm trying to—"

"It's okay. Ford's sending a couple of guys to keep an eye on her. Can you—"

"Call the hospital and make sure they don't call the cops on the goons hanging around her room," he said, ending on an exhaled laugh. "Yes. I will."

Her gaze dropped. "This is linked, Lach. When it counts, you believe in doing what's right, not being right."

"I never dismissed you. When you're ready, we'll have dinner. Take me through it. Sell it to me and I'll sell it to them."

"Call me if anything changes."

"Yeah."

"Lach?" She swallowed. "If Yvonne Ingham turns up dead…"

"I know, babe," he said, under his breath. "I know. I'll call you tomorrow."

The woman was out there. Maybe it was her choice to be at Hustle. Maybe Yvonne wouldn't wind up dead. But if she did… The guilt was already so much. How would she get through another murder? Women were dropping like flies, dying because she wasn't smart enough to figure it out. She had to do something. And fast.

TWENTY

SOMEONE WAS MAKING coffee. The scent drifted through to the bathroom from the breakroom. She wrapped her hair up in a towel and hurried out hoping to—oh.

Eight guys, none of whom were her brother or boyfriend, strewn around the room.

From then on, clothes in the bathroom were a must at shower time. Though her towel wasn't what interested the male eyes tracking up and down her form.

"I'm Ford's little sister," she said, fighting to contain an awkward laugh. "Yeah, his baby sister, so you might not want to—"

In he came, her brother and her boyfriend together.

"Stop drooling assholes," Ford said, then glared at her. "Put some fucking clothes on."

"Okay, okay," she said, holding up a hand. "Geez, you'd think none of you ever saw a naked woman before."

Said a lot about her brother's sex life. Jagg's she was less inclined to think about, unless it included her. Going into her bedroom to change, she brushed her hair and then was back in the breakroom seeking coffee.

Thankfully, Jagg was all alone, typing something into his phone in the kitchen.

Delicious and just what she needed.

Without a word, she went to stand at his side, resting her lips on his arm. Sleeping so close to him wasn't easy when her mind wouldn't give her a break. If they'd been able to wake up together—

He put his phone down and raised his arm to drape it over her. "You sleep okay?"

"Yes," she said.

"You forget I know when you're lying?"

"It's relative. I slept better here than I would've slept at home or at Mila's hotel."

"When we don't know what's coming, you need all the sleep you can get."

"I'll remember that when we're public and you're trying to get some at three in the morning."

"Won't be a big bad coming for you then. I'll keep you up all night long."

He kissed her head and went to fill the coffee machine again. Damn guys must've drained the first pot. Containing her disappointment, she sat on a stool at the island to pull her purse across. She really should keep better track of it if people just wandered in and out all the time.

Her notes and laptop were there too; her life reduced to basically what she could carry. She'd take it over what the victims endured.

"Where were they last seen?" Jagg's voice brought her attention up. "Each of the women, the victims? Remind me."

"Heather went from work to the bank and then into a cab. Stephanie left Mila in the apartment to go meet her boyfriend—"

"All in the same area of the city?"

"No," she said, pushing her notes toward him when he stopped opposite her at the island. The damn thing was too wide; she didn't enjoy being so far away from him. "They were all over the city." The way his brow came down in a frown was just so sweet. "You're getting it."

"Getting what?"

"The bug!" she shrieked, hopping off her stool to dash around and grab his arm in both hands. "You want to know too."

Could it be someone finally believed her? Mila lost her friend and was invested in figuring it out so someone could be held accountable. Other than being a stand-up guy, Jagg cared because he believed her, it had to be.

"Are you gonna give it up?"

"Sex?" she asked. "Yes. The case? Never."

"As long as you're on it, I'm on it. But you've gotta follow the rules."

She winced. "I've never been good at that."

"No hiding things from me. No going places on your own. You didn't follow your gut yesterday, don't do that again."

"What if my gut tells me to hide things from you?"

"Why would it do that?"

"I don't know." Look at that mouth, those lips, the incredible force of—she closed her eyes. "You distract me. When I'm supposed to be concentrating—"

"We're messing with serious forces here, no screwing around."

Mila was proof of that. "Okay, I'll be serious and follow the rules."

He kissed the top of her head and let his lips linger there. "There might be some time for screwing around." Swaying back, he met her eye. "I'm still a guy, remember that."

"How could I forget?"

"Let me see this."

Putting a few inches of space between them, he scraped up her notes. The distance felt wrong, but with Ford in the vicinity, they couldn't take chances.

"I couldn't find commonality in where they were last seen. Stephanie told Mila she was going to meet Bryan. He said she never showed up."

"We have to find Bryan."

"Yeah, that would be incredible, if he's willing to help. He reached out to Mila, or someone did, that was who she was running to in the street when…"

The accident happened. Except it wasn't an accident. No one believed the hit and run was a coincidence.

"Why did she want to meet him?"

"Why wouldn't she? Mila wants answers. This guy is either the real thing or responsible. She's desperate to get justice for her friend, to understand. If she missed something, some clue—"

"This will eat her up if she lets it." That relied on her friend waking up. "It's dangerous. This Mila should've known better than—"

"There's something else," she said, attracting his attention. "You said I shouldn't keep anything from you so…"

"So?" he prompted. "Genny, the more I know, the more I can help. And this is not like you and Mila. If something happens to you, there won't be any coming back from it, not for me."

"Because Ford would take you apart?"

"Because I'd destroy the person who hurt you, their network, and then I'd destroy myself. I'm not proud of it, Genny, but this was my world for a long time. I know how things work."

"It's not that I'm hiding from you. This is just… The woman Mila and I were investigating, Yvonne Ingham. We don't know for sure if her disappearance is connected to the other abductions. We assumed she was because her details match the victim profile but… I saw her."

His brow descended. "Saw her where? Yesterday?"

"No." Parting her lips to draw in a breath, she rested against the countertop. "At Hustle. Friday when we were in with Vex. Yvonne Ingham was in the room. I recognized her from her pictures online."

"Are you sure?" he asked. She nodded. "You think she's the next victim? The next woman who'll turn up dead?"

"Maybe." The quiver in her throat was more than just fear. "This is the closest we've been to saving someone, to stopping this before someone else gets hurt." She scooped a hand into her hair. "I feel like I'm chasing in circles. I've barely investigated one death before someone else goes missing. Maybe this is the way—maybe I'll be this way forever and I won't—"

"You will," he said, taking her arm to straighten her up. "Genny, you know you can do this. I know you can. Go with your gut."

"Why did I get into this? It's so much pressure and I… I'm letting them down."

"You're the only one listening." His conviction didn't waver. "And I've got you, baby. You've got this. Start at the beginning. You won't find Yvonne if you don't figure out how the women were chosen, how they were taken. No one saw anything? No one heard a scream? No one—"

"The cab," she murmured, making a connection. "Oh my God." Grabbing for her notes, she spread them out, checking one page and then another. "All of them were last seen going somewhere else, from the street… in a cab."

"All of them?"

"Stephanie was leaving the apartment. Mila didn't mention a cab, but neither of them had a car." And they couldn't ask Mila until she woke up. "I have to call the hospital."

"In a minute," he said, keeping hold of her. "Do you have access to their bank transactions?"

She shook her head. "But Snake Guy, that picture I have, I got it from the camera at the convenience store across the street."

"A bank would have cameras," he said. "You said that's where Heather was last seen."

"Yeah, but I show a little cleavage at the convenience store, I get a guy to help. I doubt banks are so liberal. Do tellers have access to camera footage?"

"Banks will be digital."

"So?"

"I'll make some calls."

"You can't hack banks."

"*I* can't," he said. "But there's always a guy who knows a guy."

"Oh, is there?" she asked. Another thought hit her. "I'll call Steeple. He might know someone."

"You know who else might know someone?"

"No," she said without equivocation, knowing exactly who he was implying. "I'm not calling my father unless the world is on fire."

Shoes. Hair tie. She headed toward the bedroom.

"This will come out one day," he called after her. "That you put your life on the line for a story."

Spinning on the bedroom threshold, she caught the frame. "To save other women," she said and flashed a smile. "And I'll create a distraction before he goes postal."

"You think there's anything in the world that distracts him from his baby girl's life being at risk?"

"Oh, I don't know, maybe you lusting after me."

"I'll do a lot more than that."

"Which we'll tell him and he'll forget all about the life on the line stuff."

"That the reason you slept with me?" he asked, the corner of his lips rising. "For cover."

"Yep, absolutely. Best part about it is it's more than one use. We'll just have to keep on doing it."

He shook his head as she retreated to the bedroom. Call the hospital. Go to Mila's place. The list stalled. Guilt still ate at her. Being with Jagg made her happy, but it didn't feel right to embrace that bliss.

With him on her side, at her side, the chance of figuring this out was a hundred percent better than it had been yesterday.

TWENTY-ONE

NO CHANGE FOR MILA and Steeple was out of the office. His life was his office, so it had to be something big to separate him from his desk. All the time he spent worrying about his reporters, they could do with worrying about him sometimes too.

Jagg stopped the car outside the convenience store. She put her phone back in her purse and got out not expecting him to join her.

"What are you doing?" she asked, rushing over to block his path onto the sidewalk.

"What am I doing? Thought this was the place." He glanced around. "Not a lot of birds on this block."

"We only need one bird. One bird got me that picture of Snake Guy."

"So let's go."

She swooped out of the way of the arm he tried to put around her. "Cleavage is the price," she said, tugging down her top, which he didn't miss. "Cleavage doesn't work so well when I bring a brooding boyfriend."

"You expect me to sit outside while you go in and play with another guy?"

"He won't touch me. Trust me. And you can't be jealous because you've seen me naked." She hooked a hand around the back of his neck to pull him down. "Come here."

Maybe it wasn't smart to be kissing on public streets, but Jagg didn't resist.

"You're not out in five minutes, I'm coming in. And I don't know how to ask nicely."

"Ten minutes," she said, snagging the thumb drive from her pocket. "It'll take time to copy the files."

Another quick kiss and she retreated slowly, half expecting him to follow. Thankfully, he just stood there, not all that happy, but respecting her wishes.

A sense of achievement joined her on the way into the convenience store. Hopefully, that could be the theme of the day.

The store wasn't that busy, and it was the same guy as last time behind the register. Young, not all that bright, but enthusiastic, which worked for her. On her previous visit, she hadn't considered how the situation could play out with a chaperone like Jagg. If a man like him stood at her shoulder, the clerk would probably wet himself before he'd think about so much as making eye contact with her.

On getting out of there, she expected Jagg to be waiting, though not in the exact same spot she'd left him in. The guy was ready to move, given the potential for injury and death, she wasn't too sorry about that.

She held up the thumb drive. "See, piece of cake."

Without a word, he opened her door, and she slipped back into her seat. Patience wasn't exactly her most exercised muscle. So before Jagg was even next to her, she had her laptop open to pull up the footage from the store.

"The screen's too small to pick up much," he said.

Yes, her laptop wasn't the best viewer. "It's what I've got right now, and I have to know."

Jagg drove. She didn't know where they were going and didn't even bother to look. Tracking to the day and the time, her breath stalled as she watched, waiting. People on the sidewalk, cars went this way and that.

Stephanie's apartment stoop had ten stairs from the communal door to the street. The convenience store was at street level. She didn't know the exact time and wanted to be aware of anything suspicious.

Nothing looked strange, out of place, yet she zeroed in on every cab that went by.

"Maybe it was an app."

If it was, the connection could be traced. At least that way, it could be discounted or absorbed into the timeline.

"I don't have access to their cell data, but if we find—"

Stephanie.

Straightening up, she zoomed in. Yes, that was Stephanie, emerging from the apartment building, descending the stairs, wearing her new glasses. Raising the screen to eye level, her heart thumped, waiting, watching for…

Stephanie stepped off the curb and raised her hand at the traffic and—yes, a cab! It pulled up and she slipped inside.

"Oh my God," she whispered, tracking back the footage to scrutinize the car.

"What is it?"

"She's in a cab. She gets into a cab."

"Is it waiting for her?"

"No, she flags it down and…" A random pickup would be impossible to trace. Though this wasn't definitive proof. For that, they'd need to match the cabs to each other. Prove that the same one picked up every victim. "Is that it? Is that how they get them?"

"Depends who you believe."

Details of the cab weren't easy to pick out and the single frame angle didn't help. It was almost exactly perpendicular to the opposite building. When the cab drove into view, the license plate wasn't visible and with other traffic in the way… No, she couldn't see it at all.

"Damnit, I can't see the plate."

"Look on a bigger screen and—"

"The angle isn't right."

Disappointing? Yes. But there was invigoration too. Progress. It was something and a clue she could share with Mila when the woman woke up.

"It's a start."

"Yeah, we know how he got them."

The women wouldn't have thought twice about getting into the cab. Something they'd probably done a million times before.

"No assumptions, we don't know for sure," Jagg said. "Not from one victim."

True. All the picture showed was a woman getting into a cab. Not exactly a smoking gun.

"You okay to take me to the bank? They might not give us the footage, but there could be other cameras on the block. And Langspring, her boss, should give us whatever video they have of Yvonne leaving. If he doesn't, I know you can take him."

"I shouldn't have hit the gym this morning, huh?"

"I'll always give you a workout any time you want one. And I'd love to join you at your gym."

"You a member?"

"No, but I don't need to use the machines. I'll spot you."

"Bet you will."

Another indulgent smile. "Langspring said Yvonne got in a cab. I don't know if that's what he heard or if someone told him. Do you think someone forced her into a vehicle?"

"If anyone was grabbed and dragged from the street, someone would've seen something."

Doesn't mean they'd report it though. Society was cynical these days.

"Do you think they're tracked, or is it random? The women. The victims."

"Your Bryan guy could answer that. Two of the four dated a Bryan. Could be a helluva coincidence."

"Or not." She pondered. "I wonder how they met. Maybe I could—"

"No, I draw the fucking line at a honey trap, honey. You're mine and the Manzanis know it."

"He doesn't seem like your type."

"'Scuse me?"

"Vex Manzani. You and Ford hung in his crew for years."

"We weren't his crew. We were part of the entourage, side shows to entertain him. I wouldn't trust a Manzani to have my back, now or then."

"You must've trusted someone."

"Ford," he said. "Strat."

"My dad."

"I trusted him more than Ford did. Strat's always been on the fringes, in and out of every group. A part of every crew and none of them. He's one of the few people—"

"Okay, you're going to tell me how great my dad is. I get it. You know, I remember when he used to fight. When they used to fight, Dad and Ford."

"Yeah? That's guy stuff. Nothing serious."

"Dad never yelled at me, never got in my face."

"You stood up to him."

"Not like Ford. They'd go toe to toe and never back down. Dad didn't say no to me. He didn't care enough to fight."

"That's what you think?" Jagg tightened and loosened his fists around the wheel. "You think he didn't care about you?"

"I'm his little angel; he has to love me. But care about my choices or the course of my life? Ford's the one he made in his image."

And he'd let her go without a fight. Her mom took her, choice or not, and Strat just let it happen.

"Strat can relate to Ford. You? He's fucking terrified of you."

Seemed unlikely given her dad was easily twice her size. "Me?"

"It's a battle he fights with himself. He wants the best for you, in the world, fulfilling your potential, I guess. But he's also terrified of losing you. He didn't want to corrupt you. He didn't want to corrupt Ford either. Having kids changed a lot, he says it changes everything. He wanted what was best for you. Your mom could provide more, Ted could provide more, better. Strat didn't want you to waste that chance for the sake of loyalty."

"But Ford—"

"Your mom couldn't control Ford. Even when Strat tried to send him to your mom, he'd runaway and come back, like a fucking boomerang. Strat knew there was nothing in this life for you."

"He told you this?"

His shoulder rose in a half shrug. "I know the guy. My dad? He didn't give a damn. I know what that looks like. I know what hate looks like, what anger looks like. Impatience. Fury. My dad taught me that young. He taught me how to read the room. If I didn't read him right, I could be in for a world of hurt. I knew when to get out of the way. Didn't work all the time."

"Strat never once asked me to stay. Visits with him were obligation, not a choice."

"Now I know you're shitting me. Strat cleared his schedule a month in advance for you, made me and Ford scrub the fucking floors. You were all he talked about. All he worried about was letting you down."

"My dad doesn't talk like this."

"It's his only hang up, the only one I ever read. You think he rejected you? Every time he saw you, he thought it would be his last, that you'd disappear into the world and never come back. Strat doesn't judge, he doesn't. Not you, not me, not Ford. You could tell Strat anything, any of us could. He'd be right there, shoulder to shoulder with me and Ford, to protect you. His only role as a father is to protect and provide. He couldn't provide, so he'd be damned if he couldn't protect you."

"Protect me from what?"

"Guess we'll never know." He slowed to a stop by the corner and pointed ahead. "Got a three-sixty bird right there. The bank's down the block."

Right. Yes. A domed camera on the office building. Pushing her shoulders back, she boosted herself higher to check out the reception. Big honey-blonde hair, perfectly contoured makeup... The receptionist with the phone to her ear never let her smile slip.

She sank back, her attention sliding around to him. "Looks like this one's on you, baby."

While she smiled, he shifted to recce what she'd already seen.

"Goddamnit," he said, but freed his seatbelt.

"You're not out in ten minutes, I'm coming in."

He opened his door. "Yeah, yeah."

Without him, it would be harder to stay strong, to maintain any fortitude. His dedication kept her focus sharp. And with him by her side, she had nothing to fear.

TWENTY-TWO

FOR THE REST of the day, they trawled each of the women's last known locations seeking cameras and clues. Some videos were handed over, others needed persuasion, and there were the flat nos. They got a few of those.

"We should get some food and go through the recordings," she said. "The more eyes, the better."

The laptop wasn't the optimal place to wheedle out details.

"I can drop you back at home. There's something I want to check out."

"By yourself?" she asked. "What happened to not hiding anything? Where are you going? Is it case related?"

"Could be. I don't know."

"I want to come with you. If you've had a thought, share it."

Silence. One second, two…

He inhaled. "The point we triangulated from the victims' bodies," he said, "from the location where they were found—"

"The hotel."

"It could be nothing."

"I've been."

"To the hotel? The Carlyle?"

"Yeah."

"Alone?"

"I wanted to check it out."

Oh, he didn't take that well and his face didn't hide it. "And if they were murdered there? The killers could've hurt you."

Now there was an interesting distinction. "Killers? Zz? You think there's more than one perpetrator?"

"I think if it's related to the Manzanis, looking at this like it's one crazed serial killer would be a mistake. Guys who work for families like the Manzanis don't take initiative, they don't make their own decisions." Or indulge their own obsessions, she'd guess. "They do what they're told. Someone had to give the order."

Their lenses on this didn't match up. While she sought a single murderer, Jagg's experience steered him toward something more organized.

"Bryan will tell us."

As a first step anyway. Though that would come after actually nailing down the guy, kind of an important detail.

"You don't think he's connected to the Manzanis? You got to Hustle through him. If you know Hustle, you know someone. You owe someone or they owe you. One thing links to another, cause and effect, something Silvio likes to say."

"I found the hotel. I went in and didn't see Bryan."

He shook his head. "You have no sense of self-preservation."

"You worry too much. Yes, it was a risk—"

"Did anyone know you were there?"

"No," she said. "It's my job to—"

"If Ford had any idea the risk you took, if your father knew. Shit." He swung the car around to head back the way they'd come. "They'll forgive me for screwing you before they forgive me for this."

"You're taking me with you?"

Probably because he'd concluded she'd be safer with him.

"New rule," he said, tossing a quick glare her way, "never go anywhere dangerous without me or Ford."

"Can I give you that rule too? You said if you wanted to go to Hustle, I couldn't stop you."

Just like she could go to the hotel with or without him.

"We're getting food first."

"Food? Okay. We can get food."

Not like there was any great rush. Business could be conducted at the Carlyle at any time of day. Arguing to get food after just because she was impatient would be petulant, especially given his concession. Worry though he might, at least he was giving her the respect of taking her along. If he hadn't, she would've ventured there alone, most likely after viewing the footage.

They stopped to pick up food and, without eating it, Jagg drove them toward the Carlyle. Less than a block away, he killed his lights. The streetlights gave them some scope, the ones that worked anyway.

On the perpendicular street, he slowed and parked at the far side, providing them with a prime view of a good chunk of the hotel's façade. She undid her seatbelt.

"Just wait, Genny."

"Wait for what?" she asked, glancing from him to the hotel entrance and back. It was a good fifty or so feet away. "You want to watch? For what?"

He reached into the backseat to retrieve their food bag. "If we walk right up there, we'll only learn what they tell us when they're on the defensive." He passed off her sushi tray. Not something he'd ever be caught eating. "We sit here a while, we do some learning of our own. You know what this Bryan looks like?"

"Sort of," she said. "Mila has a picture of his profile."

"Think you'd recognize him?"

Settling back, she opened her food box. "I guess we'll find out."

"If he shows."

An hour went by, they ate and watched. A few guys went in, a few departed. Ones they hadn't seen enter left too. Another hour. And another. Women came out to smoke or talk, one argued with another. So far, nothing newsworthy.

She shifted in her seat, stretching her spine. "I don't think I've ever just sat in a car this long."

That his gaze remained intent was impressive. "Never parked in high school?"

"If we were doing that kind of parking, I wouldn't be so stiff. Are we going to sit here all night?"

"I can take you back to the garage, if you want."

And possibly miss their target. "No, I'm not complaining. I'm just curious what happens if we don't see him."

"What do you think will happen if we do?"

"We'll grab him or—"

"If he's connected to the Manzanis, we back off." What? No! Why—"Do you recognize him?"

Following the line of Jagg's nod toward the hotel entrance, the new arrival definitely wasn't Bryan. The tall, solid-built guy talking to the smoking women was partially turned, so a back view was all they got.

"No," she said. "Should I?"

His lips thinned before parting. "That's your Snake Guy."

Her jaw dropped. "Asshole," she said, socking his arm. "I knew you recognized him! I knew it! Who is he? Should we go get him?"

"Get hi—fuck, no. We don't get in his way. No one gets in his way. The guy's got nothing to lose and nothing but cojones."

"He could be a serial killer."

"Oh, he's killed. Bet your sweet ass on it. He works for the family, when it suits him. He's the only guy you'll hear saying no to Silvio and getting away with it."

"Why? Does he owe him for something?"

"Something? Maybe."

"Who is he?"

"Alotta bullshit flying around out there. No one knows the whole story."

"Would you just tell me? Don't and I'll grab your dick next time we're alone with Ford."

"Inside or outside the pants?" he asked like she was serious. Her growl challenged that assumption. "Word is he's one of Silvio's."

Okay, that made exactly zero sense. "One of Silvio's what? Minions? Goons? Favorites?" Nothing. "His friend? His partner? His brother? His blood enemy? What?"

"What's the worst kept secret about Silvio Manzani?"

He said it like she should know, like everyone did. Nope, not her.

She just shook her bewildered head. "What?"

"It's not really a secret, not like he's shy about it. It's just not talked about openly, not in the ranks, or while Manzani ears are close."

"What is it?"

"He's a breeder."

The words went in, but she shook her head. "What's that? A breeder?"

"His thing is getting women pregnant." Still Jagg's attention stayed on the hotel. "Fuck knows how many kids he has out there, dozens, maybe hundreds."

"Do you mean like having affairs? He cheated on his wife?"

"It's not cheating when Silvio Manzani does it." No, the don would think it was his right. Arrogance wasn't in short supply in their city. "Affairs. Strangers. One-night stands. Fuck buddies. His friends' wives. His wife's friends. Doesn't matter who it is, he just wants to knock them up. It's what gets him off."

"I don't get it."

"People out there are into all kinds of kink. It's his thing. Hell came first, at least that's what they say. I don't know. Silvio got high on the power, high on watching Daphne carry his child. Since then, he fucks around every chance he gets."

"And doesn't use protection? Women let him—"

He laughed and scooped up her hand. "Baby, come on, it's Silvio Manzani."

"That's no excuse."

"Not a lot of women say no to him. No woman says it more than once."

"Does he support them? These hundreds of babies?"

"Never asked. Some of them maybe, if it suits him. Others are just out there, probably don't even know he exists. Silvio doesn't care about seeing them, just makes him feel like a stud to know, whatever."

It was kind of disgusting. No, not kind of, completely disgusting. "Just when you think a guy can't stoop any lower."

Snake Guy went inside. Conversation over.

"If you think that now, don't ask about Silvio's dolls."

"His dolls?"

"Swerve will know what's going on. He's pretty good at relaxing people before going in for the kill. I can talk to him, but if he knows I'm interested…"

"We could draw attention to ourselves. Swerve is Snake Guy?" After a single nod of confirmation, she sat up straight. "I'm going over there."

"No, you're not. With Swerve in the building, it's more dangerous. You want me to go talk to him, I'll talk to him, and keep your name out of it."

She hadn't considered for a second that Jagg would ever drop her in it with anyone.

"Why would you go over there? What reason could you have for going into that hotel except for sex?"

"Shit, baby, I'm not gonna—"

"That's what men go in there for. That's what you said in the diner. Besides, I already have cover."

"Cover?" he asked, narrowing his eyes. "You went in the last time, didn't you?" She nodded. "What did you say? Because if you fucking tell me anyone tried to put you to work—"

"Don't freak out, it was nothing like that, I…" It was going to come out anyway and they were supposed to tell all. "I asked if my boyfriend had been around… you know, if he was playing away?"

"Your boyfriend? Fuck, in Hustle we…" He trailed off as she braced. "Me?"

"You said I had your protection so long as the Manzanis thought we were together. I needed a boyfriend so—"

"A whorehouse?"

She hitched her chin. "Something wrong with women who make their living using their bodies?"

"If they were using it for their own gain, no, but the women in there are Manzani product. What did they say?"

"Woman on the desk told me if you showed up there would be a line around the block." And damn, she believed it. "She said I should let you play away. Some guys just needed it."

He kissed her knuckles. "I don't need it."

"I know. I didn't go there intending to name you. She asked for a picture of my then imaginary boyfriend, which obviously I didn't have, so—"

"You knew she'd know who I was."

"I'm sorry if it embarrasses you, if I embarrassed you."

"I'll get over it," he said, kissing her hand again. "You want to keep watching?"

"Snake Guy, Swerve, went inside."

"Swerve's as likely to use the product as I am. Either he's in there taking care of business or he's bedding down. Last I heard, some of Manzani's guys stayed here."

"For protection?"

"They get a bed and if anything hits the fan, they're nearby. Works for everyone."

"If Swerve is one of his children—"

"Potential."

"Why wouldn't he stay with his father?"

"Swerve's welcome at the mansion. More welcome than Vex, that's for sure."

She'd bet that applied to a bunch of situations. Knowing nothing about Swerve, she couldn't judge him. Vex, on the other hand, was not a presence anyone would covet.

"So why doesn't he stay there?"

"Swerve plays his hand close to his chest. He shows up and disappears as he pleases. Does Silvio's most important work, for the right price. But he's not housebroken, baby, he's not the type of guy who sits at a table to eat. He doesn't do small talk."

Small talk in the Manzani house. What would that look like? Kill anyone special today? Rip off anyone cool?

"You don't sound sure of him. I mean, I believe everything you're saying, but—"

"Everyone should watch their ass around him. Sometimes he's like a coiled snake, and his fire is worse than the dragon's, that's for sure. Only people I'd trust less are the Huntsmen."

"Who are—"

"That's a story for another day, baby. You're wading in deep. Let's go home. Bryan's not gonna show up."

"Maybe we try tomorrow?"

"We'll get some rest and check out those videos tomorrow. My guy should have something for us by then, if there's something to get."

"Okay," she said, going with the plan.

They could sit there all night, but if they didn't get some rest, tomorrow would be a washout. Yvonne Ingham did not have that kind of time to play with. A day could be the difference between life and death.

TWENTY-THREE

"THANK YOU," she murmured to Jagg as she passed him to go into the garage.

The workshop was spooky in the night. Cast in only the dull blue light of a couple of bug traps on either wall, the vast space was cavernous. Who knew what could lurk in the dark corners?

Spooky was relative. What did she have to be afraid of? Nothing. Not there. Not anywhere so long as the men in her life paid attention.

"You okay?"

Startled by Jagg just a few feet away, she'd been gazing into nothing. "Yeah."

"Wanna tell your face?" he asked, coming back to take her hand. "You pissed we came back?"

"No, we need to be fresh for tomorrow. I…" She swallowed. "We're safe."

"Yeah, I locked the door. We have alarms—"

"No, I mean, we're not just here and safe, we're happy. We're happy, right?"

His concern deepened. "Yeah."

"And wherever she is, Yvonne…" As the name came out, his form relaxed in understanding. "She could be chained up; someone might be torturing her and—"

"You're torturing yourself with this. What's going on out there isn't on you. And we're gonna figure this out. We'll find out who's doing this."

Such confidence. "You're saying that to make me feel better."

"If I wanted to do that, I'd back you up against the wall and fuck you."

Her hormones took notice, but her guilt spiked too. Going to him, wrapping both arms around his torso, she sank against him. For comfort. For heat. For something sure and solid to hold her up.

"Wherever she is, they could be—"

"You think that's the same thing?"

"No," she whispered, closing her eyes, pulling herself against him. "What if she never knows this again? What if she never knows it can feel like this?"

"You're the only one who gives a shit. The only one who saw this and went out there to help these women. The risks you've taken, the danger you've put yourself in—"

"But I'm not in danger." Loosening her embrace enough to look up at him, certainty was all she could give. "You'd never let anyone hurt me. No matter what it took, you'd find me. I know you would."

"Baby, there's nothing in this world that would keep me from getting to you."

"I know." Doubt didn't exist at that moment. "And she's out there. Yvonne's out there, alone, with no reason to live. Any second she could give up, hurt herself or let them hurt her. What if we're too late? What if we don't find her and they take someone else? An innocent, oblivious woman in the city tonight could be their next victim."

"You're the media, baby. Write something. Warn them."

"What? That they can't get into a cab? That's the closest thing we have to an MO, and it's not exactly airtight. We know this, this tiny morsel of information. With all the legwork, everything we've tried and we're still no closer to—"

"We have the footage. We'll go through it second by second until we find something."

"And if we don't? We can't just stare at the Carlyle forever, we have to find Bryan. And even if we do, I…"

"What?"

But she didn't want to admit Bryan may not be forthcoming. Whether it was protecting himself or the Manzanis, she doubted that just asking Bryan what was going on would reap results.

What did that leave them with?

The cops, she could go to Lachlan, but if they didn't believe her, would they really charge Bryan with a crime? No, they'd let him go and he'd split town. She could play bait. Though that might be tough unless they could nail down the exact cab and where it would be. And they'd still be relying on it stopping for her.

Somehow, she couldn't exactly see Jagg just being okay with her being abducted and carted off to wherever.

"Maybe I'm not strong enough to do this. Maybe I'm not good enough. If I'm all these women have to rely on—"

His kiss silenced her. That was what she wanted, the oblivion of how he made her feel. But it was wrong, they shouldn't, not while Yvonne was still out there.

Pushing his chest, she leaned back on his stabilizing forearm. "It feels wrong to feel good."

All those times Lachlan was preoccupied now made sense. She'd chased a story before, countless times, but this was the first time her failure would sentence another person to death.

"It puts it into perspective…" His thumb traced her cheekbone. "How little time we might have, the bullshit we worry about, these tiny things we make our whole lives."

"Being allowed to surrender is an honor."

No was a word that meant something in their world, in the real world. It wouldn't wherever Yvonne was being held.

"You surrender when you're beaten." His caress continued, soothing and igniting her, pleasing and arousing her. "You'll never be beaten, Genny."

"You're the one undefeated."

"And I'll always be by your side. This is not on you. It's on us. If we're fucking this up, it's because I'm not good enough. It's because I'm letting you down."

"No!" She grabbed his neck. "You're in this because of me. We're in this, and in danger because—"

"I couldn't stay away." Gripping her waist, he guided her backward. "Because I can't stay away, Genny." Her back hit the wall. "How did I live without this? Without you?"

In a way, they hadn't been without each other. All their lives, each drifted in and out, always on the periphery.

The tighter his grip got, the shallower her breathing became. "We're against the wall."

As if that was enough, he hooked her thighs to clamp her against the cold concrete, pelvis to pelvis.

"It's risky."

Although it was late, they had no idea who might be around or if Ford was still awake.

Looping her arms around his neck, she pulled herself up to kiss him. "You really are afraid of my brother."

His gruff laugh accepted that challenge. "No one comes between me and my woman."

"Between you and getting off." Smiling, her tongue touched his lip. "I'll protect you. It's nice and safe inside me."

And if her brother walked in, God help him not them. Witnessing the act would not be as fun as participating in it.

Their mouths and hands knew what they wanted. Their bodies called to each other. Maybe they always had because this didn't feel new. Rather, it had the excitement of novelty while at the same time enveloping them in a comfort that came with security.

Jagger Dunn. All her life she'd been looking, no other relationship fit, and he'd been right in front of her the whole damn time.

"Yes," she exhaled in bliss when their mouths parted, not because they lost contact, but because their union was about to become a whole helluva lot more intimate.

When he slid home, her neck loosened, landing her face against his hard body. Each thrust moved her against him, the cool wall heated as the friction burned her back. That didn't stop her pushing to take him and easing his retreat.

No. She wanted what he wanted. That satisfaction. The need had to be satiated.

His name seeped from her throat. But, shit, they had to be quiet. Turning her face, her teeth dug into him through his tee-shirt, holding her voice at bay.

In the moment, in the now, there was no other way to be. Right then, the growing mass of pressure in her gut needed its release. She needed it. Fuck, damn, she needed it in that second.

A screaming yelp of satisfaction, muffled against him, only just got out before her head was back and her eyes met his.

Still drilling into her, his darkness colored desperation. Feral, wild, without fear or worry, he owned her and the moment, and every ounce of their potential.

What would she be without him? How could she ever be?

He slammed into her so deep, her stomach lurched as it clenched tight, aching to hold him within her for as long as possible.

"I'll tell you what feels wrong," he huffed into her hair when his mouth landed on top of her head. "Laying you down in any bed but mine."

She smiled, smoothing her palms down his arms. "We'll be under the same roof."

"Not the same."

No, it wasn't. "Maybe one day—"

"Definitely one day." Hooking a finger under her chin, he brought her gaze to his. "After we find our guy, I promise."

"I think I already found mine," she murmured, skimming her hands up to the globes of his shoulders.

"We'll go in and tell Ford right now, if that's what you want."

"Waking him up won't improve his mood."

"Don't know if he's asleep."

"It's late. Why wouldn't he be asleep? You think he was worried about us being out late? If he was, why didn't he call or come find us?"

"Guy's got his own troubles. And we don't know if he's alone," he said, backing up to set her down.

"You think my brother's getting laid?"

The audacity of her tone was kind of rich and probably why he snickered. "Might put him in a better mood."

"Who is she?" she asked as he draped an arm over her shoulders to lead her across the space. "Have they been seeing each other long? Why don't I know about her?"

"That's another mystery for you to solve another day."

"My brother goes through women," she said, going through the door he opened for her to go into the hall. She scoffed. "What am I complaining about? Bet he doesn't even know her name."

Opening the breakroom door herself, she looked back at him and the twist of his lips sparked her suspicion.

"Don't be looking at me like that." With his hands on her shoulders, Jagg eased her into the room. "I don't know nothing."

"You do know. You know what he's like. What aren't you telling me?"

"No hiding things applies to the case."

"Not our personal lives?" she hissed in a whisper, pushing back when they got to her bedroom door. "I want to know."

"I know you do." This time, he reached around her to boost the door from in front of her. "Get some sleep."

He pushed her inside, leaving her with nothing but questions.

TWENTY-FOUR

"YOU'RE DISTRACTING ME," she murmured, pushing Jagg away.

On the couch in the breakroom, they were supposed to be watching the footage he had hooked up to the wall-mounted TV. The computer was perched on his knee supported with a steadying hand, while the other kept finding its way under her skirt.

That had been distracting enough. Then he'd gone and slid closer to kiss her ear, her cheek, that soft spot on her neck that—

"Stop," she laughed, shrugging him aside. "Ford could walk in any second."

"You scared of him?"

"Funny. You're projecting." She nodded at the screen. "This is serious work. Would you pay attention?"

Though his exhale was one of frustration, he straightened to play the video again. They couldn't be fooling around while women were being murdered. But she couldn't deny it was flattering that he couldn't keep his hands off her.

And she'd thought she would be the one trailing after him with her tongue hanging out. She would be. As soon as this was over. Yet another incentive to add to the list.

Ford's bedroom door, by the TV, opened, and he came striding in. They'd separated just in time. She expected a woman to follow, but as he headed for the kitchen, no one else emerged.

"Where is she?" she called.

"Who?" Ford asked.

Jagg nudged her. Was it supposed to be a secret? She hadn't heard anything through the night. No sounds of love, giggles of romance. Did women giggle around Ford? Probably, knowing the type he attracted.

Pushing back, she raised her mouth his way, though she couldn't see over the back corner of the couch. "Nothing, I was just asking if you slept okay."

"Like a baby, little sister," Ford said. Was it just her or did Jagger shift away another few inches? "What did Ludlow do now?"

"Ludlow?" she asked as Jagg tracked the image back. "Who's Ludlow?"

Thrusting her elbows into the couch, she rose to see her brother there in the kitchen, hands open on the island.

"Fuck me," Jagg said, slumping back.

Ford laughed. "Don't tell me you missed the old jerk. Him and Dad were thick as thieves in the old days."

"Ludlow?" she asserted, looking back and forth between them. Still her question went unanswered. "Who is Ludlow?"

Her brother got discerning. Wow, who knew it was possible for him to think that hard?

He went to grab a cup and the coffeepot. "Never found out what happened. Did you ask?"

"Kinda, but he didn't say anything and I let it go," Jagg said. "Figured he'd tell us if he wanted to tell us."

"Me too."

"Hey!" she exclaimed, closing the laptop on Jagg's thighs, blackening the TV. "Who is Ludlow?"

"Buddy of Strat's. They were tight for years."

"Then he just disappeared one day."

"And we didn't ask."

Or Jagg tried to and Strat hadn't filled him in.

"You're telling me that my father... that Kurt Stratford is friends with someone you saw on there?" She jabbed a thumb toward the blank TV. "Dad? My dad? Our dad?"

"Used to be friends. What is it?"

"Driving the cab," Jagg said, meeting her eye. "He's driving the cab."

Thus far their attempts to get a plate or ID anyone had been unsuccessful. See! If Jagg had been more interested in the TV than her underwear...

No time for that kind of thinking.

She jumped to her feet. "I have to go."

"You have to go where?" Ford asked.

Purse. Shoes. "Dad's."

"You're going to Dad's?"

"Is that so unbelievable?"

"The way you've been with him recently, yeah. Him and Lud haven't spoken for a few years."

"We don't know that for sure."

And there was Jagg, right at her back.

"Can't hurt to check," she said, all innocence. "It'll give me an excuse to judge him face-to-face. A little of his own medicine."

Adrenaline fueled her certainty. Did she want to see her dad? No. But one step followed another. Talking to him was progress toward cracking the case. Her personal feelings didn't matter.

"Well, wait a minute, I'll go with you."

"Why do you need to come with me? Dad's not going to do anything to me."

"And you?" Ford asked. "What are you gonna do?"

Not flatten him. Not unnecessarily anyway.

"Fine. Come with me. But if you two start conspiring against me, I'm out of there." Her brother picked up his coffee like they had all the time in the world. "If you're coming, come now."

"I'm coming."

And yet, he hadn't moved.

Stomping around the counter, she snatched his coffee cup to pour the java away. "I will buy you a new one." His wrist in her fist, she pulled him along. "We've got to get moving."

Her dad could know where this Ludlow dude was, what he was up to, and who he hung out with. For all the issues she had with her father, the guy had his ear to the ground. He'd know something. Though when he heard about what she'd been getting involved in… She wasn't a baby anymore and wouldn't let him bully her.

They needed answers. Words. At least this time, unlike instances before, she had ammunition of her own that should dampen his urge to baby her. After she reminded him, of course.

"You need me?" Jagg asked.

Was he talking to her? They halted.

"Tav's coming over," Ford said, like that meant anything to anyone.

Her. Like that meant anything to her.

"We can't deal with that today."

"Desperate to see Strat?" Ford asked, a snicker in his words. "You babysat her yesterday. I'll take today."

"Babysat me?"

Now it was her brother pushing her out. "What else would you call it? You're chasing a crazed murderer who loves killing women, which you are, in case you forgot."

"Nice of you to acknowledge I'm not twelve anymore."

"Don't get used to it."

"With you, I never do."

Her big brother, her protector, and her aggravator. That was kind of his job and hers too in return. What else were siblings for?

TWENTY-FIVE

AT STRAT'S DOOR, Ford reached for the handle, obviously planning to waltz on in. She intercepted his hand, shaking her head.

"You knock on Dad's door?" he asked. "Since when?"

Making a point of exaggerating her knock, she waited. "You don't want to know."

"What—"

"You never know what you might walk in on. This could save you from serious mental trauma."

The door opened. Strat's jaw was loose until he took in the sight. Then a suspicious frown overtook his expression.

"This ain't gonna end well," he muttered.

He stepped back and Ford tried to go in, but the back of her hand hit his torso, stalling him.

"Are you alone?"

Her dad might not appreciate the question. She didn't appreciate its necessity.

"Yeah, I'm alone."

Her hand fell and she took the lead going inside. "Is there coffee?"

"What's going on?" Strat asked. She heard the front door close. "Which one of you is in trouble?"

"You think we'd come here if we were in trouble?" she asked. "You *are* trouble."

And he'd raised it too.

In answer to her question, yes, there was coffee. Enough for half each.

"I'd come here if I was in trouble," Ford said, dropping into the armchair by the window. "Strat knows all the back doors out of this city."

"It's not Christmas, no one's dead," Strat said. "What else gets you two together?"

She poured two half cups, but only took them as far as the breakfast bar. "You know a guy called Ludlow?"

"Way to ease in."

Their father aimed his keen surprise at Ford. "Told you not to go near that asshole. Why would you let your sister—"

"His sister is the one who asked the question." Rounding the bar, she peeked at the bedroom door. Some part of her suspected they weren't alone. "I know you know him."

"Then why ask?" Strat asked with a tinge of anger. "He's trouble. You stay away from him."

"Same might be said about you. And him there." She jerked her chin toward Ford. "When did you last speak to him? Ludlow?"

"What is this? An interrogation. I won't talk about him, and I won't let you talk to him. If he comes anywhere near you—is that why you're with your brother?" He switched to Ford. "You not taking care of business? What else I gotta tell you about him to get the message through?"

"You never told us why you cut ties. Jagg asked, but—"

"Why the fuck does it matter? Steer clear. That's it."

"You were friends, you used to be," she said. "Is that what you do with your friends when you're bored with them? Way to be loyal, Dad."

"That guy was not a friend. Maybe once, but I— he got mixed up in shit I wanted no part of. Dangerous shit. And I don't want you two in it."

"Where can I find him?"

"Didn't you hear me? I said no."

"That's not the way it works. Are you going to help me?"

"Get near Ludlow? No. Guy would see me coming."

"I didn't ask you to join me; I asked if you know where he is."

"No."

She glanced at her brother. "Well, this was a fruitful trip."

"It's important, Strat. Life or death important."

"Which one of you's in danger?"

"Not us," she said. "We're trying to help those trapped by whatever circle he runs in."

Or his web. She hadn't excluded the possibility it was just one crazed serial killer. Jagg said otherwise, and she acknowledged that. But one nut was easier to come to terms with than a consortium killing for kicks.

While shaking his head, Strat exhaled. "That's the thing, Immie. His circles are sick."

"Anyone called Bryan in that circle?"

"It's a common name. Probably more than one."

"Ludlow near a Manzani?" Ford asked. "Vex?"

Hmm, well, she had been the one to bring up Hustle with him in the beginning.

"Could be. You wanna stay away from that crap. Fuck, son, you know better." Now their dad was getting mad again. "One step into that world is one step too many."

"I'm not the one on that path. You want to look at the pretty Stratford for that."

And a second later, their scrutiny was on her. "Who do you know in Manzani circles?"

First Bryan and Hustle, now this Ludlow Cab Driver Man was connected to the family too. Somehow, she had to get closer.

"I won't let you do it. I won't let you—"

"What are you going to do? Keep me prisoner? You want to ground me, Dad? You didn't even pull that when I was a teenager. I need an in, someone who can help me figure out who Bryan is and how he's linked to the murders."

"Murders?"

"If it's nothing, I see it out and move on to wherever it leads me. Until I know, I can't give up on it."

"Much as I tried to scare her off it, she's adamant. And I can't deny there's a chance…" A chance what? Her brother didn't look her way. "If she's right, people are dying."

"Women are dying."

"And we don't want her to be one of them," Strat said. "Stay away from the Manzanis. Both of you."

"We're looking out for her," Ford said. "She's staying at the garage. If I'm not with her, Jagg is. Cutting her loose only leaves her exposed. The more you help, the faster this is over."

"Help?" she asked. "No, I don't need either of—"

"One person knows the Manzanis better than anyone." Her father's attention drifted to her, and she closed her eyes. "Only one close to the circle who I'd trust."

"You're going to say her, aren't you?"

"Her?" Ford piped up. "Her who?"

"Dad's girlfriend."

"She's not my girlfriend."

"Okay, sorry, your screw buddy."

"Who are we talking about?" Ford really wanted in on the secret. "I didn't know you were seeing anyone."

"She's not my girlfriend." That was for her. The next sentence went to Ford. "I am not seeing anyone. It was a—"

"One night thing?"

"Im—"

"She's younger than me, Dad."

"You said that already."

"Shit, Strat, you parking in the stroller aisle?"

Strat threw up his hands. "It was so much easier when I could just turn both of you over my knee." Not that he ever had. "Respect your damn elders."

"I respect elders who respect me. Does your girlfriend respect you?"

"Who the hell are we talking about?" Ford exclaimed.

"Sersha McLeod," she said. "Lachlan's sister."

"Shit, Dad, that's way above your weight." A laugh hit Ford as he pounced to his feet. "How did that happen?"

"It didn't. We're friends. I help her out. It's no big deal."

Ford squinted. "Isn't her father like—"

"Police Superintendent? Yes. He runs the damn police department and our father is nailing his little princess."

"Okay, no one who knows Sersha would call her princess. That word's cursed with her," Strat said. "And

I am not nailing her." He gestured at Ford. "I told her she should make time with you but—"

"You want me to screw your girlfriend?"

Written in disgust, the words were a tease too. She didn't find this funny.

"Doesn't matter. You stay away from her."

Ford held up both hands. "She's yours, guy. I don't want hand-me-down pussy."

"Won't be so funny when you have to see them together. I caught them in bed—"

"When?"

"Five weeks ago," she answered her brother. "Five weeks ago yesterday, to be exact. Was that some anniversary for you?"

"Immie—"

"Whatever," she said to her dad. "Are you going to call her? I can have Lachlan—"

"I'll do it, I'll text her," he said, digging his phone out of his pocket to type into it. "Then you can fill both of us in on what the hell you're mixed up with."

"I didn't come here to tell anything. I came here to get information, not give it."

"This Sersha, she's the one who wrote that piece in The Chronicler," Ford said like he was just figuring it out. "She knows all about the Manzanis. How come you didn't speak to her at work?"

"This is my story and we don't hang out."

"You dated her brother, the cop, for long enough."

"We know each other, but we don't hang out. This isn't a teen movie. We work in the same office. Not everyone is bestest buddies with their boss and colleagues."

Bringing Sersha into the conversation was a risky endeavor she hadn't intended to undertake.

"Guess you'll have to get to know her better, if she's going to be our new mom."

Okay, that was funny. To her and Ford anyway.

"You two…" Strat said, pointing at each of them before going over to slap his phone onto the breakfast bar, "don't fuck around with her."

"Protecting your FWB?"

"Protecting my kids. Any word of anyone screwing around with Sersha could be in serious trouble. Don't taunt her." She got that hit. "Don't fuck her."

And that one was for Ford. No one could say her dad didn't give them equal attention. In that room, on that day, anyway.

"What's your deal with this woman?"

Her brother did that discerning thing again, giving her the creeps. Ford was laid-back, easy; he didn't think too much about anything. Had she missed him maturing and actually giving a shit? Jagg's accusation that she hadn't been paying attention applied in more than one of her relationships.

"I look out for her," Strat said. "And I'm not the only one."

"There's some deal with her and Vex," her brother said.

"Not just him. Trust me, both of you, don't piss her off. Don't hurt her."

"She threatened us?" she asked, affronted enough to consider calling to yell at Lachlan.

"No, and she never would. She looks out for people, like you do, but other people pay attention to her life and wanna win points with her. So, again, trust me, let her be."

TWENTY-SIX

"THIS IS UNBELIEVABLE," Sersha said, poring over the pages spread on her dining table. Why was it only women who grasped the gravity of the situation? "Someone should've put this together."

When the woman looked up, it was clear she wanted agreement. "I put it together."

"Yeah, sorry, but I meant the cops. Why isn't anyone investigating? If you told Lach—"

"I did tell him, many, many times."

"He doesn't believe it?"

"Not until things got a lot more serious when a woman ended up in hospital a couple of days ago," Strat said, from his post leaning against the wall at the other side of the table. "Which I was in the dark about until a half hour ago."

Ford was in the kitchen, not doing much, just being… there. Strat didn't blame her for getting involved with something dangerous. No, that was too logical. It was her brother's fault, apparently, despite him not being anywhere close to her at the time of Mila's accident.

"Why would we tell you? There was nothing to tell. I'm fine."

"You won't be if you keep this up."

"And you're here because it involves one of the families," Sersha said, thankfully just glossing over the Stratford tension. "The organized crime families." Curiously, her dad and Sersha fixed on each other. "Which one?"

"Aren't you the Manzani expert?"

"Some might say," the beauty breathed out and straightened, putting the notes down. "They're wearing the Manzani mark, which you must know." Yeah, not that it came easy. "But they're not working women, judging by the notes on their backgrounds. These are ordinary, everyday career women, college educated with prospects. How would they get mixed up with the Manzanis?"

"Exactly," she said, bouncing a step closer. "We need the connection."

Sersha pushed around some of the papers to reveal the pictures. "And how he picks his victims. They're all in the same age range—"

"Different areas of the city, different backgrounds."

"Different physical features, other than they're all white, but that's a big net to cast. How did you get to the Manzanis? Who are we thinking? Silvio or Vex? Because if you start down the cousins and—"

"Jagg thinks whoever is doing this needed permission, that he wouldn't just kill for fun."

"It might be fun for him, but he wouldn't get away with doing this unless someone higher up sanctioned it. Some of these women were tortured for days."

She rested a hand on the dining chair next to Sersha. "That's what happens. They go missing, people notice, but no one makes a big deal of it—"

"No one makes a big deal of it because the cops are ignoring it. Because the media—"

"I don't want to spook anyone or cause mass panic. Yvonne Ingham is still unaccounted for. He could have her now. They could have her."

"You think this could be one guy? Do the targets have connections that could've put them on the Manzani radar? Is this revenge? Payback? Leverage?"

"We know at least two of the victims were seeing a guy called 'Bryan,' probably not his real name, before they disappeared only to wind up dead. Bryan is the same guy who called Mila and lured her to the spot she got hit. And the only place Mila knows Bryan mentioned to Stephanie was Hustle."

"The sex club." Said like it was no big deal. "If you go in there, they'll want a show. Evander doesn't like being told no."

Hmm, Sersha used Vex's real name. Whatever was between them obviously ran deep. How could anyone consider…? Was Sersha intimate with Vex? Shit, that was a nasty visual.

"But you know how to do it, Scamp." Strat got their focus. "You say no to him."

"All the time."

"So if you go to—"

"No!" she asserted, smacking the top of the chairback. "This is my story, you can't send Sersha in there alone."

"She knows how to take care of herself and has been fighting off Vex Manzani for years."

"I can go in there," Sersha said. "It's poking the bear, but I can do it."

Strat folded his arms. "Vex been leaving you alone since…?"

Sersha shrugged. "As alone is alone with Vex." She shook her head. "He has other things on his mind right now."

Sersha McLeod, daughter of Police Superintendent, granddaughter of a beloved alderman, and sister to Lachlan McLeod, vice detective. Also known as her last boyfriend. The woman should be about the great and good, like the rest of the family. Yet she talked about one of the most dangerous men in the city like a friend, a benign entity, like they were talking about a store clerk or bank teller.

"Vex Manzani's a killer."

As Sersha's attention rolled around to her, a smile formed on the woman's lips. "Yes, just like his father and brothers and everyone else in that world. They're all capable of it, if not already guilty. This is a dangerous road."

"Yeah, everyone likes to tell me that a lot. You don't shy away from it."

"An odd confluence of relationships gives me a kind of safety net."

"Because your dad runs the police."

"That and…" Sersha again glanced at Strat, "and other things."

Ford chose that moment to come over and get involved. "Sersha can go in there clean, talk to Vex, find out what he knows. There's no reason for you to go to a sex club."

"What the hell is with the men in my family—"

"No one has to go to Hustle," Sersha called over her rising irritation. Everyone silenced. "You want me to ask Vex, I'll ask him. But if I open my mouth and tell him you're on this, we're on this, whatever, I don't have to name names, then it's out there. I ask, he'll know someone's watching."

"And they might shut up shop," Strat said. "Good. Contact him."

"I don't want them to shut up shop." That sounded a whole lot like Yvonne's death knell. "Shutting up shop means getting rid of evidence. It means never getting justice or tracking those responsible."

"Or…" Sersha drew out the syllable. "Vex dishes out the punishment." That didn't sound like a daughter of law and order speaking. "If this is on Evander's order, yeah, he'll clean house. But this isn't like him. It's too… complicated."

"What the fuck does that mean?" Ford asked.

"Evander doesn't apologize for who he is and would never feel guilt or shame. If he wants to kill a woman, or a bunch of them, he'd slit their throats in a club full of people and never blink. No one will roll on him. No one's going to the cops with that."

"Could be well known on the street."

"And you're who I go to for that," Sersha said to Strat. "You can call around."

"He's already refused to help," she said.

That startled Sersha. "Why would you refuse? You got skin in this game?"

"Yeah, right, Scamp," he said. "I'm the killer."

"Don't doubt you're capable."

"Everyone is capable in the right circumstance."

"Or the wrong one."

Her dad and Sersha's familiarity was kind of jarring. Their ease was blatant, their trust, their understanding. Did they keep each other's secrets? Confide in each other. Commiserate? Yes, it was nauseating to think of her dad with a woman younger than her, but it was nauseating to think of him with anyone.

"I'm not calling around on this."

She groaned. "See, refusal."

"Because I like you alive, Immie."

"Tell them I'm asking," Sersha said on a shrug. "It's not like our association is a secret anymore. If someone asks why you want to know, use my name."

"Why would he be okay using your name and not mine?"

"I don't have to use anyone's name. I don't want my little girl mixed up in this."

"I'll take it if you want," Sersha said and briefly sucked her lips around her teeth. "But if anyone tried to take my story out from under me…"

"No one is taking this," she said. "Help, don't help, that's up to you, but I am not letting this go."

"Do you want me to call Evander?"

"Call him?" she asked, flabbergasted. "You have his phone number?"

"He has me on speed dial. Some nights he doesn't let me sleep."

The opening was too good to ignore. "Do you have sex with him?"

Amusement bubbled out of Sersha. "He wishes."

"And has been wishing for a long time." Strat didn't miss the opportunity. "These guys get obsessed, Immie. That's what I've been trying to tell you. I don't want you on their radar."

"But it's okay for Sersha?"

"You're my daughter."

"And she's your… what? Fuck buddy, friend with benefit—"

"He knows I can handle this," Sersha said, interrupting again. "And he's right. If you want someone to deal with Evander, I'm already in his field of fire."

And since they were there anyway, she asked, "You know a guy called Ludlow?"

Sersha's brow creased. "Yeah, low level, not a Manzani by blood, he used to run with—"

"Ludlow is bad news." Her father was just stuck in a groove. "Neither of you should go near him."

Sersha laughed. "Oh, if that was a challenge, I'll pick it right up, old man. You're afraid of Ludlow? I've seen you stand up to the scariest sons-of-bitches this city has and you draw the line at Ludlow? Ludlow?" The woman just couldn't believe it; her head shake carried incredulity and laughter. "One phone call and we can have him trussed up on a platter or behind bars, take your pick. I, for one, wouldn't be calling in those favors on a nobody like Ludlow. Hell, I'll kill Ludlow for you. That's as much as anyone's paying attention to him."

"These women are paying attention." And it wasn't quite so funny to her. "He's involved."

"Ludlow?"

"He drives them. Each of the women was last seen getting into a cab. One of those drivers was Ludlow."

"Just one of them?"

"So far he's all we've ID'd," Ford said like he'd be around for a while. "City isn't as well covered as you'd think."

"We don't have access to the city cameras."

"Lachlan could get you that," Sersha said. "You never told me why he isn't chasing it down for you already."

"He didn't see the connection, and it's not his department. The hit and run shook him up though, I think. I haven't spoken to him for a couple of days." Because she'd been too busy with her new boyfriend. "I was supposed to have dinner with him, but we haven't got it together yet."

"He's not Homicide; those guys can be territorial."

"The victims don't care who catches the asshole, or assholes. They care they stop getting away with it, that no one else dies."

"Ludlow does make it more interesting," Sersha murmured. "What do you know about him, Strat? Tell me, pretend your kids aren't here."

Like that would work. Her father kept his secrets locked up tight and never—

"Porn. He's into porn."

She couldn't believe it. Her mouth dropped open, though her father only saw Sersha.

"Who cares?" the woman asked. "A lot of guys are. A lot of people are."

"Not like this, not watching it."

The two chatted away like they were shooting the breeze, putting pieces together, tossing around ideas. It was… unfathomable.

"Making it?" Sersha asked. "Is that what you mean?"

"It's an easy area to break into, cheap, quick cash."

"For the men holding the cameras," Sersha said. "What happened?"

"When I found out what he was doing, how he paid his Manzani dues, I walked away."

"It wasn't so simple. Walking away is not a choice most men get."

"Ludlow was like me, our allegiance was more fluid than anything. We dipped in and out of deals or schemes as they came around. But he was into this, like I've never seen, and the better he did, the deeper into the Manzani world he got. He wanted me in, tried to get me involved…"

"The women weren't willing, were they?" Sersha asked, now solemn.

That was going around.

Even Ford shared the thought. "Hookers?"

"Who signed on, maybe, at first, but they didn't know what they were getting into. It was a meat market until they eventually…"

"Eventually…"

"They were selling them off. Guys paid to star in their own film. Nothing was too much. Any fuck with a fistful of cash abused the women night after night."

"Now we're in Lachlan's arena," Sersha murmured.

"This was years ago," her dad said, shaking his head. "I haven't heard about it for years. If they got too close to the—"

"Russian dolls." What the hell did that mean? She frowned at a distant Sersha. "A few weeks ago, Evander tried to bring in a shipment of women, the cops intercepted them. Got them out, got them help." That was something. Though anything better may not be awaiting the women if they got deported back to wherever they'd come from. "I thought his plan was to distribute them around, Lachlan thought that, at least that's what he said. Steeple mentioned you were into something. How long has this murder spree been going on?"

"I don't know," she said, searching for a specific list. "Could be a year, could be more. Without knowing how he chooses his victims, I can't ID every one to pinpoint it."

"It's a computer search. All the women who match the profile and are wearing the Manzani mark."

"The cops think the mark means nothing."

Translated, Lachlan thought it meant nothing, just like Jagg.

"They're not seeing these women for what they are. They see the Manzani mark and toss them aside, assuming they're prostitutes." Which deserved a whole story of its own. "The method of death is different, the dumping of the bodies—where did they make these porn movies? If a john was willing to pay for a more respectable woman… Supply and demand."

"A computer search," she said, jerking like something jabbed her spine. "If they are making these movies, would they be online?"

"Could be."

"Who wants to trawl through porn like that?" her brother muttered. "You said these women are tortured."

And at that, she scraped together the pictures of the victims and held them out to him wearing a smile. "You want to make yourself useful?"

"No," he almost groaned. "Why would I want to—"

"You wouldn't want your sweet, innocent little sister to sully herself watching that filth, would you?"

Though he sneered, he snatched the pictures. The guy was there anyway, might as well take on the cause.

"If it's for private collections, it won't be online. The johns want confidentiality."

"I get that. It's worth a shot."

"It's worth a shot," Sersha agreed. "And maybe if we can get a look at the location background of the Manzani porn that is out there, we can figure out where it's being filmed. They'd be keeping the women close to the set I'd bet. Doesn't help without a point of reference though. Manzanis have sites all over their territory."

"Maybe it's not in their territory."

"Outside it, they don't have protection. They're targets. It will be somewhere they feel safe, somewhere with protection. Ideally, with lots of loyal eyes and not a lot of questions."

"There's a hotel equidistant from where each of the bodies was found."

"You're talking about the Carlyle," Sersha said. "That's a building full of selfish indulgence. There were whispers about things going on in there. Less of the simple sex for cash transaction, but that was about blackmail, not murder."

"Maybe the two go hand in hand."

"We can't eliminate the possibility. It would be perfect for privacy. Sex is already going on, so people don't react to anything they might hear. It's fully controlled by the Manzanis and has been for a long time."

"Good, so we have a plan. Ford's on the porn. Strat's going to call around and—"

"Can I talk to you, Scamp?" Strat asked, striding toward the bedroom without waiting.

Saying nothing, Sersha left the table to follow him.

They couldn't be intending to do anything intimate, could they? With the door perpendicular to the breakfast bar open, the bed made an ominous sight just as the door closed. A plan. A team. Focus. The story mattered, not her dad's sex life. The Chronicler. Murders. Her job, at least, was straightforward... sort of.

TWENTY-SEVEN

WHILE SHE WAS AT SERSHA'S dining table, Ford lay on the couch somewhere in the living room behind her.

"I don't want to hear you enjoying that, whatever you're watching."

"Ah, bite me. This is your bullshit."

So far there hadn't been any sex noises. While Strat and Sersha were still in the bedroom, if there was any moaning or grunting, she'd tell herself it was Ford's porn. Not that thinking of her brother having sex was appealing.

Lach strode through the front door, his tee-shirt half off over his head. When his arms dropped, fabric in hand, he spotted her and stopped.

"Im." No one could claim Lachlan was a stereotypical donut munching cop. Not with a physique like that. Distracted by it, she just sat there, staring. "Immie, what are you doing here?"

Snapping out of her daze, she shook her head. "Working. What are you doing here?"

"Did something happen? I thought you were staying with Ford, if you need somewhere—"

"He's back there," she said, tipping her head back. "Somewhere."

"Over here, so quit taking your clothes off in front of my sister."

For so long, their intimacy was a given. They'd both taken it for granted. How odd it was to have full entitlement over something one day, and absolutely none the next.

"I came here to change and I was going to call you," he said.

"About dinner?"

"Yeah, but they're weaning Mila off the sedation. It's possible she'll wake up soon."

She leaped up. "Oh my God. You should've called me!"

"I was going to," he said, crossing the room to grab a holdall that he dumped on the back of the couch. "We don't know for sure. The doctors are happy the swelling is going down, but don't know if there's been any aftereffects."

"Like what? Like a concussion?"

Lachlan opened the holdall to grab out a clean tee-shirt. He discarded one to don another. "Maybe. I don't know, babe, I'm not a doctor. We can find out when we get there."

"Okay, good." Immediately, she headed for the door. "Come on."

"Hold up a second…"

Not what she wanted to do. "We have to get over there."

"We will." He came over to cradle her face in both hands. "You look tired."

"Thank you. Just what every woman wants to hear."

"Are you taking care of yourself? You know I'm here if you need anything."

"Her brother's still in the room, asshat," Ford called, "dial it back."

"That wasn't what he meant," she called to her brother. "Get back to your porn."

"Porn?"

"It's a long story," she said. "Why are we waiting?"

Her father and Sersha appeared from the bedroom.

"Lach, you're a jerk," Sersha said, barely pausing for breath.

"Good to see you too," he said, his hands dropping from her face. "You holding meetings here now?"

"It's my apartment," Sersha said. "You don't like it? Leave."

"Why are you here?" she asked, knowing it was unusual. "Are you staying here?"

Better than a hotel. He'd left her in the apartment they'd shared. They'd paid the rent for the year, and she was at Jagg's, shame for it to sit empty.

"Sersha had her heart broken, she needs a keeper."

Like she was some kind of zoo animal. While Strat regarded Sersha as an equal, Lachlan morphed into Ford when it came to the way he treated his sister. In some respects anyway.

"I do not need a keeper, a minder, a bodyguard, or a therapist," Sersha said. "You're a squatter. An unwelcome houseguest who won't go away."

"Like you said, I'm at Ford's. If you want to use our place, I won't be back there for a while."

That was as specific as she could be. Living with Jagg wouldn't be a bad thing, but if she hung around too long, she'd cramp Ford's style and he'd have no problem telling her that.

And that posed another question. Would she and Jagg ever live together? She couldn't see him leaving the garage and he wouldn't kick his oldest friend out. Living with her brother might not be so bad. Though living with him while in an intimate relationship would be a whole other matter.

"Yes, go live there. Anywhere but here."

"I know how much you need me, sis."

"Yeah? And where were you when Imogen needed you?" Sersha gestured toward the dining table. "You knew about all this? The cops knew, and they didn't do anything? You didn't do anything? You're a jerk."

Hence the woman's opening statement.

"We're picking it up now."

"Picking it up?" That sparked optimism. "You're going to investigate?"

"Not me, homicide, but, yeah."

"Who in homicide?" Sersha asked.

"Wanstead."

She glowered. "He's a bigger jerk than you. He might get the award for it."

"Yeah, but sometimes it takes a jerk to find a jerk."

"That's touching, Lach, real pretty," Sersha said. "You come up with that yourself?"

She took Lachlan's hand. "Can we talk about this more in the car?"

"The car?" her father chimed in. "Where are you going?"

"I'm going with a cop, Dad. Not a serial killer or a gangster."

"It's been my experience they're the same thing."

Whatever bug was in her dad's ass, he was not letting it go.

"Not my experience," Sersha muttered absently. Strat glanced at his friend and she shook it off. "If there's been a break—"

"It's Mila. They're going to wake her up."

"You think she'll remember anything?"

"I don't know."

Shit. What if Mila didn't remember her or that her friend was dead? Could they miss vital clues? Could the poor woman have to experience the grief of losing her friend all over again?

"One step at a time," Lachlan said, always steady and calm. "She's alive. Her health is the most important thing. You can't rush her or scare her. She won't be up for much."

And may wonder why there are people questioning her and guarding her, if Ford's friends were still at the hospital.

"Have you spoken to her family? Do they know what happened?"

"So far, no one's showed up," Lachlan said.

That chilled her. "She's by herself?"

"Do you want us to come with you?" Sersha asked.

Ford got to his feet, putting her laptop on the coffee table. "Someone else can take porn duty."

"No, I don't need you. I'll be okay."

"You need someone with you. You go poking around in Manzani business—"

"Lach's with me. We'll be at the hospital where your guys are anyway. Nothing will happen to me."

While her brother and father looked at each other, pondering this and having a silent conversation, she grabbed her purse and dragged Lach out of the apartment.

"They care about you and want—"

"Please don't," she said, hurrying down the stairs, her hand still in his. "Let's get to Mila." In the car, they rode in silence, which was not like them at all. "I appreciate it, okay? That you all care about me, it's just..."

"You don't want to be babied."

"No one does and maybe my upbringing was more sheltered than Ford's, but it seems..."

"What?"

"It's so unfair."

"What's unfair?"

"Everyone in my life backs me up. Even when I don't want anyone dictating to me or coddling me, you all do it anyway. And there's Mila, in pieces, literally, and there's no one there for her."

"Sometimes life works out that way. It's sad, but there's nothing we can do about it."

"There was something I could've done. I should've realized when she came to me that I was the only one she had, her only support. No one would've noticed if she'd just been erased."

Like Jagg said. The Manzanis would push Mila beyond sanity and take her out. That would be bad enough for anyone who noticed, but worse that no one noticed at all.

"You noticed."

"Did I?" she asked his profile. "I went back to her apartment and found her gone."

"See, there, you went to check on her."

Rankled by her own discomfort, her mind wasn't so sure. "Did I go to check on her? Or did I go for the story? Did I go there to use her, just like these maniacs used her friend?"

"You were there," he said, firm. "No one else showed up and you were there when she needed you. I believe you cared because you do care, but even if you didn't, what does it matter? Your goal was to get justice for her friend, that's what Mila wanted. That's what she wants."

"So many people care about me, and so few care about her."

"You want to see her, don't you?"

"Yes, but why do I want to see her? Do I give a shit or am I just hoping she saw something that helps the story?"

"This is about more than a story for you, it's always been about more. If you wanted sensational headlines and pats on the back, you would've gone to print with your hunch."

"Steeple doesn't print hunches."

"He would. For this. For you? Immie, you are a tenacious woman, a persuasive woman. Isn't that obvious by now? No one was with you. No one saw what you did. Now we're all on your mission."

"Because you believe in it?"

"I believe in you, Im." Reaching over, he squeezed her knee. "I'd do anything for you. Just like your dad and brother, just like Steeple. We believe in you."

As he threw her a smile she intended to return, her purse rang. Digging inside, she answered without reading the screen.

"Hello?"

"How you doing, Genny?"

Jagg. Her muscles loosened as relief left her in a sigh. "Hi." Except, huh, the detective next to her probably knew her tells. Getting it together, she aimed for neutral. Whether she hit it or not was another matter. "I can't really talk right now."

"My guy got back to me."

Ah, progress? "And?"

"Don't know if it's what you want to hear." That could go either way. "He pulled more from the city cams at the time of the disappearances."

Impatience quaked. "And?"

"False plates and… Ludlow's driving."

"In all of them?"

"So far," he said. "He sent us the footage."

"Okay." She sighed. "Thanks."

More to trawl through. The answer was one she expected and it strengthened their case. It also gave authorities something to look for. Any other women getting into that cab would be at risk too.

"I wanna be with you."

Her lips reacted. Was that "with" her like sleep with her? Be with her while the investigation was going on? Or could he mean with her like to be with her? Be together? With Lachlan in earshot, she couldn't ask. Not that the phone was the best way to have that conversation.

Even after a few days, instinct wanted answers. She wouldn't push, couldn't, shouldn't. But, damn, if he could just hold her for a minute, everything would be better. She would be better. Stronger.

"We're making progress."

"You've got Ford on porn duty?" So he'd talked to her brother before he talked to her? "How come that wasn't an option for me?"

If Lachlan wasn't within earshot, she'd ask if she wasn't good enough, but teasing was too risky. Her ex knew her too well.

"They're waking Mila up; I'm going to the hospital with Lach." Her way of telling him who was with her. "I really want to talk to her."

"Give it time. Don't rush her."

"I won't—"

"I don't want you to be disappointed."

"She's alive. That's all that matters."

"Want me to come be with you?"

More than she could express, but there was just no way. Ford thought he was babysitting, and she'd told him it wasn't necessary. She couldn't now call Jagg in to take over the task.

"My dad took us to Sersha. She knows a lot about the Manzanis."

"That's good. You want me to let you go?"

"Yeah," she said while every atom of her being begged him to stay. "I'll call you later."

"I'll see you later," he said. "For some off the books stakeout duty."

She wouldn't mind an official stakeout. Watching the hotel had been helpful. Though that wasn't what he meant. Some of the unofficial kind could be exactly what she needed.

The line died, and she put her phone back in her purse.

"Sorry about that," she said to Lachlan.

"No problem."

And he didn't ask. Not so long ago, she'd have volunteered the information of who was on the phone and what they said. Now it was complicated for so many reasons.

"I don't want to lie to you," she murmured.

"I didn't ask. And know better than to ask questions I don't want the answers to."

"You're a detective. I thought you wanted all the answers."

"Immie, I'll always be here for you, no matter what..."

She didn't need to be a genius to divine that there was an exception.

"But...?"

"If I ask, either you lie, and I know you're lying, or you tell the truth… and I'm not ready to hear the truth of what lightens your voice like that."

"I didn't—"

"I know you, Im." Damn, did he have to be so perceptive? "Just be careful."

"Because I'm weak and vulnerable and I can't take care of myself?"

"Because all those people you complain about protecting you, they have to be ready too."

Did he mean him or her family?

"Who broke Sersha's heart?" she asked, backing away from the murky subject of her own love life. "Did you arrest him?"

"Might if she gave him up. Sersh can be a closed shop on this kind of stuff, with me anyway."

"I didn't realize how much she and my dad trusted each other." And she hadn't told Lachlan about the bedroom incident. "I'd say I'm jealous, but it's just surreal. They vibe with each other. It's freaky."

"Came out of left field for me too. He was the first person she asked for after the attack. After kicking my dad and Henry out of her hospital room, Strat was who she needed."

"For what?"

"I don't know," he said, sliding his hands up the wheel. "He showed up and she asked for privacy."

Which he would've given them. Seeing his sister torn up like she had been wasn't easy for a brother like Lach… or like Ford either. She sighed. People cared about her. Instead of seeing it as stifling, she should appreciate their concern. Wasn't always easy in the moment.

"I'm sorry about Sersha, what she went through. She looks great though."

"Everything bounces off. Even when it doesn't. You know what she's like."

Because throughout their relationship, his sister had been part of conversation. She'd never taken the time to really get to know her though. Maybe that had been a mistake. People had busy lives. One went this way, the other that, it wasn't easy to match up sometimes. That was an excuse, one that relieved her of responsibility. They worked in the same damn building, in the same department. Okay, so their jobs didn't involve riding a desk all day, but if she'd wanted to take the time, she would've.

Damn, was she a bad person?

She got blinkered and everything else disappeared. Not disappeared exactly, just slipped down her list of priorities. People liked to say they had busy lives, but they made time for what was important.

Like murder.

If she needed to make right any wrongs, to rebalance karma, the people responsible had to be stopped. By her. And her team. Mila might be alone, but she wasn't. That couldn't be taken for granted.

TWENTY-EIGHT

WAIT.

The doctor's instruction was simple, if infuriating.

Laid out in the hospital bed, hooked up to machines, Mila looked small. Bruised, patched up, and vulnerable, the woman hadn't opened her eyes.

Lachlan had left her under the protection of two of Jagg's guys. Not guys she was familiar with, but Mila hadn't been harmed, so they'd obviously been doing their job.

"You're going to be okay," she said, squeezing Mila's hand that had been in hers since she sat down.

An hour ago. Maybe two. Her tension came with a peace. Being there meant something. Maybe her imagination got the better of her, but the proximity of her vigil held weight.

"I'm sorry," she murmured. "I should've been here. I should've stayed with you." Being with Jagg, free and safe, was an insult to what Mila endured. "The doc told us you haven't talked to your mom for years. They couldn't find your brother. You shouldn't be alone. Stephanie would be here... if she could be."

Great. Yeah. Talk about her dead friend. If there was a choice, wherever Mila hovered in limbo, maybe staying there with Stephanie was an appealing option. But what did she know? Tomorrow, the afterlife, never solved mysteries. It was beginning to feel like no mystery could be solved.

"We're making progress—"

The door behind her opened. Was it a doc or...?

Snake, dragon... Snake Guy. Swerve.

Standing fast, she put herself between him and Mila. "What are you doing here?"

Without a care in the world, he sauntered over and pulled the curtain around the bed, blocking out the door.

"Mila's a good friend of mine."

"Mila is not a friend of yours," she asserted. "And I will not let you hurt her."

"I didn't come here to hurt her."

Menace lingered, though he didn't frown or growl. His intimidation came in his height, in his size, in his tattoo and the uncomplicated ease of his arrogance.

"We're in a hospital. People know I'm here. They'll look for me. Hurting me won't—"

"Why do you think I came here to hurt you?" He came closer, but she held her ground. "Can't I just be here to check on my friend?"

"No one has visited since she arrived." Including her. The day of the incident didn't count. "You went to her apartment to scare her, to threaten her. I know what you did, who you are. The woman's unconscious, warning her won't make a lot of difference."

"Now you're getting warmer." His shoulders loose, his eyes intent. Could this guy feel emotion? Could he understand fear and hate and grief? "This warning isn't for Mila, this warning's for you."

Ah… Maybe she should've figured that out sooner.

"You know I'm asking questions."

"Questions? I don't care about questions. I don't care about you running all over town for kicks with Jagger Dunn. Yvonne cares. Marcie too. And Janine."

"Oh my God."

Others. The confirmation that there were other victims was a surprise. The surprise was them being held together. More than one victim at a time. How had she missed that?

"You're chasing ghosts, Miss Stratford. The women who are gone, you can't do anything for them. The women still here will pay for every step you take down this path. Do you want that on your conscience? How deep do they want you to dig when every ounce of dirt causes them pain?"

"How can you do this? How can you hurt innocent women? Torture them?"

"I never laid a finger on any of them."

Someone else may do the dirty work of that variety. That didn't exonerate him. Knowledge was complicity, action or not.

"You're involved. Every person who knows about this sick, sordid scheme is involved. If you're not doing anything to help, then you're hurting them."

"Here's the thing, Miss Stratford…" He moved right up close. Her shoulders rose as they tensed, each breath got harder than the last. Mila needed her to stand strong. "Alotta what I do hurts someone…" Not that it seemed to bother him when he said it so cold and plain like that. "What you're looking at is a tiny piece of the puzzle. Just a tiny piece." He showed a gap between the end of his thumb and forefinger. "But it's an important piece. Crucial." When his heavy hand dropped onto her shoulder, she gasped. "If you fuck with the system, the system fucks with you."

"I thought you weren't going to hurt me."

His voice deepened. "Hurting them hurts you." The back of his fingers rose to her jaw. "Who knows? Maybe a little firsthand experience will show you how important these women are to the bigger picture."

Their bigger picture wasn't so rosy. Every other abducted woman had turned up dead.

"What will it take for you to let them go? Right now. Just open the door and let them walk."

He laughed. "You're funny, Miss Stratford." He ruffled her hair. "Funny." As he turned, he whipped back the curtain and carried onto the door. "See you around, Funny."

He disappeared into the corridor and the air left her lungs. At the same time, her legs buckled, and she dropped to the bed.

"Oh my God."

A hand on her chest, the thump of her heart slammed against her. A headache, dizziness, adrenaline was doing its work. What was she supposed to do? How could she…? She'd promised to get justice for Stephanie and the other murder victims. What about the victims still alive? As the Snake Guy said, Swerve, according to Jagg, she couldn't do anything for the dead. Now the living depended on her too.

"Steph?"

The croak of a voice spun her around.

"Mila, honey." Sinking onto the bedside chair again, her hand sought Mila's. "Hi, it's Imogen Stratford. Do you remember me?"

"Imo…" Mila coughed and winced. "What happened? Where's Stephanie?"

Oh, God, no. "You don't remember?"

With her eyes closed, Mila's brows came closer together. "The car, I remember." Her eyes opened. "Stephanie's dead."

"I'm sorry." So many times she'd said that word. Never once had she meant it more. "I'm going to get your doctor. Stay here."

Only a couple of steps toward the door, she faltered. Stay here? What a stupid thing to say. Going into the corridor, Sutherland appeared through the doors at the opposite end with Coakley. Better late than never.

The nurses' station was the other way. So walking away from them, she went to the desk.

"Mila woke up," she said, getting their attention. "Can the doctor see her?"

"Yeah," one woman said and departed.

Drumming her nails on the desk, she peeked over her shoulder. Was Swerve still around? Did she need to be watching her ass? Depending on how this played out, she could be doing that for the rest of her life. The Manzanis… from no risk stories to maximum risk. No one could say she started out small.

TWENTY-NINE

"IMOGEN?"

Sersha walked toward her from behind the nurse's station.

"What are you doing here?" she asked.

Sersha took her arm to guide them to a quiet corner. "Does Steeple know about this?"

"About what?"

"What road you're on. How deep you're getting. He'll want to know if there's a risk to your safety. The Chronicler can provide security."

"You never have security and you're mixed up with the Manzanis, way more than I knew. Does Steeple know you have Vex Manzani's phone number?"

"Yes. My brother knows too. That doesn't put me at risk, it protects me. Evander protects me. My father protects me. My brother. My gran—"

"My father?"

"Yeah," Sersha said, dropping her arm and backing off a little. "Strat looks out for me. We're not sleeping together. I know that's what you think."

"My dad is an adult, you're an adult—"

"He told you we didn't have sex."

"And I should trust that?"

"Trust him."

"Like you do?" Imogen asked. The hostility in the word jarred her hard. What was she doing? She exhaled. "Look, I'm sorry, okay, there's a lot going on and—"

"Why don't you trust him?" The discerning air around her spoke of true intrigue. "Because your parents split up? A lot of parents do, and he hated letting you down. Strat would never hurt you in any way."

"He would never let me out given half a chance."

"He loves you so much. It blinds him. All he wants is for you to be safe and happy. That's something to be grateful for. Take it from someone who knows. It's better to have a father who's too protective than one who doesn't give a shit."

"Your father's Police Superintendent."

"Yes," Sersha said on a sort of exhaled laugh. Maybe because she'd said that before. "And I stand by what I said."

"My father's a better man than yours." She got a single nod. "How can that be?" Exasperated, her curiosity blazed. "Your father protects the whole city."

"My father protects what's important to him. His reputation. His standing. Everything else comes a distant second. Including family."

"It broke my heart, the way Lach tried to be everything to him, tried to win his approval, his pride. Your father never saw it."

"No, he wouldn't, he won't. Won't stop Lach trying though."

"It's an engrained behavior now."

"Exactly."

Giving Sersha a hard time, her father a hard time, was her vent of the pressure she'd been ignoring.

"Your piece was amazing. The Manzani exposé."

"Yeah, so people like to tell me." Leaning on the wall, Sersha folded her hands flat at her lower back. "Feels like forever ago now."

"You didn't follow it up. You could've hit the big leagues with that piece."

"Everyone's opinion of the big leagues varies. Going global was never my goal."

"What was your goal?"

Still leaning, Sersha shrugged. "Probably to piss off my dad."

When she smiled, she reciprocated with a laugh. "That I can identify with."

"It's hard to piss off your dad. He gets grumpy, but he's always a defender. Trust me, he's got between me and some pretty big fish without caring about his own safety."

"He has?"

"Sure. He'd do the same for you if you ever let him."

"He wants me in a glass box. I've never seen him with anyone like he was you… like he is with you, respectful, open, approachable."

"You think your dad isn't approachable? Damn, when I walk into his apartment it's always with some crazy story or seeking information I'd never dream of asking anyone else for… And he's saved my ass, plucked me up when I didn't even see the danger. There's nothing I wouldn't do for your dad, just like I know there's nothing he wouldn't do for me… or for you."

She wet her lips. "He said you had a boyfriend. That day I came over and you were…"

"In his bed? Yeah, he did."

"Lach said you had your heartbroken too, is it true? You were with someone?"

"Sort of," Sersha said, pushing off the wall. "Did I hear you say Mila's awake?"

"Lach and I were just too easy." The woman wanted a subject change, she got that. But this was a chance she may never get again. "We were in this place, like it was comfortable and—"

"You don't owe me any explanations. I know my brother's hurt; I know he wanted to be with you. But what goes on between a couple is their business, no one else's."

"Lach's a good man."

"He is. And not one good with failing."

"He didn't fail. Our relationship just… broke. It wasn't angry or hateful, just not in the right groove."

"I get it. Sometimes love doesn't matter. Sometimes respect and passion don't matter either. There are reasons people aren't suited to be together. Reasons that can't be overcome. Some people don't fit."

If she'd had her heart broken, she hid it well. Though the hurt was definitely in there, peeking out from beneath the façade. A glimmer of sorrow at the corner of Sersha's eye betrayed some piece of her was missing. She and Lachlan fitted as a couple and hadn't worked out. If Sersha and whoever she'd been with didn't fit each other and it hadn't worked, what hope was there for their futures?

What was the key? Were people supposed to be righteous or selfish? Do right or do wrong? Follow the presumed path, the expected path, or were they supposed to do their own thing? Sometimes no one could win.

Opening up might be the first step to learning more about the woman she'd overlooked for so long. And she couldn't deny a fascination with Sersha's position within the city's family elite. On both sides of the aisle, apparently.

"These families, like the Manzanis, do they ever…?"

"Ever what?"

She squirmed. "Make false threats?"

"Someone threatened you?" Sersha asked, instantly serious. "Who threatened you? Was it Evander?"

"No! God, no, I'm too small a fish for him to care about." She hoped. "I'm just worried that Yvonne might… be…" Her nerve faltered. She couldn't say it without saying it. "Never mind."

"Talk to me, Imogen. Whatever it is, it's okay. If I can help, I'll help."

"I don't want to damage your relationship with my dad and—"

"I don't tell Strat everything or my brother, believe me on that. Tell me. Don't take this on alone. I can only be an ally if you let me in. Let me help."

"I don't think anyone can help."

The confidence of the woman next to her was enviable. "I'm your best bet. I have the ear of them all and don't think you'll break if someone looks at you sideways."

Like the men in her life did.

"Do you know… Swerve?"

"Swerve approached you?" Sersha asked, her eyes growing. "That's not good. Not good at all."

"He said if I kept going, Yvonne would pay. And he… he said there were others."

"Others?"

She nodded. "Women. Two other names. Whatever's going on, Yvonne's not the only one in trouble."

"Okay, do you want to back off?"

"I don't want anyone to be hurt because of me."

"They'll kill them either way. If that's the MO, the process, Yvonne and whoever else they have will be murdered no matter what you do. Women will continue to be abducted, tortured, and murdered. Unless, of course…"

"Unless of course, what?" Hope. Don't snatch it away. "Sersha?"

"You take down whoever's responsible first."

Dissuaded, she sagged. "Like it's that easy."

"You're not going to take down the whole Manzani family and wouldn't want to. You'd be on the run for the rest of your life. Ask the Gambattos how that works out."

"That was them turning on themselves, like the McDades, though somehow they got through it."

"These families protect themselves. So unless you've got a big cache of info to dish to the feds, you can't protect yourself from their wrath. Trish Gambatto couldn't do it. No one trusts officials in this town, that's why she hired private witness protection. You got a secret billionaire ex?"

"No," she said. "And no information that would bring down a family."

"I can ask Hell, but that will take time. And God only knows how receptive he'd be."

"Hell?" Shock winded her. "Helios Manzani? Isn't he in prison?"

Sersha's head dipped up and down. "Yep. We write. The relationship's embryonic. For a while it was just me writing, now it's a two-way street. We're getting somewhere. Haven't figured out where yet, but somewhere."

"And you're telling me Steeple should get me protection?"

"Helios can't hurt me from prison. Evander hurts me in his own way. Always has and probably always will. I can always play the daddy card if anyone tries to disappear me."

"You got beat up. Bad. Not that long ago. How are you still so calm about this?"

"Maybe I got hit on the head too many times." The joke fell flat. "You want the story and you want justice. What does that look like? Robes and lawyers and the witness box?"

"Someone has to pay."

"Someone will," Sersha said, pondering. "We just need a little insider information."

"From who?"

The beauty's chin rose a little. Thoughts dashed behind her narrowed eyes. "We need something they want. Something to bring them to the table."

"You want to negotiate with them? You think you can talk them out of—"

"I can't talk anyone out of anything. It's about self-interest. Everything is with these men, with these families. What's good for the guy is good for the family. Make the most money, grab the most territory, live your life on top." Her gaze widened. "On top! Yes, on top."

Sersha took one stride, and she grabbed her to a halt. "On top of what? What are you talking about?"

"Find out how Mila's doing and if she remembers anything. I'll meet you back at my place whenever you're ready."

"You're not going to tell me? It could be dangerous."

"I'll be fine. Don't worry."

She tried to leave again, but she didn't let go. "If my father knew Swerve came anywhere—"

"Our secret," Sersha said and winked.

Her fingers dropped as the woman rushed off. Progress? Maybe. She had to talk to Mila.

THIRTY

SERSHA WASN'T AT the apartment when she got there. No one was there, but the door was open. Though going into the apartment alone was strange, the isolation only lasted a few minutes.

Strat and Sersha came back in together. Did they go everywhere together? How did they hook up? No, hook up was the wrong phrase. Another bad mental visual.

"Why are you here alone?" her father asked. Was she supposed to wait in the hall? Was he accusing her of something? "Where's the cop?"

"Lachlan had work to do."

"He abandoned you? How did you get back?"

"Sutherland gave me a ride." And she'd deliberately neglected to tell him the other guys had dropped the ball on guard duty and let Swerve by. "Coak stayed at the hospital. It's fine. I'm safe. And I know better than to get in a cab right now."

No guarantees Ludlow was their only driver. No one could be trusted. And, in truth, she didn't trust her ability to ID Ludlow on a quick glance given her only reference point was a grainy movie taken from several yards away.

"He shouldn't have left you here alone."

"I've been here less than five minutes."

"Tell her what you found out," Sersha said, doing her diversion thing again.

"I don't know that she—"

"If it's about—"

Sersha's phone interrupted, but it was just a message. "Come here…"

Grabbing both of their wrists, Sersha pulled them across the room and into her bedroom.

"What's wrong?" Strat asked.

"Nothing, Lach's on his way back. I don't want him to overhear us, or for us to shut up the minute he walks in." Yeah, that would be a beacon of guilt. "It's not that I don't trust him. I don't like to put him in any position where he might hear something he wants to report. He's a cop and it wouldn't be fair of us to test his integrity."

"We shouldn't test Imogen's either."

Again with the double standard. "So it's fine to test Sersha's integrity?"

"Sersh's integrity sways into the gray zone."

"Of its own accord," Sersha said. "Sometimes circumstances steer me in odd, unexpected directions."

The more she learned, the more fascinated she became. "Do you ever feel compelled to share what you know with the superintendent? In your research, you must have learned things that could be helpful to authorities' investigations."

"I've made it clear to my father that my professional integrity is not up for debate. If we start dropping a dime on our sources, we lose our ability to do our jobs."

"Yeah, and your sources appreciate that," Strat teased.

"Tell me whatever it was you learned. Please, just—"

"Guys say Swerve has been seen at the Carlyle," Sersha said, raising her brows in a silent signal. With that reveal/cover, Sersha could talk about Swerve without betraying her confidence of the threat. Smart. "Your father's sources say the frequency of his visits has caused some… upset."

"Because no one knows why he's there," Strat said. "The guys think he might be checking up on them. Reporting back."

He wasn't. No, that building held a bigger game, a tastier prize. If the men on the street didn't know it, Silvio was playing his cards close to his chest.

"Swerve changes things," her dad said. "Swerve doesn't do bullshit work and certainly not at ground level with guys like Ludlow."

"So he's, what? Working on his own?"

"One thing Silvio hates about Swerve is his lack of control over him."

"Is that because…?" she asked, reluctant to reveal what Jagg told her about Silvio's kink in case others didn't know. "Is he…?"

"I think so, though I've never seen hard evidence."

Sersha got it right away. At least, she thought the beauty did. What evidence would there be? A birth certificate could be doctored or faked. Hell, so could a DNA test with the right access.

"What did you mean by the top? Where's the top?"

"Rumor is, again, it's not somewhere I've visited, but the rumor is Silvio has a space he uses for anything he won't do at the house or the mansion. And it's rumored that's where he auditions his willing… you know."

"What?" Nope. No idea. "His willing what?"

"The willing dolls," Strat said.

"What he calls willing anyway. Desperate and destitute is not the same as enthusiastic. I can't even— never mind. Okay. So if there's a place Silvio uses for the less savory aspects of his lifestyle—"

"Are there savory ones?" she asked.

Sersha smiled. "With Silvio? Doubtful."

"His dolls?"

"Forget that. This private space has a viewing screen. A projector and widescreen, life size—"

"Just what you'd want to immerse yourself in the experience."

"Isn't he selling the movies?"

"Movies like that… with the torture, they go to high-end clients. No way he lets any joe-schmo off the street pay twenty bucks for a ride. If they're high-end clients—"

"They're blackmailable clients!" She gasped. "He keeps copies!"

"Of course he does."

"Shit." Turning his back, her dad went a few steps. "That's evidence."

"Evidence Imogen can use."

"The cops can use."

"We'll never be allowed to just waltz in there." Her father was back with them. "Where is it?"

"I think it's in the Carlyle," Sersha said. "Always have. I've just never been that deep in there."

"Why would you be? Only hookers and johns go deep there."

Hopefully, no pun intended.

Back and forth, her dad and Sersha focused on each other.

"And Silvio's guys." Sersha edged closer to Strat. "Putting my hunch together with what Imogen said about the locations of the bodies. The Carlyle is worth a look."

"Do you want me to play the other side?" Strat asked.

"You wanted me at Hustle."

"I'm in, but we'll scrap at the other side of this."

"I know. We'll deal with it."

"Always do."

Waving an arm between them, she reminded them they weren't alone. "Hello? If anyone's going in, it's me."

"If anyone's going in anywhere…" The masculine voice drew their attention to the bedroom door. Jagg. God, it felt like a lifetime since she'd seen him. "It's me." He closed the gap between him and their group. "The Top Room, that's what you're talking about, Sersha. Usually just called 'The Top.' No one gets in there without a personal invite."

"You think you'll get one?" Sersha asked. "You've been out of the game for a long time. Don't think anyone would believe a guy like you would pay for sex… unless you want to pay for something on the edge of a hard limit."

"Could be the way to put eyes on the girls."

"No, it's too risky," she said, desperate to hold his hand, to touch him, to persuade him not to step into the line of fire. "What if he's in there and they ask him to prove himself? To hurt someone or… perform. He'll be stuck in a Manzani building crawling with thugs who'd love to go up against Jagger Dunn."

"I'd be more afraid of the guns than the fists," Sersha said, "if it was me."

"I don't have to be afraid of anything. I'll tell him I want a conversation, away from the house. That place gives me nightmares."

Sersha and Strat enjoyed the tease. Shame she couldn't be so casual.

"You'll still be stuck in a room with Silvio Manzani. Crazed lunatic gangster Manzani."

"Silvio doesn't do his own dirty work," her father said. "Not this kind anyway."

"Yeah," Sersha agreed. "He's more of a voyeur than a doer."

"Why would he even agree to meet? It doesn't—"

"You'll tell him you'll fight for him," Strat said. "Are you in shape?"

"No! Oh my God, that's literally going looking for a fight. No, you can't do it. He can't do it."

"How do you like it when your family baby you?" Jagg asked. "My choices are mine." Damnit, did he have to go there? "I can handle this. I've been dancing with guys like Manzani my whole life."

"I can handle running away from a fight. Protecting myself. You walking in there for—"

"It's a distraction." His attention went to Strat and Sersha. "While I'm in there talking, keeping him busy, someone needs to be inside checking things out. He won't produce the women at a first meet, and he sure won't let me walk out the door with anyone."

"Especially not if he's being paid good money for her."

"You could get lost on the way out," Sersha said.

"And just start opening doors?"

"No cameras on Silvio's floor, not if his paranoia continues there like it does everywhere else."

"But he will have security. Besides, no one would believe me getting lost. I spent too much time there back in the day."

"When you were Silvio's prize fighter," Strat said. "Drove Vex crazy."

"What floor is it on?" she heard herself asking, almost unable to believe she'd ever agree to the madness.

"The Top? Ten."

"Not the top floor?" Sersha asked.

Jagg shook his head. "Too obvious. Easier to sneak off the tenth."

"If there was ever a raid. Smart."

"There's a problem with the plumbing on ten."

"How do you know that?"

"From my visit there."

"You went to The Top?" her father all but roared. "What in the hell?"

"To the hotel. Just to ask questions."

"No one ever got hurt asking questions," Sersha said with unmissable sarcasm.

"What is the problem?" she asked. "You're all standing there talking about Jagg going in there alone."

"He won't be alone," Strat stated.

"He won't? What do you mean he won't be alone? Who's going with him?"

"Ford," Jagg and Strat said together.

"Those boys watched each other's tails in that circle for years."

"They'd be less likely to believe it if I went alone."

"They'll expect Ford."

It defied belief. "Wait a second, so you get mad when you find out I went to the hotel, but you're sending your son in there?"

"These boys are both my sons, and I trust them to get each other out. You went alone. Without backup."

"Sersha and I will go too."

"What?"

"Why not? We can watch each other's asses."

"Silvio won't want a posse of people going in there."

"Can we have a second?" Jagg asked, fixating on her. "I need a second with Genny."

What did he think he was doing? Obviously her dad and Sersha didn't think it was weird. They filed on out of the room without resistance.

When the door closed, Jagg stepped in front of her. "Ford and I have a shorthand. We've been in these setups alone so many times. There's nothing to worry about."

"That's not good enough. I know you're trying to protect me, that everyone's trying to protect me, and I appreciate that. Can't I want to protect you too? What's wrong with that?"

"You want answers. Risk is required."

Oh, damnit, they weren't supposed to hide things, she wasn't supposed to hide things. Without even thinking it through, she'd known telling Jagg about the Swerve conversation would be a bad idea. Now withholding it could get them both, Jagg and Ford, in hot water.

"You… can't." Though her heart hammered, her throat shook. Pain between the two was acute, quivering, anxious. "You can't go to Silvio Manzani."

"I can. There's no reason—"

"He knows."

Jagg frowned. "Knows? Knows what?"

She swallowed. "Silvio knows you're helping me."

"How do you know that?" His lips barely moved; the growl in them tightened her muscles. "Imogen, how do you know Silvio knows?"

"Well, I guess I, I don't know that Silvio knows, but… Swerve knows."

"The fuck," he snarled. "He came to you? How the fuck did he get near you?"

"This is not something to be angry about, it's good, we know he knows and—"

"Yeah, it's fucking good," he barked and whirled around to go storming out of the room.

"Jagg!" Going after him, she couldn't keep up. "You don't—please—"

Without hesitating, he slammed out of the apartment.

"What happened?" Sersha asked, coming around the breakfast bar.

She sighed. "I told him."

"Oh."

"Told him?" her father demanded. "Told him what?"

"Nothing I'll tell you."

"You will tell me. If he didn't want to do it, why did he volunteer?"

"We can't. I can't let him and Ford go to Silvio for a phony meet."

"You're worried about them? Sweetheart, they—"

"Silvio knows," she said, making eye contact with Sersha. Maybe with an ally, she could stop her father having the same reaction as Jagg. "Swerve knows Jagg and Ford are helping me."

Her brother's name hadn't come up, but it wasn't a leap. As had just been said, they were peas in a pod back in the day. Well, not just then. Things hadn't changed much.

"How do you know Swerve knows?" he asked, coming a step closer. "Swerve approached you?"

Her father was bringing his own bubble to a boil.

"Don't," she said before he could vent any steam. "Don't explode like he did. I wasn't going to tell you because I knew you'd freak out. Why ask me to be honest and then explode when I am? That's no incentive for me to tell you the truth."

Sucking in a nasal inhale, his spine straightened, and his eyes went to Sersha's. Did he want an ally too? Wasn't great that she was in the middle.

Rather than shout or scold, he pushed the air from his lungs, muttering something. Then, like Jagg, he went stomping toward the door.

She hurried into his path. "Where are you going?"

"You want Jagg and your brother in jail?"

"No!"

"Then I've gotta put the pin back in the grenade." He swept his head aside in a nod. "Outta the way."

Putting her palms together, she stepped aside and he left.

Sersha went to retrieve a bottle from a kitchen cabinet. "Whiskey?"

Hard liquor was just what she needed. "Why not? I can't screw up this day more than I already have."

"How did you leave things with Mila?"

"I'm going back tomorrow. She was tired and disoriented. The doctor said she needs rest."

The front door opened. Though she expected her dad, Lachlan came in.

"Where was Strat going in such a hurry?"

"Don't ask."

"We're having a drink. Want to join us?"

"Starting on the hard stuff, huh?" He hung his jacket up by the door and came over to kiss her head. "You eaten something today? Either of you?"

"Stop taking care of us," Sersha said, handing her brother a drink. "And if you're going to take advantage of your ex tonight, don't do it on my couch. You have an apartment."

"That neither of us are living in."

"Life isn't exactly normal at the moment," Sersha said, giving her a drink.

Swallowing down the burning liquid, she put the glass on the counter and went looking for her purse. "I have to call Ford."

Someone had to tell her brother what happened. No doubt Jagg called him. Please God, let Strat calm the guys before they engaged with anyone and got themselves in trouble.

No answer. Voicemail.

Somehow, everyone around her, every time she opened her mouth, they got hurt or in trouble. Swooping back to Lachlan, she swept the drink from his hand just as it was about to touch his lip.

"What's wrong?"

Discarding the glass, she looped her purse strap over her shoulder. "Will you drive me home?"

"To our place?"

"The garage," she said. "Jagg's." How quickly that had become home. Wait, did he think she'd been asking him to follow Sersha's instruction? "I want to be there when they get back."

"I can't leave you alone."

"Just drive me. We'll talk about it on the way." Ford could still be home. Maybe Strat was wrangling the guys there. "Please."

They said their goodbyes to Sersha and departed.

Lachlan still wanted them to be together. Wasn't that what Sersha said? Maybe she'd meant in the past Lachlan wanted them to be together. Their breakup had been mutual. As far as she knew, they both understood forever wasn't in the cards for them, didn't they?

THIRTY-ONE

FORD WASN'T THERE. No one was. The light in the breakroom suggested someone had been there until not long before. After checking out the rest of the place, just in case, she made a call.

"Dad?"

Thank God he picked up.

"It's okay," he said, anticipating her concern. "I'll drop the guys off and come—"

"I'm at the garage. Lachlan brought me back. Is everyone okay? Did you see Swerve?"

"No. Take a breath, Immie. We'll be back soon."

And the line died.

Damn, so much for the relief of him picking up. Everyone was alive, which was great. They hadn't confronted anyone, fantastic. But how had it gone down? Was Jagg okay or still angry? What concession—

"Swerve?"

Damnit. Lachlan.

Glancing over her shoulder led to her turning around. She hadn't been thinking.

"Forget it."

"You know I expect Sersha to keep things from me. I expect her to jump in headfirst. It's not like you to take risks like this."

"People are dying—"

"I know."

"And you denied recognizing Swerve when I showed you his picture, but you did, didn't you?"

"I'm not saying you shouldn't take risks. You're right, that would be hypocritical. I take risks. My sister does, though I worry about her too."

"All my life I've played it safe. Going with my mom. College close to home. The Chronicler close to home in the easy local section. Even us, both of us, being together, we played it safe."

"You wanted it to be riskier?"

"No, I mean I... We made sense. From the outside, it made complete sense. And I love you, I'll always love you. It's just..."

"You want more," he said. "I get it. Settling down was next for us. Home, car, kids. The dog and the annual vacations. Normal was next. And we'd have done it because it was what was expected."

"You can't want to live that way. Just fulfilling others' expectations. What about you? What do you want?"

He sighed. "I don't know, Im. It's one day to the next, one foot in front of the other, you know? I haven't thought about the big picture."

"You should. You're a big picture kind of guy."

"I put it aside and focus on others because it's easier."

"And because you've always done it," she said. "With your dad, your grandfather, you knew what they expected of you, and you do it. You followed in their footsteps without stopping to wonder if it was what you wanted."

"I wanted you. Our life together, us, that was the purpose to my day."

"We were good together, Lach. We weren't incredible. Don't you want incredible?"

"I want you to be safe. Pay attention to what's up ahead."

"What are you saying, Lachlan?"

"Look both ways," he said, certain in his confidence. "Don't let your family's objection to what you do blind you to danger. Swerve can be brutal and doesn't think twice. Some say he's worse than Vex. At least Vex plays with people, which gives them time to dig themselves out. Swerve doesn't. Once he decides that's it, then that's it. No time or hesitation."

"How do you know him?"

"Through work. Through legend. Swerve's one of those guys who pops up now and then. He's never around all the time. He'll disappear for a while and then show up from nowhere linked to some kind of mess. Swerve isn't diplomatic but can put on an array of faces depending on his mood. He gets what he wants."

"So the rest of us shouldn't? He can't keep getting away with what he's doing. Just because he wants it doesn't make it a foregone conclusion."

"What you see is not always the truth of him. Does Sersha know he's involved?"

"Yes." Because what was the point of lying? "Your sister is not what I expected. When we were together, we only hung out a few times. Always for a reason and with other people, we didn't have the opportunity to really talk. I had no idea she was so close to Vex Manzani."

"Not as close as he'd like." The same thing her father said. "They have history."

"And you're okay with that? Your family is okay with it? You always said your dad didn't support Sersha's career. Is this why?"

"Her history with Vex isn't linked to her career. That's not where it started. I'd rather he wasn't in her world, but I can't live Sersha's life for her any more than I can live yours for you."

"We have to make our own mistakes."

"Yeah." Somewhere beyond the room, a door closed, and muffled voices approached. "I'll get going."

"Lachlan," she said, stopping him after just a few steps. Words weren't enough. Going to him, she used his arm for balance as she rose onto her tiptoes to kiss his cheek. "You're a good brother. A good man."

"Just not enough of one."

As the trio piled in, Lachlan slipped out with only a nod of acknowledgement.

Not enough of one. What did that mean? Why couldn't people just say what was on their minds rather than being cryptic?

"This madness has to stop now." Strat. Damn. Trust him to be so forthright. She had to be careful what she asked for, even in her own head. "All of you running around the city like cowboys, like some damn white hat gang. Let the cops handle it."

"The cops wouldn't be handling it unless Imogen chased it down."

Jagg. Why couldn't he look at her?

Ford grabbed beers from the fridge and tried to offer her one.

She refused with an open hand. "I'm going to bed."

"You don't want to talk?" her brother asked.

Strolling away, the ache in her muscles begged relief. "We've done enough talking." Nothing anyone could say would change where they were or her intention. "Thank you for your help, everyone. I need to sleep."

Talking hadn't got them far, not that day. Something else was needed, something more definitive. Instead of ifs and maybes, they needed confirmation. Certainty. The other side was bold. Maybe it was time for her side to adopt that methodology too.

THIRTY-TWO

SHE SLEPT. For a few hours. After waking with a start, getting back to sleep proved impossible.

Ludlow. Low level, and a driver, relied upon to get the right woman for the murderer. The right victim. Did he go out with a name, address, and picture or was the grab much more random than that? Those picked up from work or coming out of apartment buildings in nice neighborhoods could just fit the general description of the appropriate target.

Except the grab wasn't completely random if "Bryan" was seeing the marks ahead of the abduction. Did he date every victim? After learning they held more than one woman prisoner at a time, it seemed unlikely. One man could only date so many women. Although he only dated them for a short time; no one mentioned a long-term partner. Was that the point? Bryan's job was to scope out who could go missing with the least amount of fuss?

Or it could be more sinister. Did the johns paying to star in these films give criteria? Did they ask for a type? Maybe the Manzanis just sent out a newsletter listing who they had available. Yeah, that sounded despicable, but what else was it?

Evil. That's what it was. Women used for the pleasure of men and why? For nothing more than a cheap thrill. These women weren't dying for a reason. Not a valid one. It wasn't war or glory, it was degrading and sordid.

Somewhere in that city Yvonne, Marcie, and Janine languished in fear. Were they being abused in that minute? Were they a comfort to each other or did hearing the screams of their comrades only ignite their own terror?

She couldn't just lie there.

Sitting up, she took stock for just a second before jumping from her bed to get dressed.

Night was when the white hats slept, and it was when the criminal element did their most business.

Just like the first time she went to the hotel, she chose dark clothes, a hooded pullover, anything to blend in. And sneakers, in case she had to run.

Danger. All day people told her to avoid danger, and her plan was to visit the hornet's nest. That didn't stall her. No, she didn't stop to think until her bedroom door was closed at her back and her eyes fell on Jagg's just a few feet away.

When he found out about her previous visit to the hotel, his first question was if anyone had known her location. No, they hadn't. If she went tonight and got caught up in something, or abducted and tortured herself, no one would know her last movements. They wouldn't even know she got out of bed to go there voluntarily.

Their rule not to hide anything thrummed in the back of her mind too. That was why her feet took her into Jagg's bedroom rather than out the door.

The scent of him, the warmth of the space, even in the dark, beckoned her closer to the sleeping form in the middle of the bed. She could just slip off her shoes and climb in there. Forget all about the evil of the world and submerge herself in Jagger Dunn.

She sat on the bed, sliding a hand onto his stubble as her lips touched his. Instinct could be the only drive behind him responding. How awake he'd been, she didn't know. Only a second later, his hand was in her hair and he pulled her down, further onto the bed, the demand of his tongue tempting hers.

Pulling back wasn't easy. Her own instincts wanted to explore his and where their expedition would lead.

"You okay?" he whispered into the night, his fingers, still tangled in her hair, stroked her scalp. "Can't sleep?"

"I woke up." Keeping their voices low should prevent waking Ford, she hoped. Going out was one thing. Explaining why she was in Jagg's bed was a whole different ballgame. "I'm going out."

"Going where?"

"The hotel," she said. "The Carlyle. Ludlow and Swerve are both—"

"Shit, babe." They sat up. "It's dangerous over there."

As he got up and flicked on the lamp, she flipped around, catching just a quick view of his naked ass as he pulled on a pair of sweats.

"We need answers. We can't get them from each other—"

"So you thought you'd march on over there and demand them? Of who? Swerve?"

"The women might talk to me. It's happening there. It has to be."

"We don't know that." He put on a tee-shirt and pulled on a hoodie of his own. "It's a possibility."

"And I am sick of possibilities. We need to know. Those women could be over there now." With his back to her, he retrieved something from the dresser. "They could be in pain. If it was me over there, would you be lying in bed sleeping like nothing was going on?"

"I'm not lying in bed sleeping," he said, rounding the end of the bed, extending a hand to her. "Come on."

"Come on where?" she asked, leaping up to grab his hand. "Where are we—"

"What did I say to you? I'm not interested in changing you or making your choices. You're gonna do this whether or not I want you to. My say is you're not doing it alone."

They crossed the dark breakroom together and got outside into his car. Within a minute, they were on the road.

"Thank you," she said, reaching over to caress his thigh. "You didn't have to do this. To come with me."

Sersha had spoken of her safety net. Jagg was fast becoming hers. She just hoped to God he wasn't injured on her behalf.

"My choice."

"If they already know we're asking questions, we should take advantage of that, not shy from it."

"How? By asking more questions? The women at the Carlyle will have been told not to talk."

"Not if this is as much of a secret as we think it is," she said. "If Swerve's involved, the circle's small, remember?"

"We'll watch, just like we did the other night. Get a lay of the land, figure out what's happening and who's there."

"Will they kill them? Swerve said if I didn't let it go that the women would pay in pain."

"Women?"

"Three of them. He gave me three names."

"They have more than one woman at a time. That's interesting."

"Why?"

"You don't start big, you start small. Like Strat said, he broke with Ludlow years ago because of the product. Back then, it was hookers and testing the boundaries. Escalating to respectable women who'd be missed would've taken time. Now we find out they're cocky enough to think they can control three?"

"They've been doing this a while."

"Which means more victims. A lot more victims."

"And you've got to wonder," he said, glancing her way. "What will they progress to next?"

Not a pleasant thought, but someone had to have it. From three women, would they go to five? Go to more upper-class women? Instead of making home videos, would the Manzanis let their asshole customers take the women home?

Wow, just a hop, skip, and a jump to human trafficking. Something the Manzanis did engage in, if Sersha's intel was correct.

They got to the Carlyle and parked on the same street as before.

"Will they see us here?"

"If they're looking for us, they'll see us wherever we are." He cut the engine. "The big leagues play with different stakes."

"It has to be Silvio Manzani, right? He has to be the one behind this."

"Hell's in prison. Vex is too caught up in himself, and Atlas took off long ago. Don't blame him for that."

"Did you ever think about it? Leaving the city?"

"Leaving it for what? To get away from this shit? Strat always told us to maintain our independence, never to ally ourselves. It happens slow, being in deep like that. And it's a high to be included, involved, admired."

"You were young."

"Yeah. Walking away wasn't easy. Not a lot of guys get away with it."

"How did you?"

"I took a risk." He glanced her way. "A calculated risk."

"And it paid off?"

He raised his hands from his lap. "I'm here, right?"

Yes, back on the fringes of the Manzani world at her behest. "I'm sorry I brought you back into—"

"No more apologies," he said, taking her hand. "We're doing what needs to be done. I'll always be with you for whatever you need."

"My safety net."

"Yeah."

Man, she wished that were true. Leaning in, she intended to show her gratitude, but something caught his eye in the wing mirror and he sank back.

"Shit."

A body appeared at the side window, a knuckle rapped on the glass.

"Who is that?" she whispered, almost afraid to ask. "A cop?" But there was no uniform. A plainclothes cop? If only wishing made it so. The guy bowed, revealing himself. Swerve. Again. "Jagg."

She tried to grab for him, but he reached for the door. "Stay here," he murmured back to her, slipping the key onto the center console. "Don't get out of the car, no matter what happens. If it goes south, leave. Take the car and go, get back to Ford."

"I can't just—"

But he was already out of the vehicle.

"Nice night for a walk, huh?"

That was all she heard Swerve say before the door closed and the guys started down the sidewalk. A good ten feet away, they paused. What was going on? They got a little closer to each other. Was that aggression? If they fought… She couldn't call the cops or Jagg might get arrested.

Ford would race over there, and a fight would be inevitable.

Strat.

Slipping her phone from her pocket, she scrolled to her dad's number and pressed call on speaker, volume low. Putting the device to her ear would be risky. If Swerve saw it, he might assume she was calling the cops.

"Immie?" Her dad's gruff, tired voice came before a cough. "What's going on?"

"Sorry," she whispered into the phone. "I forgot the time."

"I don't care about the time. What's wrong?"

"I don't know, maybe… nothing. I don't—"

"Sweetheart, whatever it is, tell me."

"You won't get mad?"

"I won't get mad. What you said earlier was right. Getting mad gets us nowhere."

And provides no incentive for her to be honest. "I came to the Carlyle."

"Alone?" Movement on the line suggested he was up, maybe getting dressed. "Are you inside?"

"No, I'm outside. Jagg came with me and—"

"Put him on the phone."

"No, you can't get mad at him either. He came to look after me. He came so I wouldn't come alone. But he's… Swerve appeared at the car. They're outside talking. What do I do? Call the cops? Lachlan?"

"Are they fighting?"

"No, they're just standing there... talking." Neither guy's expression gave away much other than they were talking tough. "What if he hits him? What if he does something else or other guys show up and—"

"I'm on my way." A door closed. "Did you call your brother?"

"No, should I? I didn't want to escalate the situation. I should've called him, shouldn't I? Damnit."

"It's okay. You did the right thing. Are you in the car?"

"Yes."

"Can they see you?"

"They're not looking over here, they're looking at each other. He's not going to get shot, is he? Someone could be in the hotel and—"

"Are the keys there? The car keys?"

"Yes." Where Jagg left them, right there, for her. "He told me not to get out of the car."

"Don't. Good. Stay there. Slide over to the driver's side."

"I'm not going to leave him here or run anyone over."

"You can be ready to move, to—"

"Oh, he's coming back."

Swerve fixed on her for a few seconds, then turned his back to head for the Carlyle. Jagg got back in next to her.

"You okay?" Jagg asked.

"Am I okay?" She couldn't figure him out. Men were infuriating. "You were the one—oh my God!"

"What happened?"

The voice from her lap caught Jagg's attention for a second until it rose to hers. "You called your dad?"

"I'm smart enough to know I'm no help in a fight."

"You didn't call Ford?"

"Because he'd have made things worse. I trust my dad to deescalate and my brother to jump in and get dirty."

"Swerve had a message?" her father asked, calm, collected.

"How do you know that?"

"Because if the order was to kill him, he'd be dead. If it was to bring him in, he'd be dead. And Swerve would know better than to try scaring Jagg off. He's not a guy who scares easy."

"Easier to scare when your daughter's in the mix," he said. "Where you at?"

"A couple of blocks away. Meet down at Merv's?"

"Yeah."

Her father disconnected.

"We're meeting my father?"

"You called him."

"Because I was scared. If Swerve tried something—"

"I can take care of myself, babe," he said, laying a hand on her leg. "But it's okay. Won't hurt to strategize."

"Strategize what exactly?"

"Silvio wants to meet."

"You?" she asked.

"Yeah."

"Why? Why does he want to meet? Does he want me there?"

"No."

"But I started this. This should be on me."

"Silvio doesn't give women much credit. He prefers to think of them as weak and submissive."

"What an—"

"It works for us, babe." Because he wanted to protect her. "It's better if I handle it. If me and Ford handle it. Let them think we're the power behind the pen. We're an enemy he can exploit."

"He'll want something from you, won't he?"

"Maybe." In barter for her to drop the story, or for her life? "You'll like Merv's. Great pie."

From her father, she expected nothing less. Pie wouldn't salve this ail. Things were heating up. They were getting closer to the fire. Silvio Manzani. If he was responsible, bringing him to justice wouldn't be easy. No, it would be impossible.

THIRTY-THREE

A MEETING. One they barred her from.

In the breakroom after the sun had set, her family prepared to go out there alone. Without her. Nothing in the trio of men was fazed. They exchanged information, ideas, like this was an everyday occurrence. Maybe once they'd been mixed up with the Manzanis, but back then the crime family was their allies. They'd stood up for the Manzanis, not against them, Ford and Jagg anyway.

Jagg. Why had she done this to him? Why put him in this position? What would he have to give up to keep her safe? The worst part was she couldn't even ask. She couldn't go over there and hold him or kiss him or ask him to be careful. Singling him out against her own father and brother would be too telling.

But, damnit, she didn't want anything to happen to him. To any of them. If something went wrong, all the people she loved most could be taken away from her in a snap. All it took was the wrong word, upsetting someone, and a quick trigger pull would end them.

"Doesn't matter if we're armed," Ford said. "They'll take whatever we carry."

Bringing guns would lead to others showing they had firearms too. Introducing them wouldn't be smart, yet she couldn't deny wishing they had some form of protection. Especially protection that could be used from afar and didn't require them to get close to anyone.

"We'll leave a weapon in the car."

Sitting on the couch, Sersha at her side, helplessness invaded. "We've got to be able to do something." It wasn't right. It didn't feel right. Sickness churned in her belly. She stood up. "Dad, I'm coming with you."

"That's worse than you asking me to take you there," Ford said, breaking from the trio. "Dad's going to Hustle."

"Man can get distracted in there," Sersha said, rising at her side to tease. "You going to keep your eye on the ball, old man?"

"I'm parking outside, not going into that insanity."

"You don't have the best opinion of Evander," Sersha said. "Don't let that get in the way."

"I don't have the best opinion of any of your men, Scamp. Still keep breathing every day."

"I can come with you." Sersha folded her arms. "Evander would come in his pants right there if I walked into his sex club."

"We're not going anywhere for fun." Strat snagged his keys from the island. "I'm sitting there to check Silvio doesn't call on reinforcements. Every Manzani guy with a pulse goes to Hustle on a Friday night."

Which was probably exactly why Silvio chose that night for the meeting. Fewer bodies at the Carlyle meant fewer eyes and ears. The don apparently wanted to keep his secret, too much to hope that he was ashamed. Arrogant idiots like Silvio Manzani didn't know the meaning of the word shame or of guilt.

"If you see them leaving Hustle en masse, you'll know this is an ambush."

"We can get out of there if it goes south," Jagg said. "We're on alert. We'll figure it out."

Winging it didn't sit right. A plan, something concrete, would be reassuring. Knowing was better than mystery. Though it was exactly that kind of thinking that got them into the debacle.

"This is happening because of me."

The men were talking to each other again. Grabbing jackets, talking signals and boundaries.

A hand slid into hers. Sersha's.

"Trust them," she said. "They know this world."

And she didn't. She may be Kurt Stratford's daughter, that didn't give her insider knowledge on how the night would go down. Her limited experience meant nothing. Hearing the stories, reading the newspaper, it wasn't the same. She'd been such an idiot. The danger was real. How had they lived this life for so long?

They'd been right all along. Parentage didn't matter, she didn't share the nerve of the brave men ready to go out there and defend her.

"I should be there," she murmured to the woman at her side. "What if they get hurt because of me?" They'd never forgive her. She'd never forgive herself. "They're paying the price for my ambition. We shouldn't be sitting doing nothing."

"We won't be sitting doing nothing," Sersha murmured, squeezing her hand before leaning in. "We just let them think that's the plan."

Lachlan said he expected his sister to jump in headfirst. Maybe tonight she'd experience some of that for herself. Obviously, the woman had a plan, or at least an intention. Anything that would get them closer to the truth, and get the men out of danger, she'd follow the enigmatic McLeod.

Midnight. Of course that would be the chosen time for the meeting. In the dark, existing in the shadows while shade invaded their world.

"We'll call you if anything happens," her dad said, heading to the door with Ford and Jagg. "Look after each other."

"We will."

Strat's eyes narrowed on Sersha. "Be good."

"Aren't I always?" the woman drawled, innocent and insincere.

"Hmm," her father hummed, full of doubt.

The time for questions was short. The men had places to be and so they left. After the sound died and they were sure the men had gone, Sersha crouched to sweep something out of her fabric tote.

"Whiskey," Sersha said, opening the top and slapping the bottle into her hand. "One slug each."

"For? Dutch courage? What are you thinking?"

Without waiting for an answer, she complied. The liquid burned hot, catching the back of her throat in a cough that kept going.

Sersha captured the bottle and enjoyed some herself before returning it to her bag.

"We give them a half hour."

"Then what?"

"What is your goal?" Sersha asked. "The story, I get that. You've got enough to print now, but you haven't. Why?"

"Because lives are at stake. Poking around is one thing, but if I put words onto paper and send them into the world…"

"They'll take that out on the women."

"And get rid of the evidence." Which the women were. "Is it worth the risk?"

"You have to eliminate their leverage. They're using the captive women against you."

"What do you suggest?"

"That we remove that ability. Think about it. Silvio is busy with Jagg and Ford. Your dad is watching Hustle, so no Vex to worry about. I guarantee Swerve will be at the meet. He wouldn't want to miss it and Silvio needs his hench-child to take care of business if things go sideways. You think the victims are in the Carlyle?"

"If they're filming there on ten, it would make sense to have them in the building. Transporting them around the city would be risky. They might get free or someone could see something and report it."

"So we're going to look."

"For the women?" she asked. Sersha smiled as she nodded. "In the Carlyle." Another nod. "You want to break in?"

"We create a distraction and slip in a back door or something. You in?"

"Have you done this before?"

"Freed captive people?" Sersha asked and semi-shrugged. "Sort of."

"Will it work?"

"Only one way to find out," Sersha said and grabbed her hand to pull her a few steps.

"Wait," she said, pulling back. "Isn't our job to report on what happens? To find the story and share it?"

A broader smile slunk to Sersha's lips. "Sometimes you have to make the story, be the story."

Be the story. That was one option. Shit. This was getting real.

THIRTY-FOUR

"YOU CAN ONLY stand on the sidelines for so long," Sersha said as they drove toward the Carlyle. "Sometimes we have to take matters into our own hands."

The car they'd commandeered at the garage didn't belong to a Jagg's Auto customer, she didn't think. It had been there a while, and the keys were on the board. Despite her hesitation, Sersha persuaded her it wasn't stealing if they intended to bring it back. True. And they wouldn't damage it. Also, they may need a quick getaway vehicle.

God, how did she get into this?

Real was right.

They stopped in the street, facing the entrance. Deep breath.

"How do we distract them?" she asked. "You want me to go in and make a scene?"

"We need something more unexpected. I'd bet they've dealt with crazy before."

Wives, pimps, drug dealers. Yeah, and they probably had little patience for the shit that drew attention to their business premises.

Extracting her phone from her pocket, Sersha tapped the screen. "Stay close and keep your head down, hood up."

As her hood went up, Sersha propped the phone on the dash, video recording, and reached into the back to grab her tote.

"Why are we recording?"

The woman tossed her a sly, almost sinister, smile and got out. Together, they crossed to the other side of the street with purpose. Women on a mission. Thankfully, at that moment, no one was outside to spy their approach. Sersha put on a ball-cap and pulled it down over her eyes, then her hood went back up.

Getting to the corner of the building, her newest friend produced the bottle of liquor and ripped off a section of the tote.

The plan was a mystery. Sersha stuffed the fabric into the bottle and wrapped the rest around the glass. When the woman retrieved a lighter from her pocket, clarity hit.

"Oh my God, you're not going to—"

"Walk past the front," Sersha whispered. "Keep going if there's no one there. We don't want to hurt anyone. No one innocent anyway."

"And if there is someone there?"

"Keep walking, but look back here, I'll wait." Sersha breathed in then murmured, "Damn, it had to be the good stuff…" She got a push. "Go on."

After another prod, she got on her way. Casual. Walking. Going past the hotel like it was just a building on her route. This was a new kind of terrifying high. Adrenaline filled her fired heart. Checking the coast was clear wasn't so bad. No one hung around. The reception woman wasn't even at the desk, as far as she could see. This was on her; all she had to do was walk.

Opening her lips to get more air into her lungs, at the opposite corner of the hotel, she spun around to hug the edge of the building. Sersha was there. The spark of a flame started small but quickly grew.

"Oh, shit," she whispered to no one as Sersha, calm as anything, walked toward her, flame in hand.

In a languorous split second, Sersha lingered at the edge of the doors just long enough to lob the bottle into the lobby. An instant smash and the woof of a flame came before a scream. Sersha was already running toward her, grabbing her, pulling her into the shadow of the side of the structure.

"Come on," Sersha hissed, trying a door to find it locked.

She even had the presence of mind to wipe the prints with her sleeve before going to the next one.

"My brother is in there with his best friend, I—"

"They'll be fine." She tried another door. "They're smart enough to get out when—"

The building's fire alarm blasted the air. Were they always so loud? The whole block would know. Cops would be called. Fire people. Crowds would gather.

They rounded a barrier and Sersha ran up a few concrete stairs to another door and… voila! That was exactly what Sersha's smile said. Gesturing inside, the woman entered.

She hesitated.

This was important. Necessary. Yes, it was dangerous, but fuck it, hadn't she been saying all along that risks were for the greater good? The greater good.

Sersha poked her head out the door again, red light pulsing in the air behind her. "Get in here."

If for no other reason than Sersha needed backup, she ascended the stairs to enter a darkened corridor. Someone, Sersha, caught her wrist to jerk her through a door and down a flight of stairs.

The alarm wasn't as loud down there. What did that mean? Well, that she could think straight, sort of. Like they were on a submarine or something, the ominous red bulbs at regular intervals signaled danger. Of fire or the Manzani goons who could catch them skulking around.

"Why do you think they're down here?" she whispered, following her into the labyrinth. "Do you know this place?"

"Not exactly. Kind of. It's worth a shot." Sersha tried doors and peeked through windows. "Everyone above will clear out." The area would be flooded with people. Great. Nice. "And if the fire guys come, they might evacuate."

"The entire building?"

Official authorities could save their victims.

"Shh!" Sersha landed a hand on her stomach, halting them. "Shit."

Whatever she heard, Sersha bundled her back into a perpendicular corridor, flattening them against the wall.

Shit. Shit. Shit. Her father would go crazy. Ford would—Yeah, but that was nothing to how Sersha's father and brother would react if they were caught breaking and entering. Skulking in the shadows of a known criminal's semi-lair wasn't what the superintendent's daughter should be known for.

Footsteps thundered by, sounded like the corridor they'd been about to turn into. People. Foes not friends.

Sersha peeked out.

"Aren't you afraid?" she asked, glad she wasn't the one literally sticking her neck out.

A wide smile on the woman's face seemed more exhilarated than hesitant. "Of what? If they kill us, we'll be dead, we won't care."

That was one way to look at it.

"They could put us in their videos."

Sersha's distracted eyes met hers. "You don't have to be afraid. Be smart, sure. But when you're with me, you don't have to worry about what they'll do to us."

Because her father was the police superintendent. And Lach… she'd used her connection to him at the precinct too many times to count. Being with him gave her some reassurance, but she'd never done anything like this, never anything dangerous.

"I didn't know you were so fearless."

"Fear gets you nowhere." More footsteps passed, but the woman didn't acknowledge them. "My father, grandfather, brother, yeah, they give me cover."

"That didn't stop you being attacked."

"And I came back from that. You learn a lot about yourself when you go through something like that."

"A trauma."

"An awakening." Switching the mood, she laughed. "Besides, Evander would cut off his own cock before he'd let any other man have first go at me in Manzani territory."

They linked hands and crept out. "You were attacked in McDade territory."

"Mm hmm," Sersha said, checking the next corridor before heading down it. "They came from this way, right? They had to be coming from somewhere."

So maybe the people, almost getting caught, had worked out for them.

"Was it McDades that attacked you? Were they trying to send a message?"

"It wasn't McDades," Sersha muttered.

"One of the guys was killed, wasn't he? It was horrific. Was that Vex? Was he mad the guy hurt you?"

"It wasn't Vex." Sersha let her go to start trying doors again. "Help me find the right place."

Some rooms were dark, lit only by the intermittent pulse of those lights. Some contained furniture, boxes, no people, no chance of… The next door was black and heavy, not like the others.

They made eye contact, sharing the thought. A different door could mean different contents.

The handle gave. The light inside was still red, but there was something else too. Half a dozen lit candles flickered on the floor around the perimeter of—

"Oh my God," her words came out on their own.

The shock was just too… A woman, bent over, locked in something akin to medieval stocks. Naked. Squirming and mumbling.

"Hey," Sersha said, rushing over to crouch by the woman's face. "It's okay. You're okay." Sersha removed a blindfold and then a gag. "We're going to get you out of here."

"How?" the stranger's voice rasped. "Who are you? What—"

"We're the good guys," Sersha said, rising to full height, glancing around. "Does it need a key?"

Springing to action, she went to examine the end of the contraption. "No, it's just a…"

Sliding back the bolt, she raised the heavy wood with Sersha's help.

"Who are you?" the woman asked again, struggling to stand straight, squeezing her bruised wrists.

"We're here to help," she said.

"We have to get out of here."

This wasn't Yvonne. The brunette didn't match any picture she'd seen. Maybe she wasn't one of the abducted women. That didn't mean she didn't deserve to be saved.

"What's your name?"

"Marseille," she whispered, moisture filling her eyes.

"Do you know where they're keeping anyone else?"

"There are other women upstairs. I don't know what floor, I…" the woman said, her dry voice breaking. "They make these videos and…"

She wobbled, her eyes closed, and she grabbed the stocks for balance.

"It's okay," Sersha said, catching the woman in a sheet from… somewhere. "The building is on fire. We have to get out."

"The others?" she asked.

"One at a time," Sersha said, guiding the woman to the door. "Get moving, Stratford."

The others. Yvonne. Finding this woman proved focusing on the Carlyle was justified. Torture happened there, why not murder too? But, as a structure, it was too big, too much for them to search while people were scrambling. On their own anyway.

Going with them, she helped hold the rescued woman up to keep her moving.

"We should find a back way out."

"Yeah. Away from the chaos out front."

If the fire was small, no big deal. Authorities would put it out and everyone would move along. Maybe the Manzani people would extinguish it; they wouldn't want anyone poking around.

Except the fire alarm was still going. This was an old building. The electrics were probably shot. Turning off the alarm may not be so easy. At least, she hoped that was the explanation.

Seeking the back of the building took them to a loading dock, perfect to sneak out and down the back path while sirens blared behind them. Slipping into an alley, she followed Sersha, followed their intention, stuck with the momentum. She didn't look back.

She should've looked back.

THIRTY-FIVE

THEY GOT THE SURVIVOR to the hospital. Staff were so overworked and harried, they didn't delve deep. They'd skipped over finding her. Randomly. In the street. No story here, as it were. Marseille didn't add any details. She didn't say anything and went with a nurse.

"She'll be okay," Sersha said, sitting next to her in the waiting area. "At least she's free of the Manzanis."

Would it last?

"They'll just take someone else," she said, her forehead landing on the heel of her hand. "Why did I think I could stop this?"

"You're doing something. You saw the pattern when no one else did. Would it have been better for anyone if you ignored it?"

"I haven't helped Yvonne, have I? We didn't find Janine."

"Look, I…" Sersha shifted to angle her body toward her. "Shit goes on in the world. We can't stop all of it. We help when we can. What you did tonight, it meant something to Marseille. Even if she's the only woman saved, it's better one than none. The Carlyle was full of desperate women. Full of women who once dreamed of a future and now just barely make it through the days. Kidnapped or not, we can't save everyone."

"Does that mean some people are beyond saving?"

"That means some people don't want to be saved. You can rush into these situations full of good intentions, but people are who they are. We can't live their lives for them."

Lachlan had said the same thing, a similar thing. In a lot of ways, the siblings were complete opposites, as tonight had proved. In others, they were exactly alike.

"Some people never know safety," she said, reality weighing her conscience. "They never know choice or opportunity."

"No, they don't."

"How do you help those people?"

"Do the best you can. Be the best you can. And be open to putting yourself out there. In a non-relationship type way. Don't be fooled that disappointment won't follow though. More people than not will let you down."

"You persist. The McLeods persist. Your family does so much good. You're respectable, wholesome people who make a huge difference to—"

Sersha laughed. "No wonder my dad loves you. That's exactly what he wants the world to see. He's a man in power, a man as fallible as any other. He's not perfect. None of us are."

"You try."

"So do you. What do you think tonight was?"

Sitting straight, she shook her befuddled head. "You take it all in stride. How are you so calm?"

Shrugging, Sersha sank against the back of her chair, observing the room. "You build a kind of tolerance to it. We weren't in any real danger."

The ambulance bay doors burst open. Someone was wheeled in as the paramedics reamed off facts and figures. Such purpose. Such simple complexity.

"You committed a crime tonight," she whispered. "You started that fire."

"And? Got us in, didn't it?"

"Your father is a cop, every man in your family—"

"So by association I'm wholesome and respectable too?" The twist of her lips failed to conceal her amusement. "Sometimes right is right, and that has nothing to do with the law. Saving that woman was right. You won't hear me apologize for what went down tonight."

"And if someone finds out? A Manzani?"

"No one will find out. How would anyone find out?"

Her gaze cooled with a prickling intensity. Sersha McLeod's dark thread glowed from beneath its shroud.

"You're not like Lach. You're not like him at all," she said, just getting it. "He believes in the system. He has limits."

"And he'd thank you for noticing."

"You don't believe in it? What your father, your brother—"

"Have dedicated their lives to? Not recently. You'll find me more cynical. Good isn't all it's cracked up to be. People are complicated."

"You grew up surrounded by it. It should be all you know."

Wasn't that her problem though? Being ensconced in suburbia growing up, she hadn't acquired the shell her dad and brother built as a shield against the threats coming from all sides. All she knew was safe and secure, yet that was what she fought against. Sometimes just being related wasn't enough to imbue someone with the same values and limits. The men in her family knew what made sense. They understood the darker side of life that had passed her by.

"I've come a long way from being the woman who wouldn't deliver an envelope," Sersha muttered.

"What does that mean?"

"I've always known I would never be good enough. Lachlan desperately wants to be, so he falls in line. I do my own thing. I am not a model McLeod, believe me."

"You can't live up to your father's expectations and I can't shake my father's expectations of me."

"Seriously, you're overthinking it with Strat." The doors banged again. One person was wheeled in with another hot on their heels. "All you have to do to make him happy is show up. He's a low maintenance guy. What do you expect of him?"

What did she…? What did she want her father to do? That was a good question. Thrust her into danger, encourage her to leap into the unknown? Being protective was a father's job. Oh, wouldn't he be thrilled to hear about that night's antics?

"I should probably call him before he gets back to the garage to find us gone."

"Yeah, he'll worry." A group of people came in, talking, shuffling, coughing. It went on and on, people and people. "What the hell is going on?"

When Sersha got up, she was quick to follow. The door banged again.

"Move! Move!" someone called out.

The endless gang parted, and she jumped out of the way with Sersha.

That was a fireman on that gurney.

The people, the gang, skimpy tops, barely there skirts, heavy makeup.

"Oh my God," she whispered.

Sersha slapped a hand on the admit desk. "What's going on? Where are these people coming from?"

"The hotel." Despite whispering it, Sersha's head snapped around. "They've come from the hotel."

"Old Carlyle went up," the guy behind the desk said, dealing with something else. "Still going they say."

"Oh, shit," Sersha said, pulling her along to the end of the desk, out of earshot. "Call Strat."

"Ford and Jagg were in that building."

"I know. Call him. Call your dad."

"Sersh?"

Spinning around as her head went up, they both landed on Lachlan about the same time.

"What are you doing here at this time of night?" Sersha asked her concerned brother.

"London called. I was on my way to pick her up." Whoever London was, someone who worked there, no doubt. "Want to tell me what you're doing here?"

"No, I don't," Sersha said, folding her arms. "Who's London, Mr. Fifth Date?"

He glanced at her and back to his sister. A love interest? Weird? Yes. But also a blessing. When the truth came out about her and Jagg, it would be easier if she wasn't the only one moving on.

"I'm going to call," she said to Sersha and retreated to a quiet corner.

Quiet being relative. She dialed and held her breath, waiting for her father to answer. Five rings… ten… Oh, God, what if he was—

"Immie? Jesus, girl, where are you?"

"The emergency room," she said. "We're fine. Sersha's with me."

"What you doing at the hospital?"

"Have you spoken to Ford? The hotel—"

"Yeah, I know about the hotel. It's a fucking mess. Silvio being in there can't be a coincidence. Someone set that fire for him." Maybe, could be. Okay, so he was right, but the aim hadn't been to hurt Silvio… not exactly. "Someone who knew he'd be there. I'm trying to find out what happened with—"

"Have you spoken to Ford? Did they get out?"

"Yes, shit, sorry, sweetheart, yes, they're out. Tell me why you're at the hospital. Did you get hurt? Is it Sersh?"

Cringing, she braced for revealing the truth. "We were in the Carlyle." Silence. "Not in any danger, we… After you left, we took one of the garage cars to the hotel." Oh, the quiet killed her. "With everyone focused on the meet upstairs, we thought it was a good time to search for the missing women."

"We?"

"Sersha and me."

"Shit, what if something happened? Something did if you're at the damn hospital. Sersha should know fucking better. She's spent enough time in the hospital recently." Something she hadn't thought much about, but her father had a point. Was the woman a masochist? "Which one of you is hurt? I'm on my way."

"No, it's neither of us. You don't have to come here. We found someone. We found a woman they were keeping captive. We rescued her."

"You rescued her?" Strat's voice got uncomfortably calm. "You took a woman out of the Carlyle?"

"We couldn't leave her there."

"You took from the Manzanis."

Which meant what? Something serious judging by the gravity of his tone.

"Dad, I—"

"I'm on my way."

The line cut off.

Sersha knew the families and hadn't said anything about taking from them. Going back toward her and Lachlan, she was just a couple of feet away when a nurse intercepted her.

"Excuse me, you're the woman who brought in the Jane Doe?"

"I am," Sersha said behind her, bringing the woman a step back to include her in the circle. "I brought Jane Doe in." That assertion wasn't about credit, not with Sersha's expression so hard. Was her father's friend protecting her? "Is there a problem?"

"She refuses to answer questions and…" Despite obvious apprehension, the nurse focused on Lachlan. "I'm sorry, Detective, but it's very apparent a crime has been committed."

"Oh, I'd say so," Lachlan said it plain. "Can I have a minute with my sister?" The woman nodded and backed off. She didn't know what to say, but it didn't matter. Lachlan was set on his sibling. "Where did you find her?"

"On the street," Sersha said in an obvious lie. The sister didn't sweat under her brother's scrutiny. "I'm a good Samaritan."

"Sersha," she said, not ready to let her ally go down alone. "I'll talk to the authorities and—"

"No, Imogen, you will not," Sersha said. "You keep your damn mouth shut."

"Hey," Lachlan snapped. "What the fuck is going on with you?"

"You should thank me, not question me. This is a delicate game. Everyone has to trust me that—"

"Trust you threatening Imogen?"

"It's not a threat. I can only protect her if she follows my lead."

"I can protect both of you—"

"No, not tonight, not this," Sersha said. "This is one of those sibling moments when you look into my eyes and understand it's best to trust me. Don't quiz me. I am doing what is best for Imogen, our Jane Doe, and what's best for you."

"Because if I know—"

"Then everything gets messy. If the truth comes out about this publicly, you can't be in three places at once."

"I'm talking to your Jane Doe," he said like it was a foregone conclusion.

"Good, yes," Sersha said. "You make sure this lands on your desk, brother."

"Because another cop won't be as understanding. Nice, Sersh, thanks for putting me in this position."

"You're welcome!" she called out as her brother passed to go join the nurse.

"Why can't we tell the truth?" she asked, moving in close. "If we expose—"

"Expose what? That we found a naked woman in a hotel full of hookers? Only Marseille can decide whether to tell the truth. Whatever that truth may be. We don't know what the hell went on in there or how she got there."

"The nurse said she wasn't answering questions."

"Would you? Seriously?" As they talked, Sersha kept scanning the department. "After what she's probably been through and with the insurmountable wall of the Manzanis, would you tell the truth? She tells the truth and she's dead within twenty-four hours. Guaranteed. Set your watch by it. The only chance she has of surviving is to keep her mouth shut."

"That's crazy! They'll just keep—"

"It's self-preservation. Something you should consider practicing yourself."

"The point was to expose this. To stop it."

Still on alert, Sersha smirked. "You can't stop it. You can't stop the world turning, Imogen. Women are subject to hellish sexual crime the world over. They're taken, abused, exploited, and cast aside like trash."

"Yes, but these women are—"

"What? Respectable? That makes a difference? They're not hookers so they deserve our intervention? That's an arbitrary distinction, don't you think? Sort of elitist. Is one woman worth more than another depending on her economic status?"

"No. No!"

"If you land in the Manzanis' sights, they won't come after you. Hurting you isn't enough. They take everything you love. Everyone you love." Sersha leaned in and lowered her volume. "They will turn your life inside out and punish anyone who tries to protect you. Know what that means? That means your father and my brother are in the firing line."

"Lachlan and I split up."

"You think that will stop him trying to protect you? Don't ask him for help. Keep him out of this. Don't go to him for advice. Don't cry on his shoulder. Because, so help me God, if anyone touches him because you couldn't keep your mouth shut—"

"I don't want anyone to get hurt."

"Good. Then we're on the same page." Something caught her eye and she nodded that way. "Hey."

Looking over her shoulder, her father barreled toward them. When he got there, he put an arm around her, kissing the top of her head.

"What the hell were you two thinking?" he hissed.

"No one got hurt," Sersha said. "No one on our side anyway."

"You got someone out of there? You took from the Manzanis."

"Marseille's her name. Jane Doe to anyone who asks. She's not talking."

"Good. You better hope it stays that way," her father said to Sersha. "Have you called him?"

"No." Sersha shook her head and took another look around. "I won't."

"You've gotta meet force with force, Scamp. You know that. He'll help. You need him."

"Don't ever say that to me. You have no idea what he would do for me."

"It's time to find out," Strat said. "He'll step up."

"I won't do it. I won't pull him into… No, war is not an option."

"Sersh, he will—"

"Yes, he will," Sersha snapped, frowning at her friend. "I won't do it. I will not invoke… No."

"I can—"

"No means no, Strat. That's it. Final. You don't go near him."

"Threatening me now?"

His concern was etched with amusement, no doubt meant to defuse the tension.

It worked enough to soften Sersha a fraction. "I need you with me, Strat. You know I can only do this if we're united. I can't do it alone."

In the times Sersha spoke of Vex, it had never seemed the woman cared much for him, but he could be the only man her father referred to. Other than someone with Manzani blood, who else could protect them? They didn't know anyone on equal or better footing than the Manzanis. In comparison, their allies were weak. Could Vex Manzani be their only hope?

"What do you need?" Just like that, her father clicked with Sersha. "How do we do this?"

Sersha licked her lower lip into her mouth, holding it there a second before letting it go. "We keep this in house."

"It will cost you."

"Yes, it will. I'm the only name attached to this and we're keeping it that way."

"The cops will want to talk to you, to ask questions."

"Lachlan's got it," Sersha said. "He'll run defense for us."

"You're taking this from every angle. It's a heavy load."

"Not for long." Sersha and Strat made eye contact. "What is it you say? Always make friends with your enemy."

"You want to go toe to toe with him?"

"We want something. That means we have to give something in return."

"What do we have that he'll want?" her father asked.

That was a question she wanted answered too.

"A megaphone," Sersha murmured. "Take Imogen home."

"What about you?"

"I'll wait for Lach." When Strat hesitated, Sersha smiled. "Honestly, I'll be fine. Take your daughter home."

"You're not invincible," Strat said, stern in his concern. "Didn't you learn anything from the last time you wound up in here?"

"To fight for your life, you first have to value it. If they want to take me down, they can do it. What do I have left to lose?"

Backing off, the woman walked away, disappearing into the Carlyle crowd.

"He really hurt her," she muttered. "The guy who broke her heart."

"You have no idea," her father said under his breath, sliding an arm around her. "Come on. We need to check on your brother."

And on Jagg.

Their posse was apart, each concerned for the others. If this didn't teach them they were strongest together, she didn't know what would.

THIRTY-SIX

"DO YOU WANT to stay at mine?" her father asked for maybe the tenth time. "I know you said no already. Are you sure? I can turn around."

"You don't have room," she said. "I don't mind being at Ford's."

Though she might go crazy if she didn't lay eyes on Jagg soon.

Her heart rate picked up as they rounded onto Jagg's block. Play it cool. Keep calm. She couldn't fly out of the car and run to him. Oh, why did they have to be secret? How long could that secret last when their lives were being endangered?

They stopped and she took off her seatbelt. "You don't have to come in," she said. "Everyone's tired. We should all get some rest."

Or do their best to try.

"I'll come over in the morning," he said, leaning over to pull her head to his lips. "Try not to get into any more trouble until then."

"Will you check on Sersha before you—"

"Yes," he said. "I'll call her."

Good. On another reassuring smile, she left the car. The vehicle stayed there, waiting until she opened the side door and gave her father another wave. Yes, she was fine, but it was his job to worry. Something she was coming to terms with gradually. Moving through the dark corridor, she mustered her strength to maintain composure. Be relaxed. Be…

In the breakroom, Jagg was alone. And her poise dropped in a snap.

"Oh my God," she exhaled, hurrying to him as he strode over to pull her against him.

All thoughts of reserve vanished when he grabbed her head to tip it back and plant his mouth on hers. He'd needed her. In his urgency, his desperation matched the explosion of need within her. Need to be together, to see the other. Separation was a weakness. At that moment, she found strength.

"What were you thinking?" he panted, breaking the kiss to shake her head once. "Everything. You tell me everything."

Just managing a nod, she bounced up to kiss him again. He boosted her onto the kitchen island and pulled her closer. Angling her back, pushing, taking, forcing, as she grabbed, squeezed and pressed in return. Eager to express her fear for him, her legs caught his hips and pulled him in close. Not close enough. She needed to be joined with him, to have him moving inside her and—

A door slammed and they broke, freezing for a second, their mouths just a millimeter apart. It could only be—Jagg eased back and twisted around to… Ford, right there, glaring at them.

Oh, shit. They'd talked about keeping them quiet. They were a secret. Well, no, not anymore.

"Ford…" she said, bracing for a reaction.

Her brother didn't respond and flipped the turn to stalk toward his room. She tried to push Jagg away, but he set a hand on the counter beside her thigh.

"Leave him," he muttered.

"Leave him?" she asked. Ford's bedroom door slammed. "What the hell…? Why didn't he—"

"Because he doesn't want to say now something he'll regret in the morning. It's been a long night."

Of all the reactions she'd considered her brother may have, none was not on the list.

"We can't let him think this is adrenaline. If he thinks we're screwing around for—"

"He needs time to process." Stepping back, he took her hands to slide her off the counter. "Whatever he thinks, and if he wants answers, he knows where to find us."

"I don't want to hurt him."

"You can't pressure him. Your brother prefers to think, then act. Got me out of trouble more times than I can count. Opposite of Strat, he must get it from your mom."

"Oh," she said, her breathing getting deeper. "Will he call my dad?"

"I don't know. Maybe. Do you care?"

"Yes, I care. I—"

"Everyone is safe, everyone is alive. Tonight could've gone a different way for all of us. If he calls Strat—"

"My father will come racing over here and probably wrap his car around a pole in the process. If he's mad—"

"He won't call Strat. Why would he?"

"We should go in there," she said, worrying her lip. "We should speak to him. Explain it to him."

Jagg smiled. How the hell could he smile? This was a disaster.

"You don't want his knee-jerk reaction. Trust me. You harass him and he'll only shut down. No one forces Ford to do anything. Give him space. Give him time."

"How much space? How much time?" His easy smile poked at her. "How can you be smiling?"

"Because he knows. It's out there now. This is a blessing. We'll take whatever he wants to give out, but we don't have to worry about keeping secrets."

"No, just making amends," she whispered. "What if he tells us to end it?"

"Don't upset yourself thinking about things that haven't happened yet. It is what it is. We are what we are."

"I don't know what that means."

"It means relax. Take a breath. And see the positive."

"What's the positive?" she asked, going with him when he moved, their hands still joined. "It's positive if he accepts us. It's not if he tells us to break up."

"The damage is done, Genny. We've crossed the line. We can't uncross it."

"That doesn't mean he won't ask us to," she said. "Are you sure we shouldn't go talk to him? If he's up all night—"

"If he wants us, he'll find us," he said, opening his bedroom door. "Tonight's been enough of a headfuck. I'm betting he just crashes."

The meet, yes, they hadn't talked about Silvio, about what happened before the fire or how they got out.

Though he went inside, she stopped on the threshold. "I want to hear about tonight, what happened with you and Ford."

"And I want to hear about your unscripted adventure with Sersha, but let's do it lying down."

She honestly didn't get it and looked around until—there was that smile again. "You want me to come to bed with you?"

He lightened. "Ford knows. You wanna sleep alone when you don't have to?"

No. And not after a night like that. "No."

"Then come on," he said, dropping her hand to go inside, leaving the choice hers.

If Ford knew, what harm could it do? There was no point getting caught kissing Jagg if she backed away from the relationship at crunch time.

Exhaling, she went inside and closed the door. Jagg was already stripping off. Oh, sex would be a bad idea. A very bad idea. Talk about rubbing salt in Ford's wound. If he heard them…

"We should probably keep things cool tonight," he said, reading her mind.

"All I want to do is lie with you. I was so scared and…"

"Tonight could've ended differently," he said, naked as he pulled back the covers. "I know. Come 'ere."

She shed her clothes on the way to the bed and climbed in before he joined her, laying the sheet over her body.

"You didn't know we were in there."

"No, I didn't. I would never have left the building if I'd known there was a chance you'd be in it." Jagg's fingers sank into her hair, pushing it back in a calm combing motion. "Why would you take that risk?"

"You were taking a risk upstairs with Silvio. We got a woman out. Not the one we were exactly looking for, but she's safe tonight because of us."

"Sersha." His admiration stayed on her locks. "It was her idea?"

"It was the right idea." And one she should've come up with herself. "Sersha's better at this than I am."

"No, Sersha's better protected." His eyes narrowed. "You can't go racing in without a plan like that. What would you have done if you didn't find someone to save? What if the fire never happened?"

The fire was a foregone conclusion as part of Sersha's plan, though it did get far out of hand.

"I don't know. You can't anticipate every eventuality."

"You can, or you should, before jumping in like that. All Sersha's potential outcomes are positive. She threatens someone with her father or Vex's obsession with her, no one lays a finger on her. You—"

"Belong to you and the Manzanis know that." She wriggled closer, her fingertips drifting up his torso. "Isn't that what you said?"

"Were you gonna tell them that in front of Sersha?"

"I don't know, Jagg," she said. "Maybe instead of pulling apart the maybes of what I did, we should talk about the definites of what you did. You walked into that building, into a meet, knowing exactly who was going to be there. One of the most dangerous men in the city. In the state. What if Silvio tried to hurt you?" Except, huh. "Did he hurt you?"

"If he wanted me dead, he wouldn't do it over bourbon. No, he wanted to send a message."

"Which was? Don't mess with him?"

"In an ideal world, he wants to keep doing what he's doing and for others to stop poking around in his business."

"Did you say we would?"

"I said nothing. We barely got started before the fire broke out."

"So you'll have to meet again? I don't like it. I don't trust him."

"Me either, but Silvio Manzani can be a reasonable man, sometimes. He'll give us something if we give him something in return."

"What does he want from us?"

"Assurance that you'll print his truth."

"What truth is that? The women weren't really abducted and murdered? They were all meth-whores who got what they deserved? I can't print lies."

"He'll give us the murderer."

Her hand caught his, stalling it in her hair. "He'll give us the... I don't understand."

"You want someone to go down for this. Justice. You need a man in prison for—"

"Is it the real murderer? This is linked to the Manzanis, the Carlyle is their hotel. Are you trying to tell me that someone, one man, is responsible for killing these women on Manzani property and it wasn't sanctioned by Silvio? If that's true, why doesn't he kill the guy himself? Punish him for operating in his territory without permission? Punish him for drawing attention to a Manzani operation?"

"We didn't get to all the details."

"But that can't be it. Can it? Is he saying someone brought each of the women there and, what? Reserved a room and went to town torturing and murdering them while Manzani women went about their jobs in other rooms? Is that even possible?" These women were held, kept alive for days or weeks, before being killed. Do the Carlyle rent rooms by the hour? By the week?"

"I told you some Manzani guys stay there. Or they did. Depends how sound the building is after the fire if they can go back."

"If they can't, the streets will be flooded."

His fingers twined with hers to bring them down between their bodies. "Someone would be in prison for the crimes."

"But is it the person responsible?"

His gaze searched hers. "I don't know that there is justice here, baby. I could lie to you and say there is but, the Manzanis will keep operating no matter what. They'll offer up as many sacrificial lambs as they need to, and those people will go along with the guilt."

"Why? Why would someone risk spending their life in—"

"Because it's the Manzanis," he said and actually smiled, though it seemed more pitying than amused. "If they don't have something on you, they find something, or they threaten whatever you love. I want to tell you there's true justice and the good guys always win…"

She sighed. "But they don't. Sersha said something similar tonight."

"We'll keep going after them, as long as you want to, but Silvio's giving you a win."

"And only we'll know it's a lie. How does that save women from going missing in the future? Will they keep taking them and murdering them?"

"Like I said, we didn't get all the way into it before the fire."

"If nothing changes, if women will still be killed, what does the win matter? I don't want glory. I want justice." An impossible goal if she listened to those around her. "Is this why?"

He frowned. "Why what?"

"The cops wouldn't put them together, people at the paper, on the street. I thought I was the only one who noticed. Was I the only one stupid enough to speak up?"

"You weren't stupid. You thought you were doing the right thing."

"It is the right thing," she said with almost petulant frustration. "The bad guys aren't supposed to win."

"It's the way of the world. I'm sorry, Genny. Sometimes the good guys win, sometimes we have to back away slowly. You losing your life, or the lives of people you care about, won't save those women."

"I can't tell Mila that we're just giving up. That we're letting the killing continue."

"I'll talk to Silvio again. We didn't hash it out. The fire will distract him, which could work for us. At the very least, he's a venue down. If the Carlyle's deemed unsafe, he'll have to find somewhere else for his women to work or his revenue will tank."

"It's more than a little sickening that women's bodies are only valued for the income they can attract."

Something else that had been the way since the dawn of time.

"And tonight accomplished something else."

"What?"

"If the Carlyle was your victims' jail, it's been taken out from under the perps. Now they're scrambling for a new base." And possibly dragging the prisoners with them. "Fire will investigate the Carlyle, who knows what they'll turn up."

"Silvio Manzani will have the influence to silence officials."

"Some of them, yeah. But maybe what they find is undeniable."

"Like the charred remains of missing women? Do you know if anyone was seriously hurt or killed?"

"I think we'll have to wait until the dust settles to know that. No offense, but the media can turn a tragedy into a circus. I'm betting your dad gets the truth before the rest of us."

"He said he'd come over in the morning," she said, her eyes closing. "Now I don't know if I want him to."

His digits lost themselves in her hair again. "Why?"

"What if Ford reacts or blows up about us? Can we handle both of them at once?"

"We can handle anything so long as we're together," he said. "Get some sleep. We'll figure everything out tomorrow."

Tomorrow. What wonders would the new day bring? Was she strong enough to face another day?

THIRTY-SEVEN

MORNING.

Oh, she shouldn't be nervous about seeing her own brother. She'd have to play it cool, be calm. There couldn't be a fight. They couldn't face each other with hostility. Usually with Ford, if he was giving her shit, she'd give it right back or let it roll off. With his discovery of her relationship, deference was the word of the day. It wouldn't be easy to let him jump on his high horse and judge her, but she'd take it to keep the peace... if that was even a possibility.

She'd woken up in Jagg's bed alone. Alone! Wherever her guy was, it wasn't in his room. Had he tried to head off the argument by getting in front of Ford first? Maybe. Maybe not. Screaming and ruckus hadn't woken her. Hopefully, that was a good sign.

Whatever happened, Ford didn't scare her. He'd never hurt her. Still, pushing her luck was a bad idea. Her clothes were in her bedroom, not Jagg's. Shoot. If she went out in Jagg's clothes or in nothing but a sheet, and Ford was there, it could inflame his opposition.

Last night's clothes would have to do.

Maybe it was her imagination, but smoke hung in them. The scent was a harsh reminder of the previous night's events. Not that smoke hounded her during their rescue. Maybe the smell hung in Jagg's clothes rather than hers, that could be the source. He'd skimped on the details. How close had the fire come to him? How close had she come to losing him?

Despite worrying about her brother's reaction to her relationship, her mind was clearer than it had been the previous night. Conclusions were still a ways off, but her determination had shifted.

The case would come after breakfast.

After all the mental build up, exiting Jagg's bedroom was a huge anticlimax. The breakroom was vacant. Relief… or delaying the inevitable?

Huh.

Had everyone just gone on with their lives? No fights, no arguments, no face-off? Somehow that didn't seem right.

At least the seclusion gave her a chance to shower. She walked out of the bathroom after cleansing herself still pondering.

Until she saw Jagg there in the kitchen.

"You…" she said, tucking her towel in as she marched over. "Left me in bed!"

"What was I supposed to do?" He gulped down half a bottle of juice. "Carry you out?"

"Wake me up! What did Ford say?"

"Haven't seen him yet."

Leaning in, he put the bottle down on the counter, forcing her to back up against it.

"Is he here?" she asked, her arms dropping to her sides.

"Haven't checked his room." Untucking her towel, he started to open it. "I'm not that kind of boss."

She grabbed the edges of her towel. "What are you doing?"

"I'm twitchy about last night."

"The Carlyle?"

Stooping, he nuzzled her hair. "You spending the night in my bed."

"You invited me."

When his hand found its way beneath her towel, she kept hold of the material, but let him fondle.

"I should've violated you," he mumbled.

She laughed. "I don't think it's a violation when I'm willing."

Dipping lower, he kissed the side of her neck. "Want to be willing right here?"

"Jagg," she said on a laugh, sort of pushing and pulling him at the same time. "We don't know if Ford's home."

"He is."

Her brother's deadpan voice drew their attention.

"Fuck, man. You're worse than a McDade. Wear a bell, why don't you?"

"To give you time to take it out my sister and put it back in your pants?" he asked and wandered over. "Is there coffee?"

Jagg glanced back. "Maybe."

She tucked in her towel again and pushed at Jagg while Ford poured coffee into a mug. Someone had to say something. Their actions, what he'd caught them doing, couldn't just be left without answer or explanation.

He'd referenced them sleeping together, so obviously he got that—

"Ditzy Daisy is coming in later," Jagg said.

"Oh, yeah?" Ford drank some coffee as he propped himself in the vee of the units. "Big job?"

"Could be," Jagg said. "I told her you'd fill her in later."

"She still in the Firebird?"

"Yeah, the fucking beauty."

"You going to take another swing at buying it?"

"Maybe up the bid," Jagg said, "sweeten the—"

"What are you two doing?" she asked, stepping between them, looking left then right.

"What should we be doing?" Ford asked, coffee on the way to his mouth again.

Putting her back to Jagg, she folded her arms. "You saw us kissing last night and today in—aren't you going to say anything?"

"Like what?"

"Like how you feel about it."

"'Bout what?" her brother asked.

God, he was infuriating. "Jagg and me!"

The former's hand slipped onto her shoulder. "Genny—"

"He has to have an opinion. You have to have an opinion."

"Will it make a difference?" Ford asked. Jagg squeezed her. "Am I happy about it? No. It better not be some BS rebound from the cop. You'll cause a lot of damage that won't be fixed."

"Me?" she asked, her jaw swinging loose. "You're warning me to take this seriously? Me?"

"Jagg knows better than to bullshit this. He's my best friend, but I'd have to put a bullet in him for screwing around."

"Jagg knows better?"

"Yeah, he doesn't fuck around anymore," he said, boosting away from the counter to walk away. "And you both have bedrooms. Stop screwing around in here. Keep it behind closed doors. That's my opinion."

That was it? Ford went into his room with what was left of his coffee.

"That's it?" she asked.

Jagg pulled her back to kiss the top of her head. "Go get ready. You want to visit Mila, right?"

"Mm hmm." Ford's door was just closed. The end. A period after an unexciting sentence. "And then to see Sersha if we can."

"Okay."

He pushed her toward her room.

After a couple of steps, she twisted to him. "What am I missing? Is Ford going to murder us in our beds?"

"Bed," he said. "Easier for him that we're both in one place."

"I expected… I don't know what I expected, but it wasn't that."

"It hasn't sunk in. We'll find out how he feels about it as he does. Your brother trusts me."

"But not me, apparently."

"Go get changed."

"That's it?"

"We'll just have to play this through, no other way. What does he get for freaking out?"

Always so calm and together, so damn laid-back. Why was she the only one flummoxed? He gave her another boost.

This time, she went forward, slowly. "We still have to talk."

"Who?"

Damn, now he was doing it.

"You and me. About what you left out about last night." The life or death part. "We can talk in the car."

In an enclosed space where he couldn't get away or distract her. That day, she hoped, would be enlightening on many levels. As frustrating as unknowns could be, there was an exhilaration to progress. Even incremental progress.

Dressing as fast as she could, she blasted her hair with the blow-dryer and skimped on the makeup. Given Jagg had known her since, well, forever, she didn't need to go out of her way to dress up for him.

They got in the car, drove off his property, and still his mouth hadn't opened.

"Did you speak to Ford?" Yes, she wanted to talk about the fire. She also wanted to know if her brother had been lobotomized. "This morning?"

"You saw me talk to him."

"No, before that. Before I got up."

"No. I told you I didn't."

Maybe he'd been protecting her. "How can he be so cool about this? About us?"

"We should take the win."

"It's not a win if we don't understand it. Is it a trick?"

"A trick?" he asked, almost snickering. "He knows we're together, what is he tricking us into?"

"I just don't get it."

"Let him adjust. Maybe he'll yell at you later."

"He already thinks I'm the problem. Can you believe he accused me of being on the rebound?"

"You are on the rebound."

"I am not! Lach and I broke up months ago."

"You been with another guy since?"

"Yes."

He frowned. "Who?"

"You," she said. His expression relaxed again. "I am not on the rebound. This is not a rebound. Why would you be with me if you think you're a rebound?"

"You told him about us? The cop. Have you told him?"

"Lach?" she asked. "When have I had the chance to do that? And if I tell him, he'll tell Sersha… which means Dad will find out."

"Your dad will find out eventually. He's got his finger on the pulse. You know it'll get back to him sooner rather than later."

Strat had an easy-going, non-threatening attitude that drew people in. A guy like him, everyone's best friend, people just told him things. So, yeah, he would find out. They couldn't keep them a secret forever.

"Should we get in front of it?"

"Tell him?" Jagg asked. "If you want."

"Do you think Ford will?"

"Dunno."

Breathing in, she held for a second, then let it out. "Men are so infuriating."

"Yeah, sugar, we're the problem."

"Actually, you are the problem," she said, switching modes. "You didn't tell me about the fire."

"I did."

"You didn't tell me how long you were in there or how you got out."

"We got out. What does how matter?"

"Because I want to know how close I came to losing you."

He picked up her hand. "I've survived worse than a few flames and a little smoke."

Was that supposed to appease her?

THIRTY-EIGHT

QUESTIONING HIM FURTHER wasn't an option when they pulled into the hospital parking lot and got upstairs to Mila's floor. As soon as he saw them, Coakley came storming over, halting them halfway up the corridor.

"Now might not be a good time, man."

"What's wrong?" she asked, bobbing and weaving, trying to get a better look at Mila's door. "What's going on?"

"She's… upset."

"About what?"

"Fuck knows," Coakley said. "A nurse went in there and—" Rounding Coakley, progress was essential. "I don't know that she's put together right!"

Ignoring Coakley's call, she went straight into Mila's room. Her friend was sitting on the bed, trying to get up, while a doctor and two nurses attempted to both stop her moving and lay her down.

"Imogen!" Mila called, reaching for her between people. "Help me!"

"What is going on?"

"She wants to leave," one nurse said, struggling with their patient. "We can't let her leave, she's not stable enough—"

"Let me talk to her," she said and smiled, stalling Mila's struggle. "You'll stay and talk to me, won't you? We can decide what to do next together."

After a quick glance at all the faces, Mila nodded, and the medical staff backed off. They went out and Jagg closed the door, staying in the room.

Resting a hand on Mila's shoulder, she stayed loose. "What's going on?" she asked, keeping her tone calm and, hopefully, soothing.

"I figured it out. It… it hit me and… It was him driving; he was the driver. Bryan hit me with the car."

"Stephanie's Bryan. Are you sure?"

"Yes! He killed her! And he tried to kill me!"

"Okay," she said, rubbing Mila's upper arm. "Don't help him succeed. You need to rest. Recuperate."

"Someone has to stop him or he'll come back to finish the job."

"You don't have to worry about that. Jagg has his people guarding your room. I told you he wouldn't let anything happen to us, didn't I?"

"I have to do something."

That sense of duty, the urgency to help, she understood the desperation. To a degree anyway. Having lost her best friend and been plowed down with a vehicle, the need had to be stronger in Mila. But she wasn't at her peak. Letting her run around in the world wouldn't have positive results.

"You are doing something, Mila. You are. You're getting better. That shows Bryan he won't win. Nothing is more important than your health. Stephanie would say the same thing if she was here."

Mila deflated. That action needed no translator. Eager to fight for her friend, the woman wanted to bring the man who harmed her to justice. You'd think that meant being always aware of Stephanie's death. It didn't. Every time the truth thwacked Mila, another piece of her would fade.

The door opened, whirling her around, and there was Lachlan, peering at Jagg.

"What you doing here?" Lachlan asked them both. "Witness tampering?"

"If we were, my guy wouldn't have let you in," Jagg said. "This an official visit?"

"Yes, it is." Lachlan held up a file and went around her to Mila. "Can you look at something for me?"

"At what?"

"A picture." Mila's trepidation was so potent that even she gulped in anticipation of what Lachlan drew from inside the file. "Do you know who that is?"

Mila took the sheet, but the answer was already clear. After a quick blink, the picture was in her hands.

"Yes. Yes!" Mila's agitation grew again, flooding her voice with anxiety. "Stephanie's boyfriend. He hit me with the car. This is him, it's all him."

"How did you get this?" she asked her ex.

"It's a screen grab from a movie," Lachlan said, grave in the way he met each of their eyes. "And not a nice one."

"A movie?" Maybe like the ones Strat mentioned Ludlow produced? "Where did you get it?"

Lachlan hesitated, which wasn't like him. Though, in the past, when they had insider conversations, they were usually alone. This time, they had an audience, one Lachlan may not trust.

"Fire kept the Carlyle off-limits," Jagg said, scrutinizing Lach's profile. "To the public and the owners anyway. Did the cops—"

"One of the fire guys saw something sketchy and we got a warrant."

"See something, say something, right?"

Oh, wrong road.

Lachlan didn't appreciate his integrity being questioned. "It's above board."

Jagg's sarcasm continued. "Yeah, you couldn't let this chance pass you by."

Was Jagg being an asshole? Why should he care if the Manzanis were in the firing line?

"Tell us about the movie," she said. "Was it porn?"

"Why would you assume that?"

Once a cop, always a cop.

"Was it?"

"A…" Lachlan dragged it out, "specific variety of porn."

She didn't like him being cagey. "And now you're looking for Bryan. Was there a woman in this movie?"

"All I need is a positive ID." Which wasn't an answer to her question. "Mila, are you sure this is the same guy you saw with Stephanie? Stephanie's boyfriend?"

"Yes. Bryan. His name is Bryan."

Lachlan would know that the cops would have Mila's original statement. They'd also talked to him, if Mila was right. Lachlan being so thorough suggested they'd caught Bryan doing more than just being an incidental boyfriend unrelated to any crime.

"Yvonne Ingham was seeing a Bryan too," she said. "It was on her social media. No picture though."

Lachlan got closer to the bed. "Where did Stephanie meet him?"

The picture was just the opening shot. In all the times she'd asked Lachlan to take the case, he'd reminded her he wasn't homicide. Porn though, women being trafficked, forced into prostitution, that was her ex's deal. Unfortunately, in this case, one segued into the other.

"I don't know," Mila said with a head shake that prompted her hand to her crown. "Maybe I should know that. Do I know that?"

"You are still recovering." Adjusting the pillows, she eased Mila back down. "You get some rest and we'll come back later."

Opening her arms wide to the guys, she herded them into the hallway.

"You're hindering my investigation."

"That woman has been through enough," she whispered to Lachlan. "She lost her friend, her apartment, and almost her life. She doesn't know anything about Bryan, I asked her before. She said the cops talked to him. How did you find him the first time?"

"We didn't. He caught our guys outside. They talked for a minute, turned around and the guy was gone."

Great. Dead end. "Tell us about the movie. What was it?"

"That's not how this works. I don't give you information. I get information… or I should."

Not so long ago, he'd give her details. Something was different.

"Please, just help us—"

"Torture porn," Jagg said. "That's what the movies are, right? The women being tortured for the client's pleasure."

"More than that," Lachlan said, apparently giving in… a little.

"More? What's—"

"They're snuff movies."

"Snuff?" she asked. "Why do I feel like I should know what that is?"

"Murder," Jagg said, squeezing her shoulder. "They're being killed on film…"

"For the client's pleasure," she whispered, stalled on that for a second before being infused with complete outrage. "That's what this is about? Fucking movies?"

"Keep your voice down," Lachlan said, getting closer. "Whatever was going on in the Carlyle, we need witnesses to testify."

Who would do that? Mila? Marseille?

"Sersha says if they testify, they're dead."

"She threatened them?" Jagg asked.

"No, she knows how the Manzanis work."

"I'll deal with my sister. Right now, we need to track down the guy on this drive."

"How many were there?" she asked. "Movies?"

"So far just one."

She looked up at Jagg over her head. "That's bullshit," he muttered.

"Yeah, we figure that too. A lot of hard drives missing. A lot of empty shelves."

Amazing how even in the clutches of potential death, men stayed behind to clear the archives. But if others were in these movies, they'd want the evidence gone as much as the Manzanis would.

"Talk to Swerve?"

"Tracking him down," Lachlan said to Jagg. "But you know how much help he'll be."

"You think Bryan's the key to this?"

"I think he's potentially the weakest link. They left this behind, dropping him into the cops' lap. If he knows what's going on, testifying may be the only way to save his own ass."

"You can't let him get away with it. Don't accept his testimony and let him off the hook."

"Would you rather everyone was off the hook? Going after the Manzanis—"

"You can't take down the Manzanis with this. You can't take down the Manzanis."

Lachlan frowned. "You've been spending too much time with my sister. You think because it's difficult, we shouldn't try?"

"I think this is related to Silvio Manzani," she said, leaning in as she lowered her volume. "And I think he's stronger than his son."

"Vex? How's he connected?" This time it was Jagg under Lachlan's scrutiny. "Been in touch with your old pal?"

"Vex wasn't at the Carlyle when it went up."

"No, Im's right, it's Silvio's operation."

"And here I thought families worked together."

"You know better than that, Immie."

"Wading into this…" she said, drawing in a breath. "It's all so much more complicated than I thought it would be."

"What did you think tracking the Manzanis would be?"

"I didn't know I was chasing the Manzanis when I started this."

"What took you to them?" Lachlan asked. She hesitated. "You want me to solve this and bring people to justice, you have to tell me what you know."

"You knew I was mixed up with the Manzanis before I did. Jagg told me about the tattoo."

"That's it? That what put you on this path?"

No. Lying wouldn't get any of them anywhere. "Mila," she said. "I was over there, at their apartment. Bryan told Stephanie that he could get into a club, a specific club that… I don't know that they ever went, I didn't know it was relevant… not exactly. I was investigating. Asking questions, going places… following leads."

"What club?" he asked. "I want you to say Stag, but you're not going to… are you?"

"Hustle." Might as well get it out there. "Bryan could get them into Hustle."

"Which belongs to Vex Manzani. What the hell were you doing going in somewhere like that alone? You're lucky you got out alive. Why did they let you in?"

"I wasn't alone," she said, her hand swinging back to twine her fingers with Jagg's. "I was safe."

As Lachlan's focus fell to their joined hands, understanding came in a slow breath. "Right." A beat. "Got it."

And with that, he turned to walk off.

"Lach—"

"Let him be," Jagg said, strengthening his hold on her hand.

Separating her fingers, she landed the hand on Mila's door. "I'm going to check on my friend."

Damnit. She hadn't wanted Lachlan to find out that way. Had she wanted him to find out in any way? Yes, they were over, but she didn't want to hurt him.

With one perfect shot, pins were flying every which way.

THIRTY-NINE

AFTER MILA FELL ASLEEP, she and Jagg went to find Marseille.

"Do you think they'll keep her in the ER?" she asked in the elevator on their way down.

"I don't know," Jagg said, flopping an arm over her shoulder. "She might not want to talk."

"She wouldn't talk last night, according to the nurse. Sersha didn't even give her name. She's a Jane Doe here."

"Smart. It's Marseille's call. We can't imagine what she's been through."

Safety was a privilege. "Do you think they'll get her therapy and—"

"Doubt it. Treat and street. Alotta people in the world got problems."

"We can't save everyone." This story brought so much into perspective, not all of it good. "Sersha says not everyone can be saved."

"Marseille might be okay. We know nothing about her."

And they never would if the woman didn't open up. Then again, how could she help? What did she know about imprisonment and violence?

Stepping out into the emergency department, the waiting area was busier than it had been after the fire. Jagg grabbed her hand and wound her through people to the front desk. He stood there, waiting, until someone came to sit in front of them. The person hadn't acknowledged them, but that didn't stop Jagg.

"We're looking for a Jane Doe," he said, projecting his voice in a way that made it impossible for the clerk to ignore him.

"Get a lot of them in," the clerk said. "Fire brought an entire squad of amnesiacs in last night."

Right. Yeah. How many hookers and henchmen would give their real details?

"This woman was memorable," Jagg said. "Found in the street. Wearing a sheet."

"Oh, yeah." The clerk actually looked up and seemed startled to register him. "You're Jagger Dunn." How the hell did the guy know that? "Followed you back in the day."

"Can you help us out?"

"Yeah." The guy leaped up. "Yeah, just wait one minute."

Scurrying off, the clerk quick-stepped it out of there.

"You didn't tell me you were famous," she said. "Thank God for that."

Or the employee may not have been so eager to help.

"Not a good thing," Jagg muttered, turning slowly, checking out the space, much like Sersha had the previous night. "He can ID me to whoever asks. One short step from me to you."

Her eyes darted around. "What are you looking for?"

"Nothing." But that was a lie. He put an arm around her, pulling her close to kiss her head. "We're good."

"Who would ask?"

"Always assume someone wants to know what you don't want them to know."

Okay. That was beyond a level of paranoia, but made sense given how deep they were in.

As Jagg continued his observations, the clerk came hurrying back.

"She split," the guy announced.

"What?"

"Yeah, just disappeared. She was here and then... gone."

"Anyone with her?" Jagg asked.

The clerk shook his head. "No one saw anything. She just disappeared."

"Thanks," Jagg said without further question.

"Hey, uh..." Now it was the clerk's turn to be paranoid. "We're not really supposed to—"

"We were never here," Jagg said, understanding the guy's anxiety. "Thanks."

His arm stayed over her shoulder, holding her close all the way back to the car.

"Gone?" she asked as he peeled away from the curb. "Gone where?"

"I don't know. We'll probably never know."

"Do you think her family came to pick her up?"

Except if it was family and a legitimate pick up, why did it happen in secret? Why was Marseille still a Jane Doe?

"Maybe." Jagg humored her. "Could be she's safe."

"Could be she's not though, right?"

"If the Manzanis got word she was here…"

"They'd come and get her, take her back there, punish her for—"

"We don't know it was them. Could've been anyone. The Manzanis had a lot going on. The fire bought her a window that, if she's smart, Marseille took advantage of."

Every step on this path brought more frustration. Marseille was the wronged party. It shouldn't be on her to sneak out in the dead of night to save her skin. Freedom hadn't cut all the chains.

"We have to go to the Carlyle," she said before Jagg could turn toward the garage.

"Why?"

"I want to see what's going on over there. What's the damage?"

"Doesn't matter."

"What harm can it do to go check? Maybe people are around. Maybe they want to talk. Or if it's deserted, we could go inside. Look for ourselves."

"The building might not be safe. And this is a big win for the cops." Despite his objection, he missed the garage turn, keeping them on the road for the Carlyle. "They'll be swarming."

Amped up like hornets in a nest. "I know a bunch of cops."

"Still trading on McLeod's name?" he asked. "Dangerous."

She frowned. "Why is it dangerous?"

"You just broke the guy's heart."

"I did not. He was surprised, that's all. Anyway, Lachlan's not like that. He's not angry or malicious."

"Guys change in a whole helluva way when they're hurting."

"Not Lachlan. He'd never turn his back on anyone."

"Mr. Honorable."

"You say that as if you don't like him."

"I don't know him, Genny. I'm sure he's a great guy."

Though he didn't sound convinced. "Let's just get there and see how it plays out. Maybe we don't have to talk to anyone at all."

"This isn't a good idea."

"What other choice do we have?" she asked Jagg as he took a corner. "We need to know what's going on."

"They won't let us just waltz in."

"We can watch. Maybe they'll bring something interesting out."

"The cops worked fast on this." Through the night possibly. "This fire's a jackpot for them."

"Why does that piss you off?" she asked. "You were a jerk to Lachlan. Like him or not, the man is just doing his job."

"Didn't think you'd…"

"What? Tell him about us? I got that earlier."

"That why you told him?"

"I don't want him finding out from someone else. My dad, he'll find out from someone else, whatever, but Lach and I were… He'll always be important to me, Jagg. Isn't there anyone from your past you still care about?" His lack of response caught her attention. "You didn't think I'd tell him, did you?"

"I didn't expect you to do it right there." He sighed. "I've gotta talk to Strat."

"Oh, so now who's worried about Dad finding out?" she asked, ready to needle him a little until the wail of sirens razed the air. Two police cars shot past them, speeding to the junction and going straight through a red. "That can't be good."

"Always at the center of the story," he muttered, stopping at the light.

Digging out her phone, she dialed fast. "No, but I know someone who is."

He picked up on the second ring. "Steeple."

"What is going on around the Carlyle?" she asked her boss. "I'm a couple of blocks away."

"Heard you got caught up in it last night."

"I'm not surprised you heard," she said, pressing her finger into her other ear, trying to block out more sirens. Jagg didn't move as the lights changed. His eyes were in the rearview then… three more cars shot past them, sirens wailing. "There's something going on around here right now."

"Yeah, there's been tension all day. Carlyle's off-limits. Fire investigators are still inside, cops swarming everywhere. Course the Manzani guys are sticking close. Silvio's got an army of lawyers out there… Someone was bound to throw a punch."

"As long as that's all there is. We're heading that way now—"

"Don't put yourself in danger. I've got people on the way there.

"You've got people on the way to potentially the biggest riot this city has seen for years, but you don't want me there?"

"These are unofficial guys, Imogen. Guys who can watch and take care of themselves if they have to. Your father would never accept you being hurt on my order."

"It's not an order. I was going there anyway."

"Sersha's on her way—"

"You'd put Sersha in danger, but not me?"

"She's on her way in," he said, unimpressed. "I was going to say Sersha is on her way into the office."

"You want to give her the story?"

"She has the connections to find out—"

"It's a lot of pressure for just one person." She landed a hand on the dashboard when Jagg took an unexpected right. "What are you doing?" He didn't answer. Maybe he thought she was still talking to Steeple. "I'll call you back." She hung up. "Jagg, where are we going?"

"Home."

"Why home? What is—"

"You used the word 'riot,' baby, and there are cops out there. That means guns."

"And you think I'm not savvy enough to avoid getting shot?"

"Getting shot doesn't work that way. Besides, I like this car. You want to roll in front of water cannons, get your brother's keys."

Though she wanted to argue against him and her boss, she didn't have control of the car or the situation. And her worries were nothing.

Switching perspective, someone else might be in a lot of trouble: Sersha. If the Manzanis ever found out how the fire started…

"We should've asked Lachlan about Marseille."

"Guy didn't seem like he wanted to talk."

No, because she'd revealed them. "I'll call him later, when he's calmed down. Do you know if Ford is at the garage?"

"I'm guessing yes, since Ditzy Daisy was due over there."

"Do they have a thing? Is she the woman you thought he'd be sleeping with the other night?"

"No," he said, his hands sliding down to the bottom of the wheel. "Every guy and their neighbor wants a shot on that pony ride, but she's feisty."

"What does that mean?" Not that she cared exactly. "Is Hustle open tonight?"

"Think that's a good idea?"

"The Manzanis are the key to this."

"Not Vex."

"How else do I get close to Bryan? Yvonne Ingham was definitely at the club the night we went there. Why would she be there if Vex isn't involved?"

"The Carlyle might not be Vex's operation, but there's plenty of crossover of guys."

"Why wouldn't she have asked for help? Called out and come with us?"

"With that audience? Good luck. If she draws attention to herself and doesn't get out of there, it's over for her. And probably for us, for anyone who knows more than they should."

"I wasn't paying enough attention. I can't remember if she had bruises."

"Can't have been anything major if you recognized her picture. It was dark, shit was going on, I don't remember seeing her at all."

"Why would she be there?" she murmured to herself. "Why Hustle?"

"There's all kinds of explanations why she might've been there."

"So if we go tonight, we could see her there again. Maybe get closer. Ask questions."

"And then what? You want to steal her?" His head shook. "You already took from the Manzanis once. That shit doesn't go over well. Families like the Manzanis have long memories. And in Hustle, there's a hundred guys, maybe two hundred, all ready to shoot wherever Vex points."

"He wouldn't shoot you."

"Bet your ass he would. Getting shot or dead is not what worries me."

"What worries you? Having to fight that many guys? I wouldn't—"

"You starring in Silvio's next movie." Gravity thickened the air. "Carlyle was ground zero and we fucked that operation last night. You think Silvio just let the girls ride off into the sunset? No, they're working. Probably harder now there's a hotel to rebuild."

"Only now we don't know where," she murmured. "Would Vex have—"

"Vex has his own problems. Silvio wouldn't think anything of taking from his boy. He owns it all, no matter what it says on the deed. Fuck knows where the operation moved to or if your women are with the regular girls. But if Silvio's stomping over Vex's shit, guaranteed that boy's about ready to explode. Someone will take heat, the full force of it, and it won't be us. We're staying out of the firing line. Vex is unhinged, reason does nothing. If he wants you dead, you're dead. With him, it's the flip of a coin. No one knows who they're going to get. Sometimes he's playful, sometimes he's psycho. He's lived his whole life satisfying his whims and has no reason to help us out. Even to tolerate anyone asking questions."

One person would be able to extract information from Vex, potentially, without getting dead. Her eyes closed. Shit. She couldn't ask more of Sersha. The danger. The risk. It was too much. How bad did she need to know? The only way to save Yvonne, and the other women held against their will, was to first know their location.

"Do you think there's a chance, any chance, Yvonne Ingham is still alive?"

His lips thinned before he moistened them. "A slim one. Very slim. A wafer-thin chance."

"Will Silvio let her go? Her and the other women he's abducted, will he let them go if we agree to his deal?"

"To write the story his way? To point the finger at his fall guy?"

"Which has to be Bryan, right? That's why he was the only one on the tape. They want to frame him for this."

"Could be his deal."

"Would anyone agree to being set up for something like this? Sex crimes? Snuff movies? In prison, sexual predators—"

"For the Manzanis? The guy doesn't have to be willing. Silvio says it's true then it's true. You do what you're told or they replace you. Permanently."

Was that supposed to justify Bryan's actions? Any of the men's actions?

"Don't," she said, shaking her head, sinking against the seat. "I will not feel sorry for him."

"No one asked you to feel sorry for him. Silvio doesn't answer to anyone. His strategy is his own."

"So maybe Bryan wasn't smart enough to read the writing on the wall?"

"Maybe."

"He must've known something was up. Being asked to seduce those women, to lure them to wherever he wanted them to be… He got them to trust him. Was seen in public with them." Maybe. "How could he miss what that would mean evidentially if they got caught? Isn't it obvious?"

"For you, maybe. For me. A lot of these guys don't think about what comes next. Silvio Manzani, the don himself, The Director, has a job for you. Chances are the guy thought he was in the Major League. Impressing the boss. Headed for bigger things."

Could anyone be that naïve? Though intellect wasn't a mandatory quality for pawns or goons.

"What does that mean for now?" she asked. "Does Bryan know the cops are looking for him? We don't even know if that's his real name. Lachlan didn't know where to find him. Is Silvio hiding him?"

"Or he's cut him loose. Your patsy could be on the run."

"If Lachlan finds him first, Silvio's deal goes away. Bryan will tell the truth and—"

"Tell the truth?" At least he was kind enough not to laugh at her, but that tone was more than incredulous. "Your Bryan will take life in prison over shitting on the Manzanis. Promise you that."

Just what Sersha said about Marseille's choice over telling the truth.

"How will he know what to say?" she asked.

"He won't say anything. Doesn't have to say anything. Then the cops show him the evidence—"

"Him on the tape."

"And he'll know the script. Either Silvio gets him a lawyer who directs the show, or he's stuck with a public defender. That'll be the signal of how much support he's got from the family."

Support? Could it be called that in any universe? Setting him up in advance and protecting themselves over everything else didn't scream care to her.

"I don't get it."

"It's not your world, Genny."

They parked around back to walk in through the workshop. Guys went about different tasks on cars elevated on ramps, while others did things at side areas. Someone else occupied Jagg's paint room. Hmm, how would he feel about that?

Ford came to them, wiping something black from his hands.

"How'd it go with Daisy?" Jagg asked, flopping an arm across her shoulders.

Ford tossed his rag aside. "Struck out."

"As always."

"Less competition now," Ford said, smirking at his friend. "My chances are improving."

"Never had the eye for Daisy, my brother. You don't—"

When he stopped suddenly, she glanced up at him. Ford focused on something behind them. Jagg's arm dropped as he turned, and then there was a thwack. What the hell was—Jagg stumbled, bowing back, and there was—

"Dad?" she called, but he was already stomping on out.

"I expected a right."

"Yeah, you got off lucky," Ford said, shoving up the chin Jagg cradled. "Guess he likes you."

"Yeah, you think?"

"What the hell was that?" she demanded.

"Wasn't me." Ford shrugged. "Good news travels fast, I guess."

"He can't just—"

She tried to go after him, but Ford caught her arm. "Leave him."

Argh, what was it with the men in her life?

"What the—Dad punched him in the face."

"Yep," Ford said and slapped a hand on Jagg's back. "He deserved it."

Her guy cracked his jaw. "Yeah, I did."

"Beer?"

They drifted away, Daisy's name back on their breath. Her father was out of line. Not a word and…

Walking the opposite way from the guys, she got outside in time to see Strat drive out of the lot.

This was a… Nothing was going right. Lives were being lost and violence was never the answer.

It was time to negotiate.

FORTY

WHIZZING PAST LUCY at The Chronicler reception desk, questions piled up. Sersha. She needed to see Sersha and—through the glass wall panels, she spotted her target in Steeple's office.

Without knocking, she hurried inside. "What is going on?"

"Sersh says it's a distraction," Steeple said, swiveling his seat in a narrow arc back and forth.

"The riot?"

"If the only guy the cops have on tape is this Bryan, the Manzanis obviously had a clear plan in place for evacuation. They took what they needed to take and destroyed everything else… or that was the idea."

"While the building was burning around them?"

Most people might think about running for their lives, but not Manzani soldiers. Maybe that was because if they left without doing their part, they'd be tossed back into the flames and told to get it right.

"Something must've been missed," Sersha said. "Someone needed to get back inside. The fight with the cops, the scale of it, being that heavy-handed hid something else. It was misdirection."

Something they had experience of, like last night.

"So what was it? What did they miss?"

"I don't know," Sersha said.

"Is it important?"

"To someone."

"How do we find out?" she asked.

With an exhaled laugh, Sersha landed her smile on Steeple. "Is she for real?"

"Ask your brother."

"Yeah," Sersha said. "Now I know that idealism rubs off, I won't get too close to either of them."

Funny joke, she didn't appreciate being the punchline. "There must be someone we can ask."

"Yeah, there is," Sersha said, bobbing her head in a shallow nod. "You can ask around. Won't get you far but—"

"You know the world. You know people in it. Someone could tell you the truth. You can, right? You can ask?"

"I could." Another moment of eye contact with Steeple betrayed something more somber. "But why would I?"

She faltered. "Why would—"

"Asking questions uses up scarce goodwill capital. Anyone who talks is taking their lives in their hands. You don't want any piece of that, do you? Do you want people to die for this story? Do you think Marseille wants that?"

"She's gone."

Sersha didn't blink. "I know."

Huh, curious, that strong façade gave nothing away. Maybe Sersha was surprised and hid it well… or the woman could know more than she was letting on about Marseille's whereabouts.

"You don't know the distraction today had anything to do with the missing women." Murdered women. "They could be covering for something else," Steeple said. The Manzanis fingers were in plenty of pies. "Asking around could open another can of worms. Both of you have drawn enough attention to yourselves already. I don't want more bodies dropping. Enough people have died in the last twenty-four hours."

"Twenty-four hours?" she asked. "Who died—"

"You didn't hear?"

Obviously not. "No."

"They pulled two bodies out of the Carlyle."

"Two?" she asked. Sorrow welled up inside her. "Two people were killed in the fire?"

Though appealing to both of them, no one answered. And there was Sersha's mask again, tough, unyielding, impenetrable.

"Cause of death is still to be determined," Steeple said and stood up. "Put your heads together and get something on paper. We're operating behind the lines right now, and you know how I feel about that."

Sersha raised two straight fingers in a quick salute. "Under the cover of darkness, boss, you got it."

He got it? What was…? Sersha came and landed a hand on her shoulder, guiding her out of the office.

"What is 'under cover of darkness,' I don't—"

"Steeple trusts us to do our job," Sersha said, coming around to take both of her shoulders, arms straight. "And he doesn't have to know the details. No one has to know the details."

That threat was barely veiled.

"You killed two people last night," she whispered.

"Says who?" Sincerity crept in. "Beyond the fact I don't want people to know about our involvement in what happened last night, you have to watch your ass. Forget my exposure and worry about yours."

"What does that mean?"

"It means…" Sersha bit the inside corner of her bottom lip. "Look, it means that if you have an attack of conscience and you want to tell the world what happened, you won't only be landing me in hot water."

"Lachlan?"

"Yeah, and Jagg, your brother, yourself. Everyone involved last night."

"Are you threatening me?"

"Actually, no. I'm trying to protect you. Because if I'm off the street, out of contact with you and… others, I can't protect you."

She didn't get it. "Protect me from what?"

"From people who might get angry… From people who won't wait for my say-so to seek payback." Vex. Sersha's not-so-secret admirer. The man obsessed with her might take exception to the object of his affection being jailed. "And I have an alibi for last night. Do you?"

An alibi? She hadn't even considered… "You have someone who'll lie for you?"

Sersha smiled. "A couple of someones actually. Get your story straight with yours."

"But we were at the hospital—"

"Yeah, we met there. You weren't with me when I found Marseille."

"I wasn't?"

"No," Sersha said with a shake of her head. "Protection, remember? You had nothing to do with it. I found her and took her to the hospital all by myself. And if there's any doubt about that, I have insurance."

"Insurance?"

"Against any witnesses who might try to say otherwise. Insurance that guarantees certain key players will protect my ass. A hierarchy of protection, you might say."

"What insurance?"

"You wanted to know why I hit record?" Sersha asked. "You wouldn't believe the faces we have on camera running from that building in all kindsa undress and trussed up in freaky shit. I picked up my phone last night after the hospital." Unlocking her elbows, she leaned closer. "Insurance."

"How do you know all this? How do you know how to do this?"

Because she couldn't imagine Lachlan thinking the same way.

"I learned from the best."

"Lachlan isn't—"

"No, he isn't. This protects him too. It protects all of us. Ford, Strat… Jagg."

Understanding crept over her. "You talked to Lachlan today."

"Sure did."

She inhaled. "You told my dad about—"

"Yeah, and you're welcome."

"Why would you—"

"Trust me, it's better that it came from me than you had to face that conversation. He does not like to be blindsided."

"He punched Jagg in the face!"

"And you don't think that could've gone worse if he didn't have the time to process in the drive over there? I'm sorry if it was supposed to be a forever secret, but telling Lachlan suggested you wanted it out there."

Her father's reaction was his own, whether she agreed with it or not. Standing in front of him, saying the words. Yeah, that was an experience she was glad to miss. Sersha could've asked first, though the woman was closer to Strat than she could claim to be.

"You know my dad well."

"He's not a tough guy to get to know," Sersha said, smiling. "You should try it sometime."

Sersha's arms dropped like she intended to go.

"Wait," she said. "I… I need to find Bryan."

"No, you don't." With an almost eye roll, Sersha turned all the way back. "You find Bryan, what will happen? He'll be stressed, freaking out, tweaking, and here's his story: there was a woman, guys, pressure, everyone was doing it, and he fucked her. He didn't know they were going to kill her. That she was going to die, blah, blah, blah."

"He can tell us where the women are. If they're still alive."

"If. Big if. Bryan isn't the key to that. You think the Manzanis clued him in on their fallback plan? Not a chance. You want to be a white knight? Forget Bryan. Sweeten the pot for Silvio."

"What?"

"The only way you get those women back is to swear you'll never point a finger at him. Sell the Manzani version. Bryan went rogue. He's the sole murderer. No matter what you print, he'll go down for this. That's a foregone conclusion. The cops just need to find him. Think strategically, you want the Manzanis to owe you."

"Do you believe that? That Bryan did it alone?"

"No. Though I'll bet he's no saint," Sersha said with matching expression. "But if anyone asks me, I know nothing."

Infuriated, she couldn't be as blasé. "You wrote about this family. You spent time investigating—"

"The past," she said. "I never shook my rattle at the cops. Never revealed a source. And always, always, wrote in hypotheticals. There's drama and intrigue enough around these families. People read the name 'Manzani' or 'McDade' or 'Gambatto' and they're doing all the work themselves to make it salacious. Imagination is our best friend. A current investigation, one looking into present and specific wrongs, shit, Imogen, I'm sorry, but I'm surprised you're still alive. You're on Silvio's radar and you don't ever want to be there."

"You're on it."

"No, I sort of skirt and skip round the edges, just an inch out of range."

"You think he'll kill me?"

"Killing you draws attention to you. Puts your dad on the warpath, your brother, your boyfriend. That's my guess why you're still alive."

"So I'm safe?"

"Wouldn't go that far. There is a limit to their patience. Sometimes these guys just snap. Besides, there's a whole lot that can come before death. Believe me, you don't want any part of that."

Torture, like the victims had endured. A star in the movie. Jagg was right, the next one could be her, if she wasn't careful. Keeping her alive would give Silvio a way to manipulate her family.

"What about Vex?"

"Nooo…" Sersha said, drawing out the sound. "Forget you know his name."

"But Stephanie was there, at his club."

"Where?"

"Where? Hustle."

"Where in Hustle?"

"I don't know, Vex's room, the separate part of the—"

"The people who get in there are Evander's people, Vex's people. Sometimes those people bring other people. If one of his guy's brought a woman, maybe a woman he wanted to control by showing her what she could've won, Vex wouldn't bat an eye. Women, even almost naked women, they sort of don't register to a guy like him. One who has whatever he wants, whenever he wants. Why do you think he has to go to an extreme like Hustle?"

This was an unwinnable battle. Silvio in prison? What good would that do? Okay, so it would do a lot of good, but would come at a hefty price. And who would take over? Vex? The city would be no safer.

"I only want them to be safe."

"You want an opinion from the inside? A chance of keeping other women safe?"

Was that hope? She almost didn't want to embrace the morsel. "Yes. How do we do that?"

"You have one untapped source. Someone you haven't talked to or investigated."

"Who?"

"Ludlow."

Plain as day. Damnit.

"Do you know him?" she asked.

"Personally? No."

"But you could get to him? Find out where he is?"

"I'm guessing he's lying low right now, hiding somewhere the Manzanis put him. Silvio knows how to play it cool."

"That means he's in one place. Can you find out where?"

Sersha shook her head slow. "Not a chance I'm calling Evander for something like that. No way it would be worth what he'll make me pay for it."

"Is it true he's obsessed with you? How obsessed?"

Sersha took her shoulders again. "Focus. Ludlow. You need to know what he knows. It might be the only way to stop it."

Justice was dwindling in the rearview. Maybe hope was saving future women from the fate of those lost in the past.

"I don't know how to find him."

"Yes, you do."

"But I—"

"You know how to find him," she said and smiled. "Time to call Daddy."

FORTY-ONE

RIGHT THEN, the last thing she wanted to do was talk to her dad. Choice was taken away when Sersha sent a text then bundled them into a cab. The first time she'd been in a cab since finding out about the method of abduction.

"Do you want a drink?" Sersha asked when they entered her apartment.

"No, thanks."

"Strat was already in the car, he won't be long."

"He's not going to help me."

"He wants to help; he just wants you alive more. Be grateful for that."

"I can't believe that he—"

"This is not about your personal relationship." Sersha went about putting coffee on. "Forget Jagg and your family shit. This is professional."

"He's my dad."

"He's the only connection we have to Ludlow. The only chance you have for leverage."

"Leverage?"

Against Silvio?

"It's how the world works. Everything is barter. Find something, anything, that you can hold over Silvio. He will do what benefits number one. Make sure whatever you suggest is in his best interest."

If someone expected her to threaten the don… Yeah, she wasn't the best, or most intimidating, candidate to stand up to him, to anyone.

"What about the other families?"

"What about them?" Sersha asked, flicking on the coffee machine.

"Maybe one of them could help us. They must want the Manzanis in trouble, right? That serves their interest. Do you have connections in the other fami—"

Someone knocked on the door. Sersha sidestepped to open it and let it swing wide while she went back into the kitchen.

"Scamp, I—" Strat stopped talking when he saw her. "This an ambush?"

"Just us," Sersha said. "This is professional, not personal."

"You hit him!" She couldn't contain her anger. "I don't know why you—"

"What did you expect me to do, huh?" Her dad threw the door back into its frame. "Your brother know about this?"

"Yes," she said.

"What did he say about it? Bet he swung for Jagg himself."

"He's still… processing."

"Yeah, aren't we all," Strat said, folding his arms, widening his stance. "Jagger Dunn is not the type of man you want to be with."

"You love Jagg!"

"Yes, but not for you."

"What did he do wrong? What excuse do you have for violence? There's no excuse!"

"It's a language guys like us understand. He fucked our family."

"No, he fucked me—"

"Okay," Sersha said, sliding in front of Strat. "We're not going to get bogged down in this. The family stuff can happen later. Everyone, professional, not personal."

"What do you need, Scamp?" he grumbled, still frowning.

"Ludlow," Sersha said.

On a blink of surprise, Strat's attention fell to his friend. "Ludlow? Are you fucking kidding me?"

"No. I need to know where Ludlow is."

"What she means is, I need to know where Ludlow is."

"Didn't we have this conversation? No. He's dangerous."

"Less dangerous than the other options," Sersha said. "You don't want Imogen near him? I'll do the talking."

"This is my story."

Sersha raised her hands. "And my paws are off, but if it's the only way your dad—"

"Why would you do it for Sersha and not for me?"

"He wants to protect you."

"And he doesn't want to protect you? Doesn't that piss you off?"

"Sersha has protections in place," her father said.

"And I don't? What are you? Ford? Jagg?"

"Prevention is better than cure."

"What is the problem?" Sersha went to the coffee. "Ludlow doesn't breathe fire."

"No, he just makes violent porn. Why wouldn't I introduce him to my daughter?"

"If you don't get involved and help, the options get riskier the deeper we go."

"Scamp—"

Another knock on the door. Who would that be? Lachlan wouldn't knock. Her dad leaned back to open the door and her brother came inside.

"Ford?"

"How the fuck did you let this happen?" her dad asked, pushing his son. "You let your little sister—"

"I didn't let anything."

"Dad, did you really call Ford to back you up on this?" Pathetic and galling. "What do you think I'll do? Agree to break up with Jagg because you two say so? Forget it."

"Okay, we're not focused," Sersha said. "Ludlow. And he didn't call your brother, I did." What? "I texted him actually."

"Why?"

"Because you two need a mediator and he knows you better than I do."

"Ludlow?" Ford asked. "You still on this?"

"We need evidence this goes beyond Bryan."

"The cops will pick him up eventually," Sersha said.

"Yes," she said, "and Bryan could flip. He could testify to—"

"Is he made?"

"Not a fuck like him," Strat said. "Ludlow's not made either."

"He's not Italian."

"Yeah, that's the reason. And 'Bryan' is a real authentic name."

"They picked Bryan precisely because he knew nothing," Sersha said. "He might name names or tell tales, but where's the proof?"

"Went up in flames."

"Or underground," Ford said. "Silvio Manzani knows how to cover his ass."

"So what good does it do to speak to Ludlow?"

"What have we got to lose?" she asked. "According to everyone, I'm already on the Manzanis radar for poking around."

"Least if she talks to Ludlow, Manzani will be worried about what his guy might've said to a reporter," her brother said. "Splits his focus."

"You're into this? You think your sister should—"

"I think my sister should take up knitting," Ford said. "But that's as likely as you and me joining the church. I want to protect her. But I don't want to push her away either. She's supported us. All the crap we've done and she's never judged us or turned her back on us."

As Sersha smiled, a warmth spread behind her eyes. Her brother had never articulated their relationships like that before.

A phone rang. Sersha grabbed for her purse to pull it out and answered. "Yeah. Hi… Okay… Wow, uh… Are you sure… Is there—"

Strat got closer. Maybe her father read something in Sersha's countenance, but he closed in on his friend. "Scamp?"

Sersha raised a finger and… "Thanks. Honestly. I owe you."

"What is it?" her dad asked as Sersha put the phone in her purse again.

"I'll tell you later." Sersha forced on a smile that was clearly not genuine. "Are you going to help us with Ludlow or are we on our own?"

Her father sighed. "I'll make some calls." His eyes cut to her. "But I'm going with you. Me and your brother."

Which was a better option than her dad excluding her. "Okay. Thank you."

"Want me there?" Sersha asked.

"No," her dad said. "We'll go in and if you don't hear from us, activate the clover plan."

Sersha's next smile was a little more honest. "Oh, yeah, I'll do that, old man."

"All the shit I've done for you...?"

"Duck and cover?" Sersha asked.

"Duck and cover," Strat agreed and dragged in a breath. "Okay, Ludlow, this will be fun."

Sarcasm from her deadpan father was better than fists flying. Heading into a meeting with a thug while their family ties were strained may not be smart. But she had to find out, had to know if the women were still alive. In all of this, she had to save someone. A single life would be better than none.

Had everything, her endeavors to be good and righteous, been for naught?

FORTY-TWO

AFTER SOME PACING and hand wringing, Ford gave her a ride back to Jagg's. Her agitation was agitating everyone else. Anxiety and adrenaline flooded through her. She just couldn't relax. Something felt off. Wrong. Dangerous.

Before Ford had turned off the engine, she jumped out of the car to rush inside.

Jagg was in the spray booth, talking to someone else about the vehicle there. With no paint or safety equipment in sight, she went right in to link their fingers, interrupting him.

"You got a minute?"

After a nod at the other guy, he led her through the breakroom into his bedroom, enclosing them in privacy.

"You okay?"

"Dad's reaching out to… whoever. He's going to get me a meet with Ludlow."

"But he'll be there? I won't let you go alone to—"

"He'll be there. Ford too."

"Then we know you'll be safe." Scooping her closer, he pressed his lips to her hair. "I'm meeting Silvio later."

"What?" Pulling away, she frowned up at him. "Why? No. I don't trust him. It's not safe."

"We thought the Carlyle was safe and it went up in smoke. Silvio could have me wiped off the board any time. Arranging a meet doesn't change that."

"You have to take Ford."

He didn't fight. "Okay. Busy day for him."

"Is it bad that I'm dragging him into this? I dragged all of you into it. I'm sorry."

"We came willingly." He ran his fingers through her hair. "This was my choice."

Not her father's choice and he was in it too. "If Ford got hurt, if you or my dad—"

"No one is going to get hurt."

"Something's wrong. Something's… off. I don't know. I just have a really bad feeling."

"Good. Don't take any risks. Trust your gut."

"How can it be good that my gut tells me something bad is going to happen?"

"Fight or flight," he said. "Your body's preparing you to face something heavy."

"Not me. I'm not worried about me. I'm worried about all of you."

"What do you want to hear from Ludlow?" he asked.

"What really happened. Someone has to know how those women… He has to have answers."

"Answers you'll print? Silvio will kill both of you if those accusations end up in your paper."

"Sersha warned me about that. She writes in hypotheticals."

"Hypotheticals are good. They don't bring the cops to anyone's door. Is that what you want? Just to put the maybes out there."

No, that wasn't what she wanted. "This has changed, it's become… bigger. When I started investigating, I thought we had one psychopath targeting these women. But it's not a crazy serial killer…"

"It's a planned and executed strategy." Involving organized crime. "You could call the feds but…"

"That just puts us all in danger. We have no concrete evidence of anything."

"The cops might've got it from the Carlyle."

"The cops found what Silvio wanted them to find."

Gathering her into his arms, he held her against him. "Protecting the people you care about isn't a failure. Justice doesn't have to be cops and jail terms. Stopping the operation is a win."

"Has it stopped?"

"I'll ask Silvio. Make a deal. You write your story without the Manzani name showing up and he quits kidnapping women for his videos."

"And releases whoever he has now. If Yvonne is out there—"

"You don't know this woman," he said, easing her back to meet her eye. "Why does she mean so much to you?"

"Because if she's dead, it's because I caused trouble."

"They'd have killed her anyway, Genny." He stroked her cheek. "The moment they took her, she was dead."

"Doesn't feel that way." Tears blurred her eyes. "It feels like I caused this mess."

"You didn't." He bowed to kiss her. "You've saved so many women. Silvio would've just kept on going. Think about the future women, not the past."

"That's all I can think about."

A tear fell and he caught it on a kiss.

"You are good, Imogen Stratford. The best of people. One of the things I love about you."

She blinked, clearing her vision. "You love about me?"

He kissed her again. "I love about you."

Guiding their mouths together again, he took his time about tasting her, touching her tongue with his, teasing her.

"Jagg," she whispered, eyes closed as he picked her up to lay her in his bed.

All the things she needed, wanted, everything that could go wrong or be right, only one thing could soothe her.

Every part of her he uncovered, he kissed. Her shoulders, arms, her neck, her breasts, no inch was neglected. Though her hands roamed, he wouldn't let her move, and kept her on her back as he kissed lower. Her belly, her hips… her shoes were gone, her pants out of the way and as he lay back down on her, shedding his own clothes, the connection of their skin consumed her in a reassuring blanket.

The threat, the peril, it was real, for her and the women still in Manzani clutches. But this experience, if it wasn't meant to end in complete vindication, at least it taught her something else. Something Marseille hopefully learned too. Life could turn on a dime. From happiness and freedom to torture and imprisonment, they were all just a breath away. Chaos knew no boundaries. Someone, somewhere, would be willing to hurt others for nothing more than a quick buzz. The worst kind of drug. Murder for pleasure.

"Jagg," she said again, undulating against the pressure of his lips on her clit.

Her man seemed in her head. Every thought, every negative anything, disappeared when his tongue pushed into her, appreciating their seclusion while they had it.

But she didn't want to be worshipped. That wasn't the basis for them. Digging her heels into the bed, she pushed away from his gifted tongue.

"Genny?"

"Kiss me," she said, crunching up to cup his head, bringing their lips together again. "As long as I have you, everything will work out."

"Nothing could take me from you, baby."

Her heart swelled and her legs rose, coiling them around him as he pushed into her, completing her need with the pleasure of his.

Forcing her head back, her body bowed. "I want to move in," she breathed.

"Move in." Pulling back and advancing hard, his pace slowed and sped as she writhed beneath him. "No more hiding."

"No."

"You're mine."

"Yes."

"We're together."

"Yes." Heat and pulsing pressure spasmed within her. "Yes, Jagg!"

"You tell me everything."

Her eyes closed and her lips curled. "Everything. Everything for… Ah…" Her words disappeared in the pant of desire. "Yes. Yes… Oh, yes…"

Angling her hips, she rose as the breath disappeared to the clench of orgasm.

In the middle of the day, with Jagg's guys around, her brother around, she should be quieter. It wasn't her fault he—

Friction burned, thrusting her into another climax as his dragged him under with her.

Warm, loose, in bliss, she basked in the tingle of her skin and the zips of desire still quaking between her thighs.

"Thank you," she said.

He paused in scooting her over the bed. "Uh, you're welcome," he said, maybe with a glimmer of a snicker.

Bouncing up, she landed her fist on the center of his chest, resting her head on his shoulder.

"Why does everything feel better now?" she asked, exhaling her contentment. "I couldn't dial it back and—"

"You've been under a lot of pressure. Going from one crisis to the next."

For a while, they just lay there. Though sleep threatened, her thinking evened out.

"Would Ford be mad if I moved in?" Could be that was just an in the midst of sex thing they'd said without meaning it. Did she want to move in? "Is it too soon?"

"No, and all we can do is ask him."

"What's your opinion?"

"That you should live here."

"Of his opinion?"

"My opinion of his opinion?"

"Stop," she said with a whisper of a laugh. "Is it too much to ask? With everything else that's going on. We shouldn't talk about it until after this is all done and…" Would that ever happen? "Will I be looking over my shoulder for the rest of my life?"

Kissing her head, his fingers intertwined in her locks. "No."

"How can you be so sure?"

"Because I'll protect you."

"How can you do that? You'll be at risk too. If you stay with me—"

"I will stay with you and promise you'll be safe. I'll take the heat myself before I'll let you—"

"This is not you. I did this."

"You haven't done anything. Yet."

No. The words weren't on paper. Weren't on any screen. They were in her head and she had a choice to make. Ludlow might tell them the whole complete truth. Did that mean she could write it?

A tap on the door came just seconds before it opened a few inches.

Ford's disembodied voice joined them. "Got a visitor."

"A visitor?" Her brother retreated without entering. Thank God, given they hadn't worried about covering up. "Who?" Both of them jumped up to dress. "Who would be—"

"We're not waiting out here all day!"

Strat. Shit. Her father. Great. Just what she needed.

FORTY-THREE

IN THE BEDROOM DOORWAY, her apology died on her lips. Ford, her father… and some other guy.

"Ludlow," Jagg said from behind her, laying a hand on her shoulder. "You work fast, Strat, man."

"Could say the same to you." The disapproval in that frown was unmistakable. "This your priority?" Ludlow turned like he was ready to rush right back out. Her dad got in his way with one slick move and grabbed the guy's jacket. "My little girl isn't done with you yet."

Ludlow looked left, right… Not a lot of options for the guy. Twitchy, nervous, tense, yeah, she could relate.

"No one will hurt you," she said to his back. When she stepped forward, Jagg came with her, his hand staying in place. "We just have some questions."

Or she had some questions.

"I can't—Strat, man, I—"

"You do what you're fucking told," her dad said, yanking the guy hard, dragging him across to the armchair under the TV and thrusting him down.

"Answer the fucking questions." Wow, she'd never seen her dad be so… hard. "Immie."

He backed off and Jagg's hand dropped. The men were near, but not interfering. The three of them gave her space, or maybe it was Ludlow they wanted to put at ease.

"Heather Lantry." One step. "Michelle Cadlow." Another step. "Stephanie Weet." She stopped by the couch. "Anna Emin." The guy wouldn't even meet her eye. "Yvonne Ingham."

"I don't know nothing," he said and tried to stand up.

That was her father's queue to barge over and shove him down again. "You want me to let my boys at you?" he growled. "I got no problem with a little mess."

His boys. Her brother's glare was dark, precise, tough enough that even she questioned her safety.

And Jagg… glancing back at him didn't take his focus from the man under his scrutiny. The bad boy mothers warned their daughters about. Wow. That edge. The sharp shadow across his soul stretched out to shield her.

Keeping a smile from her lips was difficult. Ludlow didn't need to see that. What he needed to see was a sure woman, one completely safe and protected with her trio of soldiers.

"How many were there?" she asked, keeping her voice cool and level. "How long has it been going on?"

"Miss, I am… I know nothing, you know? The Director will kill me. Whatever I say, I'm fucked—"

"So what harm is there talking to us?" she asked. "I want to know—"

"All I did was drive," he said, smacking the arms of the chair. "I was a fucking driver. They told me where to go, who to pick up—"

"And you never thought to question why you were picking them up?"

"He knew," her father said.

"Yeah, I think he did. Because those women started showing up. Those same women you picked up, they ended up dead wearing the Manzani mark."

"They mark every woman who earns for them."

"Willing or not," her father muttered.

"They were drugged. They got in the car, doors locked, they couldn't get out, even if they wanted to." Was that a point of pride or regret? "Once you're in it, you're in. Nothing any of us can do 'cept what we're told."

"Where did you take them?"

"The hotel, you know, the Carlyle. That's where it all happened."

Words were so easy to say, but the terror those women must've endured. "Did they fight? Scream? Beg for freedom?"

"No, no way, they… I got this mask I put on, had it round my neck, you know, where they couldn't see."

"A mask?"

"I flipped a switch, I don't know what gas it was, but those—they… they were out, you know?"

Drugged. Driven to the Carlyle where they'd wake up and…

"God, they must've been terrified."

A loud buzz droned.

"What is that?" Ludlow asked, bouncing to the edge of the seat.

"We're not alone," Jagg muttered around the same time Sutherland came running in. "Swerve's outside with at least a dozen guys."

"Fuck," Ford said.

The door opened again.

Swerve.

From nowhere, Jagg wasted no time getting to her, putting her at his back, blocking Swerve's line of sight… or maybe his angle of attack.

"What do you want? You bring a fucking army?"

"Nothing to worry about, Dunn. We'll be on our way soon as we get what we came for."

Ludlow sprang to his feet. "I didn't say nothing."

"No one gives a fuck about you," Swerve said, an irritation in his voice. "Who the fuck are you anyway?"

Below Swerve's paygrade, or he was good at making a point.

"What do you want?" Jagg asked.

"Your girl there."

"Not a chance."

"I'm the messenger, buddy. If the job was killing her, you'd all be dead. She's gonna come on a little ride with me."

"I said no," Jagg growled.

"Shame. Her friend Mila will be disappointed."

"My guys at the—"

"Yeah, you have guys at the hospital. You got guys to lose? 'Cause Silvio doesn't mind a couple of his going to prison for murdering a couple of yours. How are your numbers for a game of tit for tat?" A moment passed. "Don't want to knock your confidence, but ours is bigger than yours. Way bigger."

Her brother moved a few feet closer to Swerve. Shit. No, people were in danger. It had never been so real. Swerve. An army outside. And them… Her family. The people she loved in jeopardy because she couldn't stop asking questions.

"Threatening us isn't the way to get what you want," her brother said.

Peeking around Jagg, she wanted a measure on the invader's mood.

"What is the way?" Swerve asked. "'Cause I also have to say…" Reaching back, he produced a gun from behind him, from his waistband maybe. His elbow bent, arm loose, the barrel pointed toward the ceiling… for now. "My boss's problem goes away if I put bullets in you three."

"Jagg's guys saw you come in," she said. "They'd tell cops—"

"Good luck finding me, Funny. You heard what I said about our numbers?" Someone would go down for it. Silvio valued his henchman progeny, unlikely Swerve would see any days behind bars. "She's wholesome, Dunn. Not your type."

Did everyone on the planet know about their relationship?

"I don't want anyone to get hurt."

"Then your boy there calls his boys off at the hospital and you take a trip with me."

"Why the hospital? Why would you—"

"You forget what I said? The women still here will pay for every step you take down this path. Your Mila is first on that list."

"You already tried killing her once and failed."

"If they meant to kill her, she'd be dead."

If they meant to… "It was a warning," she whispered. "Mila was a warning."

"A glimpse into your future maybe. Though…" He sighed like it was no big deal. "If you don't give a shit about her, we don't either. She's easy to erase. No one would notice if she disappeared."

She gave a shit. Silvio's people could kill or incapacitate Jagg's guys to get into Mila's room. Even if staff called the cops, they'd never make it in time to save the woman.

"I'll go."

"Not a fucking chance," her dad asserted.

"I'll be okay. He can't hurt me. Too many people know about my investigation. If I disappear, my cause becomes their ruin." The only one who could write the story, her safety was the only way to end this without further destruction. "I'll go with him."

And he'd said the hospital. Public space. Not some dark, dusky basement of a prison cell.

Except when she tried to move, Jagg blocked her like he had eyes on the back of his head.

"Give me reason to hurt you, man," Swerve drawled. "Please."

"I'm coming with her."

"Not invited."

"You walk out that door with me or my corpse. There's not a damn chance you get to take my woman without me right there with her."

"You want a fucking bullet in your brain?"

"Right between the eyes," Jagg said. "It's the only way she walks out without me."

The conviction was chilling. Her fingers found his and although his clamped tight around hers, he didn't break his stare.

"Fine, but you call ahead. Get your guys off the patient."

"Why would you want them off?" she asked. "Can't we do it there?"

"My boss doesn't like to wait around."

Silvio, is that who they were going to see?

"I'll do it," Ford said. "I'll call."

"And just to make sure everyone plays nice," Swerve said. "My guys will hang around here for the duration of our meeting."

Play nice. They weren't the ones who started the game of kill-or-be-killed.

Jagg walked in front of her, nudging her behind when she tried to move to his side.

"Sweetheart," Strat said.

The worry shimmered around her father. Helplessness, fear, sorrow.

She smiled. "I'll be okay."

As they entered the service office, Jagg's other guys were being herded down the corridor and into the breakroom. Hostages. All the people they cared about and…

"We're taking my car," Jagg said when Swerve started toward another.

"Fine," Swerve said like it was no big deal. "But she drives."

Why her? Because the men would face off right there inside the vehicle?

She found out why when, after getting in and starting it up, the gun barrel nudged the side of her neck. Swerve was right there behind her, Jagg up front too.

"The hospital?" she asked, checking to be sure.

Swerve seemed reasonable, not nice or friendly, but matter of fact. Though she didn't trust him with their lives, she trusted he'd follow Silvio's instruction.

It wasn't like they had anything in common to talk about and the weather seemed a ridiculous topic. Time passed. Road. Distance. And not a word was spoken.

"You surprise me," Swerve said suddenly.

The echo of his voice startled her. "Surprise?"

"Not you. Dunn. Dunn surprises me." The gun bounced against her neck when they hit a pothole. "You put yourself in the line of fire for her."

"Not something you'd know about," Jagg said. "Valuing another life."

"I barely value mine," Swerve said. "You've got all this time and not a single question?"

"Gave up asking about you long ago," Jagg said. "You bullshit better than the best of them."

"Thanks. I take that as a compliment."

"Talking surprises, you've dealt one of your own," Jagg said. "You'd really go to this trouble, put yourself on the line for a stupid newspaper story? You must owe Silvio big."

"Had nothing better to do this week."

To Swerve, threatening lives and intimidating people were just a way to pass the time, like a regular person might read a book or go for a walk.

"Yeah, but you've gotta worry about your own skin."

"My life—"

"Your skin," Jagg said, his voice deep. "Your kin."

"This where you threaten me?"

"This is where I remind you they you just insulted Ford and threatened his sister." A beat passed. Then another. "Don't guess that's fun. But I wouldn't know, I don't have a sister… You ever been in that boat? Someone ever threatened yours? Guess you don't know if you haven't spoken to her recently. Last I heard, she was giving her daddy the run around. What flunky's on her tail now?"

"Now I see where you get your funny from, Funny." Swerve did not sound amused. "I don't give a fuck about that bitch, and she doesn't give a shit about me. Want to do me a favor, Dunn? Find her and kill her."

"No one is killing anyone else," she said. "There's been too much killing. What is the point of this meeting? What does Silvio want? If you're taking me here to hurt me—"

"Hurting you would be easy, then we risk your paper taking on a mission. This is your last chance to be reasonable. If you don't come to an agreement, bodies will start dropping."

"Why do you still do it?" Jagg asked like he honestly wanted to know. "Run around after the asshole who's given you nothing?"

"That's where you and me are different, Dunn. I don't want anything from anyone."

"No one gave me shit, and I'm not running around after a dictator."

"You're still one of his favorites, he'll be upset to know you talk about him like this."

"You forgetting who I am? We ran together back in the day. I know what you think of that man."

"You don't know dick."

Why was Jagg riling the guy? So far the day had been fraught enough, they didn't need to go inviting trouble.

"Is Silvio alone?" she asked, trying to cut the tension.

"Need to wait and find out, Funny."

Keeping them on the back foot gave the other side the advantage. Jagg. Her own safety came second to his. He'd stood up for her, put himself in front of her.

They'd survive this, both of them, no matter the cost.

FORTY-FOUR

JAGG PUT HIMSELF between them when they got out of the car too. He held her hand tight, keeping her locked to his side.

"Vex was right," Swerve said. "You are possessive with this one." A snicker. "No one gives a damn about her pussy. You're the free toy with the meal today. What a treat for Silv."

Swerve marched on ahead and Jagg held her back.

"Should we keep up?"

"We know where we're going." He kissed the back of her hand as they crossed the hospital threshold. "I don't want you taking any risks up here. Stay behind me."

"I thought you didn't want to make my choices for me."

Swerve held the elevator door open. Despite others obviously waiting, no one passed him to go inside.

"Genny—"

Speeding up cut him off. They were with Swerve and then ascending. No going back.

The door opened to an ominous sight. At regular intervals, lining the walls were guys. Big guys, not guys she'd want anyone to bully. The couple at the end she recognized as Jagg's men.

They approached.

"Ford called," said one of them. "We didn't know what to do. It's Silvio fucking Manzani."

"You're good," Jagg said, nodding him away. "It's all good."

They backed off, leaving her and Jagg alone with Swerve.

"Everything said in this room is off the record. Everyone will deny this little get together ever happened." Swerve paused, Mila's door handle pushed down. "That's far enough, Dunn. You'll stay out here."

"How many guys has he got in there?" Jagg asked. "Are you staying out here? No fucking way. You'll have to shoot me first."

"Fine, but no fucking talking. I want this shit done. I have a date tonight."

She almost couldn't believe it. "You have a date?" What the hell would that romance look like? "You?"

Landing a glare on her that she couldn't decipher, Swerve opened the door and gestured inside. "Ladies first."

Confidence meant everything. Sersha carried herself with confidence, which couldn't be easy when dealing with such intimidating men. In that moment, she learned its necessity. Holding her head high, she strode inside, noting Mila's still form under the crisp sheet. The man at the other side of the room, sitting in front of the window, commanded attention.

Gray-white hair, still thick enough to give a glimmer of youth, there was almost a majesty about his stature. The man may have wrinkles by his eyes and a few elsewhere, but he carried it off. Men like him always did. And had she been thinking confidence? Shit, nothing she could bolster came close to his obvious superiority.

As she assessed him, he did the same, giving nothing of his opinion in his perusal of her figure. It wasn't sexual or particularly predatory. If anything, somehow, the scrutiny minimized her, reduced her to nothing more than a fleck in the atmosphere.

Only a few seconds could've passed, but the sound of the door closing startled her out of a daze.

"Very nice, Jagg," Silvio said.

Easy on the words, bold in expression, a hint of a smile hid behind his expressive lips.

"I don't give a shit what—"

"You're here to be quiet," Swerve said and stepped up beside her. "Miss Stratford, I don't suppose I need to introduce you, but this is Silvio Manzani."

"Charmed," she said like it was a period movie. God, she had to get on her game and fast. "Why do we have to do this here? Mila needs her rest."

Her friend's presence lowered her volume. Waking up to a room full of crooks would do nothing to aid Mila's recovery. And as long as they were in proximity to her, she was in danger.

"Don't worry about your friend."

Except that's all she could do as Swerve got nearer the head of the bed.

"She doesn't deserve this."

"None of us deserves this."

That was a laugh. "What exactly have you endured?" Jagg squeezed her shoulder. "No, he's saying—wait—" Swerve drove a needle into Mila's IV. "What are you doing? Stop! What is that?"

He pushed in the plunger, and then the needle was out. Medical staff, doctors, nurses, she hadn't seen any on the floor. Goons and green would scare off even the most dedicated employee.

"Something to help her sleep."

"Hasn't she been through enough?"

Swerve was bold enough to put the needle in the sharps box on the wall. "You wanted her to sleep," he said. "Now she will."

"Will she wake up again?"

Swerve's attention went to Silvio. "That, Miss Stratford, is up to you."

"You want me to lie. Everyone in this room knows what you did—what you do. Killing innocent women—"

"Dramatics don't impress me," Silvio said like they had all the time in the world. "People do what they're told or they're punished. It's as simple as that. Beg, scream, cry, I don't care. Here's what is going to happen, you're going to write a piece for your newspaper on the disappearances."

"Murders."

"Words are your choice. You'll implicate Rodney Bryant and stress that law enforcement is looking for him. Armed and dangerous, don't approach, call authorities. Usual drill."

"And everything else? The videos? The torture?"

"Law enforcement has everything they need to prosecute." He'd made sure of that. "Anything that happened to those women was perpetrated by Bryant." So Bryan wasn't his real name, but it was close. "He's a sick individual who acted alone."

"Why would I do that? Look at this woman…" She opened a hand at Mila. "This happened—"

"Bryant was at the wheel."

Even Mila said that. "On your order. Women died. Innocent women. How many are you holding now? Did Yvonne make it out of that fire? Or will her body show up somewhere else in the next few days?"

"Don't say I'm not a reasonable man," Silvio said, signaling his thug with a nod.

Swerve raised the remote control to turn on the TV. "…anonymous tip earlier today."

Cops and a crowd gathered around a car as a cuffed someone was urged toward the vehicle. To get the arrestee in, they forced him to turn to lower and…

"Langspring," she whispered. "That's Simon Langspring. Yvonne's boss. You set him up to take the fall for—"

"They order them," Swerve said, switching off the TV. "You wanted to know how the women were picked? The client selected them. Pickup was just an additional service."

Oh, God. "Ordered them?"

It was so disgusting, so outrageous and demeaning, yet she absolutely believed it.

"Some of our top clients, loyal customers, some were invited to a platinum level service."

Sickness roiled, flavoring the back of her throat. "The men knew them. It wasn't anonymous or chance, they were specifically targeted. And Simon Langspring ordered Yvonne."

"Due diligence was done. We watched the targets. Measured their suitability. Bryant was sent in to expedite the process."

"To ask questions about their lives," she said. "Find out who would be missed, who these women were close to. Their hopes, their fears, their vulnerabilities."

"We wouldn't want anyone problematic involved."

"Problematic? This is sick! How can you possibly—who thinks something like this is acceptable? It's murder. Kidnapping. Torture. Murder!"

"An indulgence that's not worth the trouble anymore. The risk outweighs the benefit."

"It's a business decision?" Another sickening point. "How do you live with yourself?"

"Very well," Silvio said, his gaze cooling. "This was a side project, a hobby. It is not worth jeopardizing our other operations for."

How much would the men pay for the service? Hundreds? Thousands? Whatever it was would be a drop in the ocean to the Manzani empire.

"Am I supposed to be grateful?"

"You've done enough to make your point," Silvio said. "Spirited women are enjoyable to a point."

"What point is that?" she asked, not sure she appreciated the description.

"To the point at which I break them."

No apology. No shame.

"You haven't broken me."

"We'll see," Silvio said and stood to stroll over. "Write the piece as directed or you and those you care about will suffer for it. You have your perpetrator and Yvonne Ingham is being picked up by ambulance as we speak."

She gasped. "She's alive."

"You don't do what you're told and she won't be for long."

He paused at her side. "Any story other than the approved version will never make it into your newspaper." She looked up. "Steeple is your boss, isn't he? He is a reasonable man. A man who understands how this relationship works."

Silvio carried on and the door opened.

"Genny?" Jagg asked, coming around in front of her. "Babe, are you okay?"

"I… maybe."

"My guys will leave the garage after we're all out safe," Swerve said.

"What about Mila?" Going to the end of the bed, she grabbed the rail. "What did you inject into her—"

"She'll be fine," Swerve said. "Though she is weak, anything could happen any time."

Still staring into her friend, so small and vulnerable, Jagg left with Swerve, but she stayed put.

Write the story or lose her life. If that was the only choice, she might take the risk. Steeple had a wife, a family. Her brother, Jagg, her dad… Was revealing a charge the Manzanis would wriggle out of anyway worth their lives?

FORTY-FIVE

EXHAUSTION SWIRLED on the ride back to Jagg's Autos. None of her choices were appealing and she didn't trust herself to decide.

Jagg killed the engine but didn't get out. "Are you okay?"

"I have to write it, don't I? His way." When nothing followed, she shifted the angle of her head to look at him. "How can I ask for anyone's trust or respect…? How can I ask you to love me knowing I'm a coward and a sellout?"

"Hey," he said, grabbing her hand into both of his, taking it to his lap. "You are neither. You're the hero in this story."

She scoffed. "Good luck convincing anyone of that."

"The only people who know the truth are people who have your back. We are in fucking awe of you and how strong you've been through this."

"None of you would be in it if it wasn't for me."

"That's not true, Genny. Ford and I got mixed up in that world all by ourselves twenty years ago, when we were kids. We've only been useful to you because we did all the fucking up in the past. You've kept us alive."

She shook her head. "You've been the ones running around protecting me."

"Because all we have is muscle, babe. You're the brains in this and could've written your story any time."

"Steeple wouldn't have run it if it put lives at stake."

"You'd have convinced him." Their eyes met. "He publishes Sersha's pieces, doesn't he?"

"I don't know how she does it. How she can peek into that world and still come out whole."

"It exacts a price on everyone." His grip loosened. "Which is why I'd understand if you wanted to get the fuck away from me and this city as fast as possible."

"No." Straightening, she caught his fingers with hers again. "Jagg, you've been my strength in this. My protector. My everything. I don't want to be without you. I want to be with you. To live with you, love you and share our lives and…" But hope quickly faded. "Is it because of Strat? Because of Ford?"

"Is what because of them?"

"You said I was the best of people. If I write this story, I won't be. If you don't want to be with me—"

"I don't want to watch this tear you apart. If you want to write your story, write it, your way."

"They'll kill you."

He smiled. "No, they won't, because we'll toss everything we could need in the back of the truck and get out of here."

"Strat and Ford—"

"Would be right there with us. We want you happy."

"I'm sorry my dad hit you."

Still that played on her mind.

"I'm happy he hit me." His smile returned when her frown appeared. "That's how much he loves you, Genny. The only people I want close to you are people who love you that much. People who love you like I do. And I disrespected him—"

"You did not! I am a grown woman—"

"I should've told him, Im. As soon as I knew I wanted to be with you, I should've told him."

Harsh light flooded them. Headlights swung around in an arc until the car went out onto the road from Jagg's lot. One of his guys, she hoped, heading home.

"We should go inside, make sure everyone is safe."

Swerve had said his guys would go, but they needed to be sure. And who knew what damage could've been done in their absence?

They got out and walked in holding hands, all the way to the breakroom, catching Ford on his way out.

"I'm gonna talk to the guys," Ford said, patting Jagg. "Want to come with and fill us in?"

Jagg looked at her for a nod, then went with his friend, leaving her to go into the breakroom alone. Coffee or wine or—Strat, standing by the TV.

"I thought you'd have gone home."

"I wouldn't do that without seeing you were okay."

She raised her hands a few inches. "I'm okay."

"What happened?"

"What we thought," she said, going to the fridge to find only beer. Ha, well, that would do. "Silvio wants us to pin it on Bryan." She twisted the cap off one beer and froze. "Me. He wants me to pin it on Bryan."

Strat came over and she offered him a beer, which he ignored. "The Manzanis pinned this on Bryan. Whatever you do, none of this is on you, Immie."

"Yeah." She swallowed some beer. "Jagg says the same."

"He's right."

She winced. "I just can't shake the…"

"Ambiguity?" he asked, wearing an almost smile, though it quickly faded. "I never wanted you to know."

"Wanted me to know what?"

"What it was like. Being in between worlds. Wanting the good while the bad is stronger."

And that was it. The Manzanis were stronger. No matter how hard she, or anyone else, fought, they wouldn't win. Hell, the feds and God knows how many cops and prosecutors would love to take the family down. Even with all their resources, they hadn't managed it yet.

"You know, I always envied Ford. For staying with you. I always assumed you sent me with Mom because I was a girl and not quite so fun as my rough and tumble older brother."

"I didn't send you anywhere." His hands rested on the island. "Immie, you're my little girl, I can't help that I want to protect you, that I want you to be safe. I want the same for Ford. I will protect him with everything I have. We've just been in situations where we had to prove that more than you and me."

"You proved it this time. I'm sorry I was difficult about it. You're so strong and Ford's so capable. I see the two of you with Jagg, and you have this like group knowledge, an affinity. Being on the outside was… isolating. It's like they got a part of you that you wouldn't share with me. Then I see the way you are with Sersha…"

"I ruined your life. I fucked it up. I know I did. Since I figured that out, I've been looking for ways to put it right again. Now I'm seeing that it's not possible."

"Ruined my life? How did you ruin my life? By separating from Mom?"

"No! You were better off with her and with her whatever-he-is guy that got you through high school."

"So when—"

"Princeton," he said, providing clarity. "You had the opportunity to make something amazing of yourself and I was such an… asshole." He banged his fist on the counter. "You didn't go 'cause I made you think you couldn't do it. Parents screw their kids up all the time. I thought Ford was my mission and then you turned your back on…"

Putting down the beer, she went to hold his hand. "Princeton wasn't because of you. Well, I suppose maybe it was, in that I… I got the acceptance, everyone was so happy, but I didn't feel it. I didn't feel what everyone else felt. A teacher said to me, life is choices. That's all it is. It doesn't have to be big pictures or forever choices. Decide what's important to you and cling to it with all that you have. I didn't want to be an outsider at some fancy university pretending to be someone I'm not. You, Ford, this damn city, you were what was important to me. Family."

"We would've supported you no matter how far away you were."

Her smile grew. "Funny thing is, I was so scared to tell everyone, Mom, Ted, teachers, everyone, but I knew—I thought… Even if no one else loves me, my dad will."

Grabbing the back of her head, he pulled her close to kiss her forehead. "I do love you, sweetheart. And I don't give a shit about some fancy degree. Your happiness is all that matters. I'm so fucking proud of you every minute."

When she looked up at him, that was the truth of what she saw. Love, pride, and maybe a little relief too.

This was another of those moments. A choice had to be made. Not big picture or forever. She couldn't see it as letting people down, she had to see it as keeping people safe. She chose family once. Nothing would stop her doing it again. The men in her life could protect her with fists. Her only weapon was a pen.

"I got an A in French," she said, her lips curling.

"In what?"

"High school. You said Ted got me through high school, but he wasn't the one to get me an A in French. I never thanked you for that."

Her dad's confusion brought a laugh to her lips.

Ford came in with Jagg just behind.

"Guys are gone and we've locked up," Ford said, narrowing his eyes on them as they separated. "What are you two doing?"

"I'll write Manzani's story," she said, drinking some more beer before handing the bottle to Jagg, who came to put an arm around her.

"Are you sure? I told you—"

"I know you support me, but this is going to keep all of us safe. Us, Sersha, Marseille, Yvonne. Maybe one day there will be a battle we can win over the Manzanis. We're just biding our time."

Jagg bowed to kiss her. "Whatever makes you happy."

Hmm, her dad just said that too.

"You're just gonna stand there?" Strat glared at his son. "Just stand there and let it happen?"

"No," Ford said and went over to get his own beer from the fridge.

"You're fine with your sister and the man you think of as a brother—"

"If you're asking me, I say it's disgusting and more than a little disturbing," Ford said. "But I don't think shouting and screaming will change anything. If I trust Jagg with my life, hers, and yours, why can't I trust him to be a good man to my sister?"

"Thanks, man," Jagg said.

"And not that I'll ever repeat this…" Ford started, "but since they've been together, I've seen more of Im than I had in the last year. She isn't so bad. Sometimes." A point she hadn't considered. "It keeps her around, which makes her easier to look after. Not that I actually give a shit about hanging out with her."

He hid an obvious smile behind the neck of his bottle and winked at her as he drank.

"You're right," she said. "This will bring all of us closer together. We'll be one big happy family. One step closer to grandkids."

"We're soundproofing your room," Ford said, pointing his bottle at Jagg.

The tease didn't hit her father right because his phone interrupted. As he read the screen, his brow descended.

"I've gotta go," he said and touched her cheek. "You okay?"

She nodded. "Did something happen?"

"No, it's good. I'm good," Strat said, heading for the door. "Look after each other."

After he was gone, they stood in silence for a few seconds.

"Was that acceptance?" she asked.

"I don't even think he was listening," Ford said, crossing the room. "We'll order pizza and watch a movie, but you two are sitting at opposite ends of the couch."

Ford was right, they would see more of each other. She'd worried about getting to know her dad, maybe it was time to learn some more about her big brother too.

FORTY-SIX

"IT WAS JUST HIM?" Mila asked, sitting up in the hospital bed. "Bryan? It was all him?"

She nodded. "The police arrested him last night. Their case is strong, they're sure it will stick. He'll be going to prison for a long time and won't be able to hurt anyone else."

Without Manzani direction, it's possible he'd never have killed at all. Choices.

Mila exhaled. "It's difficult to know what to think. It's all so… overwhelming, you know?"

"Yes, and you should take some time, relax and recuperate. The cops will want to talk to you, but look after yourself, don't let them rush you into anything."

More than a week had gone by since she'd met Silvio in that very room. With Bryan under lock and key, Mila should get some peace. If Silvio held up his end of the bargain, Mila shouldn't be at risk anymore. She'd be able to live her life free and safe, without knowing her testimony against Bryan was only part of the story.

"They arrested her boss too. Langspring was working with Bryan."

"I can't even… it's so pointless. Stephanie lost her life for nothing."

As so many did. The cause wasn't for nothing though. She liked to think that if Stephanie was around, she'd support her decision to conceal the full truth. Mila might be in the hospital for a while. With a brain injury and broken bones, she had a journey of recovery ahead. Swerve proved just how easy it was to inject something into the IV. Next time, it could be more than a mild sedative. They had to tread carefully.

Mila's lack of family was a problem for their side and a boon for the other. If Manzani decided Mila wasn't worth the trouble, she wouldn't have a family or anyone to notice she was gone. Anyone except her.

She stayed with Mila for another half hour but couldn't sit there all day. When Mila drifted off again, she slipped out and hurried to the street to grab a cab.

Steeple's Monday meeting would begin soon and she had another appointment before she was due in his office. Luckily, it was in the same building and on the same floor.

She ascended in the elevator, smiled at Lucy, and went directly to Sersha's desk in such a flurry, the woman blinked up at her.

"Hey," Sersha said. "You wanted to talk?"

"Can we go…"

Pointing over her shoulder into one of the reading rooms, she followed her finger with Sersha at her back.

"Lachlan said they picked up Bryant. He's going down for all of it."

"Yeah, I told Mila this morning."

"How did she take it?"

"I don't know, okay, I guess."

With the door closed in the soundproof room and both of them sitting down, she slipped a hand into her purse and produced…

"What's this?" Sersha asked, unfolding the paper. "Ah."

"It might be weird, but… Will you read it?"

Without a word, Sersha leaned against the back of the chair, concentrating as she read. Putting it together hadn't been easy. She'd taken out that detail, added another, then put the first one back in. This was the first time she'd written a story under the guillotine, family lined up beside her, their fates tied to hers.

While Sersha read, she fought to stay still. Triggered by every nuance on the woman's face, it was impossible to tell what was in her head. Why was she so nervous?

At the end, lowering the page, Sersha took a deep breath in. Pausing for one beat, two. Their eyes met and hers begged a response.

Sersha exhaled. "Welcome to walking the line."

"It feels dishonest."

"It's as much truth as we know. Everything else is conjecture and you make that point."

"You don't think the cops will come banging on my door? I don't want to be in your dad's sights."

"Ha, well, don't worry about that. My door would definitely be his first stop. I have the superintendent under control. As much as anyone can. Anyone asks questions, tell them you heard it from me."

Sersha winked and handed back the article. Sometimes she feared the woman, suspected her of… something. Other times, it was awe-inspiring how determined she was to protect others.

Sersha McLeod had strong shoulders, carrying the weight of the world everywhere she went and forever adding to the burden. A brother and father loved her too, but she didn't have that someone to be hers, like she had Jagg. Someone to lighten the load by taking it on too.

She'd neglected getting to know Sersha while she and Lachlan were involved. Now it felt like she had a friend. Albeit an enigmatic, gray zone friend who she'd never know completely. Sersha had secrets, more than her brother, more than other reporters. If the strain ever became too much, she'd do her best to be there for her.

"I'm grateful, for all you did and…"

"Yeah, yeah," Sersha said. "We do what we can."

Okay, she didn't want it to get awkward.

Just one more thing to… She took her apartment keys from her bag. "Can you give these to Lachlan, please? He got his stuff out already and Jagg got the last of mine with Ford. We paid the year up front, but he should try to get some money back."

"This is Lachlan we're talking about." Sersha took the keys to put them in her pocket. "He'd probably end up giving the guy more money."

She smiled. "Thanks." Clearing her throat, she stepped back. "We shouldn't miss Steeple's meeting."

"No, better to catch the ones we can," Sersha said and they both got up. She stopped by the door. "You did good, Stratford."

"Would you have done the same? Written a half-truth to protect the people you care about?"

Sersha smiled. "The people I care about make trouble all of their own. Keeps life interesting."

Yes, and terrifying. If Sersha could do it, so could she. And even if the confidence wasn't entirely authentic, Jagg's love would get her by.

TO BE CONTINUED...

Thank you for reading this tale!
If you can, please take the time to review.

~

Ask your local library for more Scarlett Finn novels!

~

For all things Scarlett Finn check out:

www.scarlettfinn.com

BOOK FOUR

SCARLETT FINN

OUT NOW!